KNIGHT

RESCUE

Rise of the Wolf Nation – Book 1

KNIGHT RESCUE
The Knights are under attack, the US Military breaks the rules, Silas breaks the law, the pack is in disarray, and that's before Silas is given his new assignment.

Sydney Addae
Rise of the Wolf Nation – Book 1

Knight Rescue, Rise of the Wolf Nation – Book 1
Sydney Addae
Copyright 2017 by Addae, Sydney
ISBN: 978-1-937334-85-7
First Edition Electronic October 2017

Knight Rescue

Something has happened to the Knights, an elite military group of full-bloods and Silas cannot find them. Once the Goddess points him in the right direction, he, Angus and Hawke leave the country to find their pack members before it's too late. Silas had no idea what he would step into or the ramifications he would face by rescuing his Knights. Join Silas as he battles for his life and those he holds dear in an untamed country where rules hold no meaning.

Thanks to all my Den-mates and admins, Michelle and Vicky, you are all the best at keeping me laughing with new creative ideas. I heart you much.

A special shout out to Vicky Z., Sally R., Karen M., and Kelly, I could not have presented this story without your help.

Thanks

Sydney

CHAPTER ONE

Silas Knight, Alpha for the North American Wolf Nation, jerked awake and sat ramrod straight in bed. Inside his head a jumbled mass of screams, and yells for help cleared his mind of the last remnants of sleep. *"Who is this? Where are you?"* he asked mind-speaking as he jumped out of bed and moved quickly into the living room to avoid disturbing his sleeping mate.

Garbled sounds continued, like an out of tune old radio. Based on the various tones he assumed more than one person called out to him, but he couldn't lock onto any of them.

"This is your Alpha, La Patron, talk to me so I can lock onto you and help." Mentally he searched through a sea of connections of those who over decades pledged loyalty to him, but there were too many. Millions in fact. He needed a specific voice or a metaphorical hand to grab the right person. *"Goddess help me to see, to find them,"* he prayed sensing time was short. The noise continued. An occasional understandable, word offered Silas hope. He would lunge for that utterance and attempt to track the wolf but the connection always fizzled.

"Damn it," he muttered as he ran his fingers through his shoulder length hair. *"Angus?"* he called to his brother and second in command after Jasmine, his mate.

"What's wrong, Silas?"

"I'm getting a SOS from someone but can't lock onto them. What did you do when you had that problem with that KnightForce trainee?"

"Searched the list of trainees, got the name of who was missing and caught his scent. You were there. Something tells me this is different. Do you need me to do anything?"

Silas would never get back to sleep without solving this riddle. *"Meet me in my office."*

"Be there in a bit." Angus disconnected.

Silas released a long, sigh as the noise abated in his head. Sorrow leached from him as he realized that likely meant he had lost those wolves. He pulled on a pair of jogging pants, tee shirt and slippers before heading toward his office.

This area was closer to his office but lacked the warmth of the residential wing where Jasmine and Renée's artistic talents had free reign. Dim lighting dotted the shiny concrete floors. The quiet in the hall, and beige naked walls suited his mood. Morning would be soon enough for the hustle and bustle of the Compound.

Once he entered his office, the noise in his head altogether stopped. His chest squeezed tight, causing him to reach for the wall in support for several minutes before making his way to his inner sanctum. Pack members just died. Their death left a hole in his heart and anguish in his soul.

Where were they? Who were they? He sat slumped in his office chair and stared at the wall.

Angus stepped into his office, dressed similarly and dipped his dark head. "Something happened. Since we talked. What?"

"They're dead," Silas met his brother's shocked and then saddened gaze.

After a few moments of silence, Angus sat in the chair in next to Silas. "Tell me what happened."

Silas gathered his thoughts. "They woke me up. I was sleep and I heard screams, yells, and cries for help. I got out of bed, and tried to find them but couldn't locate any of them." He met Angus' gaze. "How could I not find a pack member? I should've been able to do that and help. That's why they called to me, for help."

It hurt to think, to talk. He couldn't recall a time in decades when he had failed the pack so miserably.

"Silas what's wrong?" Jasmine asked in a drowsy voice.

"We lost pack members," he said.

It took a few seconds for her to respond, but her voice sounded clearer. *"When you say lost, do you mean they can't find their way? Or…"*

"Dead. They called out to me for help but I couldn't find them."

"Silas."

"No." He shook his head. *"I need to find them, bring their bodies home."*

"You know where they are now?" she asked logically.

"No," he snapped. *"I just… I need to find them and find out why I couldn't answer when they called. I should've been able to do that, Jasmine. But I couldn't locate them."*

"Let's walk through it," she offered.

"Angus is here, we're going to see what we can find. I didn't mean to wake you," he apologized.

"Your pain woke me." Jasmine walked through the door dressed in a pair of jogging pants and his long black tee shirt. She'd once told him she preferred sleeping in his shirts because they were long enough to cover her private areas and smelled like him. Whenever he was late to bed, she'd be dressed in one which he promptly removed. Flesh to flesh was the only way to sleep.

"Hi Jasmine," Angus said standing to kiss her on the cheek. "Sit here next to him, I'll sit at the desk." Angus actions followed his words, and soon they were all seated.

Silas took Jasmine's hand and covered it with his other hand, holding her captive. She leaned forward, brushed her lips against his. "We'll fix this."

He nodded, appreciative of her not absolving him of any blame. She knew him well enough to know he blamed himself.

7

"Step by step," she said in a no-nonsense tone she'd used over the years when giving their four pups instructions in the nursery. "You were asleep, so this contact had to be a strong connection to wake you. Who can do that?"

Silas glanced at Angus, who nodded while looking at Jasmine with a glimmer of pride in his eyes. "In theory, any pack member who has pledged loyalty to me can reach out for help. They've been trained to contact their local pack Betas first and then go up the chain of command." Now that the screams and yells stopped, he shut down his emotions to pick apart the problem. "I can't recall the last time a citizen reached for me instead of their Alpha." He looked at her.

"Have any Alphas contacted you?" Angus asked.

"No. Which is strange. They should've sensed the call just as I did," Silas said thinking it through.

"If it was a member of their pack," Angus said.

"Well yes. Of course." He eyed his brother. "Are you suggesting this call was from someone not in the States? Maybe Mexico or Canada?" Silas asked. Although he was Alpha for North America he focused on the United States. It had always been that way and he wasn't interested in changing.

"Not suggesting anything," Angus said leaning back in the chair. "Just throwing out ideas, hoping something might stick or stand out so we can solve this riddle."

Since that was how they normally operated, Silas nodded and looked at his mate. "This cry for help didn't feel like strangers, which it would be if it were Canadians or Mexicans." He closed his eyes, listened deeply for echoes of their cries. "I knew them. They knew me. At some point, I interacted with them. But something stopped our connection, stopped me from identifying and locating them so I could help." He looked at Angus. "I don't like that. It's not good for an Alpha to lack the ability to find his pack-mates."

Angus nodded. "True. Are you thinking about the collars we took from the Liege all those years ago?"

Intrigued, Silas turned to face him. "I wasn't until you mentioned it."

"Back then they created those bands that blocked you from controlling the wolf. It's been almost two decades since then, what if someone's been working on an improved version and used pack members to test it?"

"It's a jarring thought," Jasmine said softly.

"It's been quiet on that front for years, hard to believe they've been practicing all this time and us not know about it." He met Jasmine's thoughtful gaze. "Your group of women thwarted hundreds of researchers, rogue wolves and enemies. How'd they get past our women to take our own, I'd like to know."

"That only works in this country," Jasmine reminded him. "If this happened on foreign soil, the women would miss it. Maybe that's the key," she added.

"Or it could be someone in KnightForce," Angus said pulling out his phone. "Or one of our Knights. Cain or Abel would know. I'm sending out a roll call for all KnightForce members to check in with the office within two hours. We'll know one way or another if any are missing."

Pleased with that idea, Silas pulled Jasmine onto his lap. The closer they were, the clearer he could think. "Good idea," he said. "I'll have Cain do the same for the Knights. If this happened on foreign soil, that would be the Knights."

"Both groups trained here at the Compound, you met them all which would make a more intimate connection," Jasmine said snuggling against his chest.

Silas nodded. "Which means I should've found and been able to help them. The connection should've been stronger." He looked at Jasmine and then Angus and explained the noise, the occasional words and his efforts to find them.

"I can't think of anything else you could've done," Angus said, earning a pleased smile from Jasmine. Since she could only mind-link with Silas and Asia, he knew she hadn't prompted his brother's comment.

"Have you contacted Cain or Abel?" Jasmine asked before Silas could reply to Angus.

"No. I'll take care of it now."

"Cain?"

"Silas? Sir?" Cain added. These twins were older than Silas and were in this country before the Goddess sent him to organize full-bloods into a pack. He wasn't sure of their ages, and they never offered that information. They were excellent trainers and took over the bulk of the Knights and KnightForce instruction.

Silas told Cain what happened and then ordered a check-in of every Knight."

"That's disturbing on multiple levels. I'll send the order now for immediate check ins."

"Good, let me know if anyone doesn't get in touch," Silas said feeling better for being pro-active.

"Yes, Sir, will do."

Angus stood, stretched and headed toward the door. "I'm going to my office to set up a relay for when KnightForce checks in. I'll have the information sent to my system and here to you, is that good?"

Unable to fault the plan, Silas nodded. "Thanks, I'll breathe a lot easier once I know who we lost."

Angus nodded, winked at Jasmine and left.

"It's a good thing all our pups are accounted for," Silas said.

"How do you know that?" Jasmine asked as she leaned back and stared into his face.

"Deeper connection since they're a more intimate part of me, so are you."

Jasmine frowned. "But I can't mind link with any of them." Her limited mind-linking ability had been a sore spot for her and his pups for years. Both had petitioned the Goddess for an expanded list of contacts to include their pups. So far, nothing had changed.

"Nothing would prevent you from sensing something was wrong with our litter or the twins. As their mother, you would know in here." He tapped her chest and then her forehead with his finger-tip.

She kissed his forehead. "I wish you'd told me this before I woke up Adam to check on him and Bella, or Jackie and Quinn."

He chuckled. "You called them? This early?"

"Yeah, I knew something was wrong because you were hurting. I just wanted to be sure those two who aren't here were okay."

"Jackie's back in Texas?"

"Yeah, they're working on the clinic. Seems to be going great, she sounds happy." Jasmine rested against him again.

"No question. That project is tailor-made for those two. René still after them to set a wedding date?"

Jasmine released a long sigh.

He smiled.

"She really wants to plan a wedding, a big one. With Adam and Bella remaining overseas, and Jackie's disinterest in moving faster, Renée 's been in a pique."

"Maybe she should wait to plan her own," he suggested.

"I mentioned that but she's convinced her mate is somewhere down the road and she has so many great ideas now. Blah, blah, blah."

He chuckled. "That's my beauty, she'll run her mate a fine dance."

"Yes, she will. Have you heard any more on Sarita? Asia said she left Hawke's sister and returned to her grandparents before going back to school."

"That's all I've gotten as well. David hasn't mentioned anything to me if that's what you mean."

"Oh. How's he doing? I mean really doing? He's so closed off and has always been the hardest to read. I can't tell if he's okay with Sarita being away or furious inside."

"He reminds me of the way I was before you came into my life. Solitary, yet amicable with the right people. He's been working with Angus in his lab, and is interested in stone-work. Angus says he has a gift and may even have the sight for spell-crafting, like Amynta, Asia's mom."

"I know who Amynta is, saying her name doesn't stop me from being uncomfortable with him dabbling in those things."

"Angus created the chameleon bracelet. It's a powerful weapon we keep hidden. He used his knowledge of stones, spell-crafting and things you may not understand to help us. That gift is a part of my line, the Black Wolf. The craft needs to be taught and passed on to others so we never lose the knowledge. I thought Jackie would've been interested." He shrugged. "David is and Angus is pleased to share what he knows with him. Hopefully one of his sons will learn as well."

"That would be nice," Jasmine said after a brief silence.

He brushed her hair away from her face and pressed a kiss on her forehead. "Go on back to bed, I'm going to be here for a while."

She yawned and stood. "I'll lie here on the sofa, keep you company."

He watched as she moved toward the extra-long, dark comfy sofa and stretch out.

"Let me know when everyone's checked in so we can decide the next step," she said before yawning again.

"Will do, Sweet Bitch."

CHAPTER TWO

Hours later, seated in his office, Silas disengaged from the conversation with Lyle, his Alpha who handled many of the pack's legal affairs. None of his 50 Alphas had received the SOS call Silas had and that made him wary. Something major just went down and he stood in a blind spot with no knowledge of what destroyed his people.

"Silas, KnightForce is all accounted for," Angus said through their link. *"The last one just reported in. Have you heard from Cain regarding the Knights?"*

"Not yet. I'll give him a few more minutes before contacting him again. If it wasn't KnightForce, it's the Knights. I'll need to set up a meeting with Major General Miller and Lieutenant General Crall, I want you there. Jasmine too, although it might be good to wait to be sure who's involved."

"Jasmine has great instincts and brings a different perspective to the conversation," Angus said.

"I know that," Silas snapped. *"It's just... she's finally resting."* He didn't have a valid reason to keep her from the meeting other than wanting to protect her from anything too dark. It made no sense, even after 20 years of ruling the Nation

together, a part of him still sought to shield her from the harsher realities in their world.

"*Let me know what time you set up the meeting. In the main conference room?*" Angus asked not bothering to argue, which underscored how ridiculous Silas' comment was.

"*Yes, I'll let you know.*" He disengaged and looked at Jasmine on the sofa asleep for several minutes. She'd been his rock, his heart and he wanted to give her the world even though she never asked for more. Their initial mating had been rocky. Even now, after all these years, he cringed at his arrogance when they met. He'd thought all humans unworthy and wanted nothing to do with any of them. He'd cavalierly ordered the death of Tyrone, her son from her previous mating or marriage to a full blood. Tyrone had been in a full-blood hospital dying from a wound suffered in the military when Silas discovered half-breeds existed in his world and his life had never been the same since then.

Not that she'd known anything about the Wolf Nation at the time. He smiled in memory of his Sweet Bitch's reaction once she learned her twins had kept the news from her. He wouldn't say she was dramatic, but she'd made sure they all knew and felt her displeasure. Once she emitted those breeding pheromones he had to have her and didn't stop until she carried his first and only litter.

Love, that elusive emotion that both built and sank kingdoms, burrowed so deep in him for her, he now understood why mates didn't live if the other died. How could he live without his heart? Not only did she hold his, she was his heart in every meaning of the word.

"Stop thinking so hard," Jasmine muttered without looking at him.

He chuckled. "I'm not." He contacted Cain. "*Has everyone checked in?*"

"*No, Sir. There's a team of four we haven't been able to reach, in fact there's nothing from them,*" Cain said in a sober tone. "*I contacted Crall, he doesn't know of any jobs or missions they were on. I'm waiting to hear from Miller. He's doing some research.*" Cain paused. "*Sir, I don't know what happened, or where they are. I suspect these are the men who reached out to you. For some reason, they did not follow the chain of command to contact me or any of the others."*

"Maybe they couldn't," Silas said, angry and sad over the loss.

"If that's the case, we need to know why. It's not like them or any Knight to leave home base and us not be aware of it," Cain said.

"Be prepared for a meeting in 30 minutes. I want answers if I have to wake the entire Joint Chiefs," Silas said, in a low growl.

"Yes, Sir, we are at your disposal." Cain disconnected.

Silas ran his hand through his hair, stood and walked to the window. Anger and grief battled within. Outside the sun peeked over the horizon, bathing the morning in shades of yellow and orange. The mountain peaks sparkled as if they'd been kissed.

He stopped and shook his head. Where the hell had that come from? Sparkled? Kissed? He needed to stay out of Jasmine's head when she read those romance books.

"You like them," she said. The smile in her voice tugged at him.

"No. I love you, which means I tolerate most things you like in addition to me and the pups." He waited for her to challenge him and call them "kids" or "children" as she often did. When she snickered, he turned to look at her, "Knights are missing."

Her shoulders tensed. "How many?"

"Four. Cain confirmed it."

She pushed up from the sofa, brushed her hair back and looked at him.

Goddess, after all this time, her unfettered beauty still took his breath away. "Conference call in 25 minutes. I need to set up a few things, can you let the twins, David, Jacques, Angus, Asia and Hawke know, please?"

"Sure." She stood, stretched and walked out his office. A few minutes later she contacted him. *"It's done. I've ordered coffee and food for the conference room. Anything I can get you?"*

"No. I just talked to Crall and Miller. No one knows what's happening, I'm going to have Lyle listen in on this as well. I may need to bring in a few more Alphas after we learn something."

"Okay, see you in a bit. I'm going to change."

Silas exhaled and ran his hand through his jet-black hair. What happened to those full-bloods? Why hadn't they gone through proper channels? And why couldn't he save them?" He sat seeking echoes of the SOS calls, pulling threads until he pinpointed a general area where the call originated. Comprised of hundreds of square miles, the vicinity was too vast, after the meeting he would try to get closer.

According to the wall clock, the meeting started in five minutes. He stood slowly and left his office. His thoughts simmered on how he failed his men. Entering the room, he appreciated the somber mood. Four of theirs had fallen. He sat and explained what happened. Hawke and Asia sat across from him. She took Hawke's hand when Silas explained the SOS call and his inability to find them. Jasmine sat next to him and held his hand beneath the table.

"Cain and Abel have no idea who sent them?" Tyrese, Jasmine's son asked.

"No, we don't," Abel answered. "None of our team was notified of the assignment, if that's what it was. General Crall, have you learned anything?"

General Crall, a half-breed high-ranking officer and liaison for the Knights sat forward, clearing his throat. "The new President was briefed by the Joint Chiefs three days ago. I urged them to wait before explaining the Knights and by extension the Nation, but… they believed it best to brief him."

Jasmine's hand tightened on Silas' as he processed Crall's comments. Silas rarely paid attention to human politics or politicians because they changed all the time. "New?"

"Yes Sir. I think he's fascinated by the idea of having a separate group in the country," General Crall said.

Silas frowned. "Fascinated? Why?"

"I don't know, Sir," General Crall said and lapsed into silence.

"Are you suggesting the new President had something to do with the disappearance of four Knights?" The idea was so beyond the scope of anything he'd ever imagined, he needed to hear Crall say it.

"It's possible," Crall said. "And would explain why no one's talking. No one wants us to know how far up this goes in case you decide to retaliate."

Silas released a long breath and looked at Jasmine. "Do you think, new or not, he'd be crazy enough to send my people to their deaths?"

"Crazy isn't the word I'd use," Jasmine said in a soothing tone. "Maybe he wanted to run some kind of tests to verify their authenticity and things got out of control."

He agreed that could be the case. "But why couldn't I locate them? And why couldn't they link with Cain or Abel, or their Alpha's?"

"Maybe they've developed something that stops that. Maybe that was the test to see if they could isolate us," she said in a cool voice. Her eyes grew lighter as she looked across the table at Asia.

Sensing her anger rising, Silas squeezed her hand, hard. "Calm down, we don't know anything for sure yet." Jasmine blinked and nodded.

"Hawke, what would stop me from locating them? Have you heard of any devices that would accomplish that?" Silas asked.

Hawke shook his head slowly. "As the top Alpha, I can't imagine anyone creating something that could block that visceral link between you and the pack. If they have something we need to counteract it before the pack is separated from all Alphas."

The idea of pack members unable to connect to their Alphas sent a shock wave through everyone listening at the meeting. It was unheard of. As wolves, their very nature depended on the pack structure.

"Find out whatever you can," Silas told Hawke. "This takes priority over everything."

"Yes, Sir," Hawke said.

"Generals, knock on every door until I get a fucking answer. I want to know what the fuck happened and how. If they won't talk to you, tell them I'm coming to Washington and they damn well don't want that."

"Yes, Sir," Generals Crall and Miller said.

17

"Abel, Cain, lock down the Knights. Bring them to Compound. They're grounded until further notice."

"Yes, Sir," Cain said hesitantly.

"You have something to say, Cain?" Silas asked in a hard tone. He wasn't in the mood to be questioned.

"Having all the Knights in one location may be seen as a sign of aggression, Sir. What if we gave them vacation time, allowed them to return home until further notice but ready for immediate deployment."

Silas thought about it. A part of him wanted to show Washington he'd kick their asses for what they'd done but Cain was right. His main duty to the Goddess was to keep the Wolf Nation a secret not start a war. "Sounds good, give the order. I want them cleared out within 48 hours. If they receive instructions for an assignment they must clear it through me."

"Yes, Sir. That should stop anyone from tampering with the assignment desk," Cain said nodding.

Silas clamped down on his beast who wanted to attack their enemies. "We need the bodies of our fallen. An extraction team will go and bring them home."

No one spoke.

"Do you know where they are?" Jasmine asked the question that had to be on everyone's mind.

"I know the general area." He looked at the monitor into the gazes of his Alphas, his Generals and then his team seated at the conference table. "We'll find our pack-mates and bring them home for a proper burial if I have to go find them myself. They served honorably. I set the Knights in motion and refuse to allow this travesty to go unchallenged or without retribution."

He looked at Jacques. "Contact Jodello, put him on standby in case I decide to go that route." Once when the Joint Chiefs had lied and used his son, Tyrese, as bait for a small country, Silas had Jodello shake the economic centers of several countries by moving massive amounts of gold and monies around. It hadn't taken the President long to contact him and smooth things over. He hoped this new President would come to understand the value of having a peaceable relationship with the Wolf Nation.

"Yes, Sir," Jacques said.

"I've alerted all the Knights, Sir," Cain said. "They are in the process of packing for a long holiday. They are saddened by the loss of their pack-mates and many have volunteered to go search for them."

"I'm not surprised," Silas said glancing at Jasmine who remained quiet by his side. "I will call them when I'm ready." He spoke of a few more matters to the Alphas and Generals and dismissed them.

Silence reigned in the conference room.

"I will take two, Ethan and Damian," Angus said. "No one tracks better than Ethan, we'll find them and return quickly. In and out."

Silas remained silent. He thought over everything regarding the distress call, the men sounded weak, afraid. As if something abnormal was happening. First off, Knights didn't respond that way. None of the men he and Cain trained would call him in fear, they'd die fighting. Unless… he couldn't think of what would make them call out to him in that manner.

"Silas?" Angus said.

He looked at Angus. "I'll let you know."

"I thought time was of the essence?" Tyrese said. "I should go as back-up."

"Back-up?" Angus stared at Tyrese and smirked. "I need back-up?"

"Not really but, I just think four rounds the team better," Tyrese said.

Jasmine pushed back from the table. "Is there anything else, Silas?"

"Hmm?" he looked at her as she stood.

"You've given assignments to Jacques, Hawke, Cain, Abel and have everyone else on hold. Is there a reason to remain here? In the conference room?" she held his gaze.

"No. Hawke let me know what you discover." He looked at Jacques. "Contact Jodello. He knows what to do."

"I'm on it," Jacques said as he left the room.

Jasmine extended her hand to him. Silas took it and they walked out together in silence.

CHAPTER THREE

Jasmine stopped in front of the elevator, pressed the button and waited. They had a lot to discuss, Silas wasn't sure what direction to search for the missing Knights. When the elevator passed the floor of their living quarters, he looked at her.

"We need the Goddess. Maybe she'll answer," Jasmine said and walked out when the doors opened.

"I planned to talk to her once everything was in place," he said to Jasmine's back. She continued down the hall to the prayer room.

"We're here now," she said and placed her palm on the security panel. The door slid open and she entered. He stood in the corridor watching the door close behind her.

"Stubborn woman," he muttered and followed. Inside she had removed her clothes and shoes and was putting on a long white ceremonial dress. The dress meant serious business, because she didn't do that all the time.

He washed, disrobed and dressed in his ceremonial white pants and robe.

Dressed he took her hand and together they lit the candles and incense before stepping into the sacred circle. Still holding hands, Silas made the plea for an audience, gave thanksgiving and worshiped the Goddess with praise for her loving kindness.

They waited to see if their petition would be answered. One moment he knelt next to Jasmine in their prayer room, the next he stared into a clear body of water. Jasmine's nose was less than an inch from her reflection.

"Greetings La Patron, Alpha of the Wolves and your mate Jasmine. Rise and come forward. It is good to see you." The soft, whispery voice flowed through Silas, touching every part of his being. No matter how often he had been in the Goddess' presence, he remained in awe of her power and grace. He and Jasmine moved toward a bright light and stopped midway, with heads bowed.

"Thank you for your time," Silas said and explained what happened with the four wolves.

"What do you think of this Jasmine?" the Goddess asked.

Pleased the Goddess included his mate in the conversation, Silas waited to hear Jasmine's words.

"I'm afraid."

Startled, Silas looked at Jasmine. He never picked up fear from her.

"Why afraid?" the Goddess asked.

"The way this happened, it's dark and I think it's a trap of some kind for Silas."

Stunned, he couldn't utter a word if he wanted.

"You are wise to be concerned. There is darkness afoot. Alpha Wolf do you sense a trap?"

He had wondered at the Knights communicating fear, something he doubted they'd ever do. "I agree with my mate that there is reason for suspicion."

"Your desire to know the location of the missing wolves is granted. Remember, pack cares for pack, find our wolves and bring them home."

"Thank you, Goddess," he said gratitude filling his heart as connections were made in his mind.

"Your mate is your match, and chosen to rule alongside you for a reason. Cherish her counsel, she will see things you miss."

21

The next moment the prayer circle came in focus. It took a moment to regain his balance and center himself.

"You got it?" Jasmine asked, watching him.

He sought the echoes of the SOS call and this time he locked down on a location but didn't see the men. "Yeah, I know where they were, not where they are."

She nodded and pushed against the floor to stand. He grabbed her hand.

"Wait. Let's talk. I didn't know you were afraid." He stroked the side of her face with his finger-tip.

"Have you examined those calls? I mean really examined them?" She asked.

"Before the meeting, after you left me in my office, I went back over them. Knights wouldn't call out in fear. They'd die before letting me or Cain know they were afraid to die."

She nodded. "Which means?"

"Either someone made them do it, which is unlikely or someone discovered a way to contact me through the link I have with the pack." He cursed as that unpleasant reality sunk in.

"Or someone's holding them and contacted you without using your pack at all," she said.

That grabbed his attention. "I don't sense their wolves or their life force."

"If they can send a fake SOS, chances are they can mask a wolf's life force," she said. "This isn't the Liege, Silas. This is the U.S. government with millions of research dollars at their disposal. They've finally grown bold enough to open those back rooms where they've been building stuff for years and are running tests on our people. They have weapons we don't know about."

Silas stared at her for a few moments, shook his head and then closed his eyes. For years he and his Generals had been playing a cat and mouse game with the military. There's always been a faction that promoted building weapons to use again the Wolf Nation. Normally, that talk was squashed by the Joint Chiefs, at least publicly. What if they'd continued creating offensive weapons?

Obviously, they had, the lying bastards.

The knowledge that a single Alpha could activate millions of wolves to do his bidding in an instant scared a lot of higher ups. But if they could separate them, fix it so the links didn't work, that would render that particular threat ineffective.

Brilliant. And dark as the Goddess said. It would be catastrophic for the Nation.

"Sweet Bitch, I hadn't seen it that way. I was blinded by anger, and let my emotions clouded my reason. What you're saying makes a lot of sense. They've always played a deep game with us." He paused. "But to use our Knights?"

"How else will they know if it worked?" she asked. "I agree someone has to bring them home. Not just for the reasons you mentioned but to discover what the military developed and make them think it doesn't work."

He frowned. "Why not destroy it?"

"It's impossible to really destroy information these days. But if we can make them believe the project failed, they'll move on, or try to improve it. That'll buy us time to counteract whatever they're doing," she said.

He stared at her. "How do you think of these things?"

She shrugged.

"I mean it. You've never been in the military or fought in a war. Yet you're able to see clearly through the smoke."

"Most mothers can see through smoke to the real problem. It's a mandatory skillset. But in this case, I had a little help from the Goddess. Don't forget she never disagreed with me and encouraged you to listen to me. When I went over everything that's what I saw and it scared me."

He pulled her in his lap and held her tight.

"This is my country, I love it and the people. Both human and wolf. But what they're doing is wrong. They're undermining an entire race, their allies, for no legitimate reason," she said.

"It's offensive. Just in case they need to shut us down for whatever reason, they have this weapon," he said seeking to explain their actions.

"I get that. But to take four Knights? Men trained to give their lives to keep this country safe? Where's the honor in that?" she asked.

"Who said anything about honor?"

She kissed his cheek. "When I think of my country, honor is a given." She pursed her lips. "We need to find the Knights quick before they think the experiment's a success."

"You don't think they're dead?" he asked, once again surprised.

"No. First, what they did was wrong and they know you're going to be pissed. I don't think they're ready to push your buttons yet. If you did nothing, those Knights will return with some excuse and they'll be patting backs in offices in the Pentagon."

"What will they think about the Knights leaving?"

"That might make them pause but I don't think they'll lock those offices we need to get into yet."

"And upsetting the economy?" he asked, appreciating the way her mind worked.

"Same thing. Remember, there's probably just a select few who even know about those experiments and they want to believe they're successful. Timing is going to be everything, we don't want them to lock everything back up for a rainy day."

"Find the Knights before they're returned which will make them think the experiment failed on one level. Steal their information to counter whatever they've done without their knowledge, maybe create a back door of some sort," he said, thinking it through. "Hawke can handle that."

"Did the Goddess share anything else?" he asked after a few moments of silence.

Jasmine smiled. "You heard everything she said and didn't say."

"Yeah, but I always over-think her messages."

She smiled again.

"So, the mission is to rescue the Knights, and gather the information on their offensive and defensive weapons against us?" He leaned back and met her gaze. "Anything else?"

"Yes. Do it quickly and quietly. No one can know, except those working in the project. They'll think they failed. You can make a stink, and send them further into the shadows or appear clueless, allowing it to pass."

He laughed. "They'll be waiting for the hammer to drop every second of the day, especially with the Knights removed from action." He squeezed her tight. "I love your mind, Sweet Bitch."

"That came from the Goddess, I think," she said.

He lifted her to the side, stood and then extended his hand to help her. "Let's get started."

"Whoa. Hold on." She dropped his hand and pointed at him. "Who are you sending?"

"Not one of the twins, if that's what you're worried about."

"I've evolved. The twins are perfectly capable of taking on a mission like this." She placed her hands on her hips and stared at him.

Silas released a long breath and took her hand. "I'm going. Possibly me and Angus. That's it."

She opened her mouth.

"I need to go. I have to see what's being planned for the pack. I need to see who and what we're up against. I can't get that information second hand. This job is for me."

"I see," she said several moments later.

"We'll use the chameleon bracelets, Angus has done a lot of work improving it so we don't leave a trail of bodies behind. We'll leave by way of the mountains. No one will know who we are. They won't suspect anything. We'll get near the Soto Cano Air Base in Honduras where the distress call originated. Being closer, on the ground, I should be able to track them easier."

"You've got it all planned?" She looked at him with a wry grin.

He rubbed his neck. "No but I don't want to argue with you about me going, so I had to think fast."

"When have I ever tried to stop you from fighting for the pack?"

He couldn't think of a time. Usually, he decided to remain at the Compound to protect his den, fully believing he was the only one who could. Over the years, Jasmine had proven she was more than capable of protecting the Compound. "Not once. I stand corrected."

"You're projecting."

"Huh?"

She gave him a mocking look. "You're remembering all the times you've prevented me from leaving here and reversing it."

He stiffened. If she thought he'd take her to Honduras, a country that earned the distinction of being called the most dangerous place on earth to be a woman, she was wrong. That small country had an epidemic of femicide, countless women murdered with no justice.

"See? That's how you act when it comes to me, so you think I've done that about you. I never have." She turned to leave.

"Jasmine."

She looked at him over her shoulder. "Wolfie?"

"Just Angus and I."

"And Asia or Hawke or Me. Your choice. You have to take someone I can talk through as well." She turned and left the room.

CHAPTER FOUR

Once the decision was made where to go, things moved quickly. Only a handful of people knew of this trip, no one outside the Compound, not even the Alphas. The fewer who knew, the better their chances of surprising those who concocted this nefarious plan. Angus, the twins, Jacques, Asia and Hawke had been surprised when Silas shared what he and Jasmine determined to be the real threat.

Asia had looked at Jasmine and nodded.

Jasmine hadn't budged on her position of taking a third person she could also communicate with, which meant Hawke prepared to leave as well.

"What if the Knights have been tampered with?" Asia asked. "It's possible they've added or removed something to those men."

Silas agreed. "Hawke pack the scanning equipment. If those men have been altered, we'll bring them in through the basement tunnels where Matt and Passen can examine them." He looked at Jasmine. "If we need them, wait until we are on our way back in before they set up the exam rooms."

She nodded and returned to their lodgings.

Silas was in his office finalizing details when his son, David, knocked.

"Come in," Silas said hoping the pup hadn't come to ask to be a part of the team. Tyrese had made his case to Jasmine why he should go, as well as Jacques. She stood in solidarity with him for the small, three-man team. It would be better for Hawke to gather the data directly than relying on a relay system in the clouds.

"Dad," David said as he closed the door behind him.

Silas waited for the pup to say more and when he didn't, Silas turned and looked at him. "What's wrong?" David met Silas' gaze with eyes the same color as his mother, and apparent determination.

"This trip." David shook his head. "Mission you're embarking on... I would ask that you be really careful."

Silas took a moment to think. Of course, he would be careful, a lot of people depended on him. But David knew that, so what was he really saying? "I will."

David exhaled and took a seat in front of the desk. Leaning forward, his elbows rested on his knees and his hands dangled between them. "Maybe I'm not saying this right." He exhaled. "You're leaving mom in charge, and I can't imagine a better person to have at your back, than her... except when it comes to you." He glanced at Silas and then back at his hands. "You weren't here, didn't see her when the Goddess snatched you to fight Uncle Angus. It all worked out but the women... the women in her network still talk about how she snatched energy from them to protect the Alpha. It's a badge of honor for them but at the time, everyone was scared. Mom... she wasn't mom."

Sensing there was more, Silas gave his son his total attention. "What do you mean she wasn't mom?"

David gave him an incredulous look. "She tried to attack the Goddess."

Silas had heard about that.

"If anything happens to you, and I'm not talking about you dying or anything like that. I mean if you cannot communicate with her, so she knows you're okay."

Silas nodded.

"No dark moments. No breaks. For all our sakes, she needs to know you're good, no matter what." He stared at Silas. "I'm serious, Dad."

"I believe you." Silas thought for a few seconds. "Why? What do you think will happen?"

David snorted. "There will be a war. Right here in the States. She won't think it through. Her anger will lash out first and there will be collateral damage." He leaned forward. "She has an Army of bitches who will follow her to hell and back without blinking. So, if the men try restraint, we'll be overruled in a heartbeat. Mom is awesome and is all about pack, except if you're in danger. Then she changes into someone else." His gaze narrowed. "Kind of the same way you'd be if she was in danger."

Silas sat back so fast, his back hit the chair. The idea of his woman in any kind of danger unleashed his beast. He fought to regain control. When he could see past the red mist, he eyed his youngest pup.

"Smart. And duly noted. I promise to think how I'd react if I were the one left behind. We don't want a national crisis and I'd certainly start one if someone messed with my bitch, consequences be damned." He nodded in appreciation. "Have you heard from Sarita lately?"

"We communicate every day. She spent time with Hawke's sister and has returned to her grandparents to finish school. She's almost done."

"You're good with that?" Silas wondered if he could have allowed Jasmine the same level of freedom and admitted his son was a better man than him in that regard. He couldn't have done it.

David smiled and it made him appear more his age. "Yes and no. I didn't have a choice, the mating bug hadn't bit before she left. As long as she's committed to me, I'm okay." His smile lingered a bit. "She's worth it."

Silas had nothing to say to that and nodded. "Good. Your mom and I just want you to be happy."

David stood. "I know. It's what we all want too." He walked to the door. "Thanks for listening and understanding where I'm coming from. We all hope your trip will be short but things happen, so I prepare for the worse. In this situation, it's a pissed off mate."

Silas nodded again, as he imagined his actions if Jasmine couldn't communicate with him. Now her demand that someone she could talk to in case she couldn't reach him made sense. "I'm always here for you and promise to listen. You have a unique perspective, like your mom."

"Thanks, Dad. That's a great compliment." He left the office. Silas sat back to think over what David said.

"Jasmine?"

"Yes?"

"Where are you?"

"Packing a few things for you, why?"

"On my way."

Moments later he entered their bedroom, wrapped his arm around her waist and pulled her back against him. Immediately, he grew hard. "I love you," he said simply.

She rubbed his hands and leaned back against him. "I love you, too." She turned slightly in his arms and returned his embrace. In a few words, he told her of his conversation with David.

"Insightful," she said after releasing a long sigh.

He wasn't surprised she didn't deny anything. "One request."

"Another one?" she leaned back and met his gaze.

"Yes."

They stared into each other's eyes for a few moments.

"What?" she said.

"Don't start a war."

"Define war."

"Jasmine. You know what I mean. If something happens to me, don't retaliate against humans. That would break the Goddess' mandate of remaining unseen."

Her lips curved as she continued staring at him.

"Seriously Jasmine. Don't start a war."

"If something happened to me and it was the humans," she said using her fingers as quotations marks. "Would you violate the Goddess' rule?"

His body shuddered as he tried to keep his wolf under control. His eyes itched, no doubt changing colors at the very idea of his mate in danger.

She snorted. "I didn't think so." Leaning forward, she traced a fingertip down his chest. "I promise I'll only do what you'd do if the situation was reversed. Don't ask me to be someone I'm not, we're mated with the same set of rules, passions and commitments." She pressed her finger into his chest. "Don't insult me by asking me not to retaliate, as if my feelings are somehow less. I'll blow those bastards up and become their worst fucking nightmare if something happens to you because of them. Now, if you have a problem with that, get over it."

He rubbed his chest and pulled her close. "I love it when you get all blood-thirsty and stuff." He growled low in his chest and kissed her hard.

Her fist tangled in his hair and pulled hard, tingles raced down his spine in anticipation as her kiss equaled his in ferocity. He loved when she forgot herself and let go. If he could bottle his feeling for this one moment in time when she held all of him in the palm of his hand, the sheer joy of being one with her, he'd do it in a fucking second. He relished the plushness of her body, neither big nor small, just perfect for him. Eager for more, eyes closed he wrapped her arms around his neck and nuzzled hers, inhaling deeply.

Goddess, her scent set off firestorms of need in him. His cock hardened in recognition of her. Leaving small kisses on her neck, face and chest he pulled her tighter, wanting more contact, and yet needing to be flesh to flesh.

She pushed back slightly, wearing a naughty grin that set his beast on fire. He pulled her shirt over her head and stared at her full mounds.

Reaching behind, she deftly popped her bra open and slid it from her arms while watching him. His eyes dropped to her breasts.

"Ah, Sweet Bitch, so fucking beautiful." His heart slammed in his chest. His mouth watered as he dipped his head to capture the right nipple in his mouth. A jolt of sensation ripped through him at the taste and texture.

She cried out as he dragged his teeth along the taut buds of her nipples, her hands grasped at his hair. He loved it. Would she demand he satisfy her now? Or would he be able to draw it out, taste more of her?

His palm settled between her legs and pressed against her mound.

She shuddered.

His beast growled as he pushed her back, seconds later he removed the rest of their clothes. Naked to his touch, he brushed his lips against her nipples again. His palm returned to her mound, she was so wet, so hot, his fingers slid easily between her legs.

Moans, music to him, slipped from her lips as her legs widened for better access. He caught sight of her wet pussy and pressed his fingers in deeper, and bringing out her ambrosia. Turning aside he sucked and licked his fingers clean. Desperate for more, he squeezed and kneaded her breasts as he slid down her body, with an eye on her glistening center.

"Silas," she moaned. Her hips writhing on the bed, he sensed her need. And he'd take care of it after.

After he feasted on her sweetness. His chest expanded at the proof of her arousal, her need for him. This was all for him. Famished, he gave long, slow lick on her tender folds.

She gasped and grabbed his hair.

Pleased she needed him for this, he continued drawing out more of her juices. She gasped when he latched onto her clit with his lips and then twirled his tongue up and down it, before giving it a hard suck.

The hard yank on his hair, coupled with the scream that bounced against the walls egged him on. His cock throbbed with desire to fill her. To once again bring her pleasure that no one else could ever provide. He continued alternating suckling, licking while his fingers fucked her tight pussy.

He didn't want her to think about anything other than him, and the pleasure he gave her. She bowed up as her first orgasm stole her breath. Her walls tightened around his fingers. Once she stopped shaking he leaned forward to lick her sweet juices before they hit the sheets.

"Mine," he growled as he lapped every bit.

Her thighs trembled against his cheek.

Smug male satisfaction came over him that she responded to him this way, that he took her to the pinnacle and brought her such immense pleasure.

"Always yours," she murmured in a husky tone that shot to his cock. His mate was spectacular, so lusty and sensual. His soul craved her very essence. With one smooth move he was atop her, his leg pushing hers wider apart. She grabbed his cock, rubbed her thumb over the head and placed it between her legs. Her instructions were clear.

He pushed forward, lifting her leg slightly so she could take all of him. It wasn't until he was pressed against her that his beast reveled in their closeness. He paused to enjoy the feel of her tight tunnel holding him, then he withdrew slowly before thrusting back inside, taking her hard and deep the way she liked, no demanded, it. Over and over he thrust into her, her silken walls caressing and then tightening as her breath hitched.

He was on fire for her.

"Now, now," she screamed.

He lifted onto his hands and arched his back, increasing the pace. Her body shook, she was in the throes of ecstasy when he released a roar and shot into her tight sheath. Together they crested the waves of sweet bliss as his orgasm ripped through him, leaving him content and drained.

CHAPTER FIVE

Jasmine stood next to the window with her arms crossed over her chest. An hour ago, darkness cloaked the forest beyond the Compound. Silas and the others took the underground tunnels into the mountains and were on a plane headed to South America.

Silence wrapped around her shoulders as she continued to stare at the rising mists in the distance. Trees of all sizes and shapes stood resolute as sunlight tickled their peaks and filtered through their limbs. She released a long sigh. A new day had come, new possibilities, and new challenges. Moving slowly, she headed to the kitchen to prepare a quick meal. Someone knocked.

Frowning she glanced at the early hour on the clock and sighed. Had Silas told the kids to keep an eye on her?

She opened the door and stared at David.

"Good morning," he said with a slight smile.

"Is it?" she crossed her arms and didn't move to let him inside.

"It's a good morning for a home cooked breakfast." He rubbed his stomach.

She laughed at his antics and moved aside. "Come on, but you're helping."

"Of course." He closed the door. They hadn't taken two steps before another knock.

"That's Renée," David said as he opened the door.

"Okay," Jasmine said shaking her head as she pulled out ingredients. "Wash your hands and get in here."

"Yes, Ma'am," Renée said as she entered the kitchen.

Jasmine looked over her shoulder at her daughter and chuckled. "I like your Wonder Woman tank and shorts. Looks good on you."

Renée leaned forward and kissed Jasmine's cheek. "Comfortable too." She looked around and pointed. "Potatoes?"

Jasmine nodded and moved aside as Renée grabbed the bowl to wash the potatoes before cutting them up. David grabbed a carton of eggs and sat them next to the pancake mix.

"What do you want me to do?" He watched her stir her batter and toss in fresh blueberries.

"Grab the bacon and sausage from the fridge. Pull out the griddle and get started."

Once everyone was busy cooking, Jasmine cleared her throat. "Why are you here so early?"

"Food." David didn't look at her when he answered.

"David thought it'd be a good idea to hang with you today, we never get you to ourselves like this. He woke up early and woke me too."

"Did Silas put you up to this?" she asked.

David frowned. "Not to me. I miss when you'd fix breakfast for us and we'd come here to eat. I thought it'd be good to have it again."

That surprised her. "Why haven't you said something? We can do this anytime." She looked at him.

"You're busy. From morning to night you're handling something or doing something, just never seemed the right time. I figured you'd have a couple hours first thing this morning before things heat up and you have to go work." He shrugged.

"I'm never that busy." She looked at Renée who shrugged as well. "Am I?"

"When David said we could have some alone time with you, I jumped on it. I miss this." Renée looked around the kitchen. "We spent a lot of time here, and it just stopped."

Jasmine flipped the pancakes and shook her head. "I didn't realize. You're both busy, I hardly see either of you. I didn't want to intrude, but... I'm glad you're here. I miss this too." Later she'd think deeper about their comments, right now she'd enjoy a nice quiet breakfast with her kids.

Sitting at the table eating breakfast, talking about the art gallery where Renée worked and David spoke of his work with Angus, and his studies, Jasmine realized they'd drifted apart. How could they live in the same place and not know what was going on with each other?

"So, are you going out with him again?" she asked Renée.

"No. He's boring, just talks about stuff he has, like that's a big deal," Renée scoffed.

"Depending on where he's come from, it could be a big deal," David said. "Not everyone has rich beginnings."

Renée shrugged. "Good point. I just don't like him. No chemistry. No need to waste our time."

"True, just be polite about it," Jasmine said.

"Is this the first time you've ever been without Daddy?" Renée asked.

"Yes. And before you ask, it sucks. I miss him terribly."

"Breeders can survive the separation, right?" Renée asked, in a somber tone.

"Maybe, physically," Jasmine said not wanting to pursue that line of thinking. "Asia and Shyla are full-bloods though."

"As long as they're links are open, they'll be okay," David said.

Jasmine nodded.

"I'm off today. Is there anything I can do for you?" Renée asked.

"In addition to cleaning the kitchen with your brother, you mean?" She pointed to the bowls in the sink.

Renée laughed as she stood and took their plates to the kitchen. "Yes, anything you need, let me know."

Jasmine smiled and could only imagine what the day would bring.

"Same here, if you need me, I'm here. Lunch? Dinner? I'm free." David winked.

"Thanks, I'll let you know." She patted his hand.

"I'll help Renée." He stood, took the remaining dishes and headed into the kitchen.

Jasmine sat at the table for a few minutes going over everything Silas laid out for her last night. Tyrese would use a chameleon bracelet to morph into Silas and Asia would morph into Hawke and Angus intermittently so that staff wouldn't realize the three men had left. Asia would go down to Hawke's office this morning, greet everyone, hand out assignments and tell them he was working on a project for La Patron and return to his home office. Since he worked from home three out of six days, no one would suspect he wasn't on the grounds.

Asia would then go to the KnightForce office, sign in as Angus and handle his daily memos to his agents. She'd work as Angus for a few hours while they put the word out that Asia was meeting with Jasmine in private, something they often did.

Tyrese would walk all over the Compound as Silas most of the day overseeing the work Silas left for him to do. Hopefully, all of this would buy Silas the time he needed to find the Knights while the military believed he was still blissfully unaware of their transgression and still at the Compound.

Renée placed a cup of hot tea in front of Jasmine. "Here, Mom."

Smiling her appreciation, Jasmine took a sip, and moaned. "Perfect, thanks, honey."

Renée sat across from her. "You're welcome. Has Jackie mentioned a wedding date to you?"

Jasmine covered her mouth to keep from spitting out her tea. "No. She promised to tell you first."

Renée released a long sigh. "I know. What's taking them so long? I have so many ideas." Her dark blue eyes lit with fevered excitement. "I started a book. A wedding book with lots of ideas."

"Use it for your own wedding," David said as he sat with a glass of water. "Jackie doesn't care about that stuff, you know that. She's only having a wedding because of you."

"Weddings are civilized and sophisticated announcements to the world that a person is no longer available," Renée said in a haughty tone.

David snorted.

"Mistress, the Joint Chiefs want to talk to La Patron," Asia said. *"Tyrese just left the KnightForce office and is on his way to La Patron's office, so is Jacques. He asked me to tell you so you can meet them there."*

"And so it begins," Jasmine said marveling at the early hour. *"Tell them do not talk to anyone until I get there. I'm finishing breakfast and need to get dressed."*

"Yes, Ma'am."

"You may need to be Silas, I'll have to think about it."

"Whatever you wish, Mistress," Asia said.

Jasmine pushed away from the table. "We should do this again; your Dad would enjoy it. This may come as a surprise, but we miss having you guys around." She leaned forward, placed a kiss on each of their foreheads and turned toward her bedroom. "Lock the door on your way out, I have to get dressed for a meeting."

####

Jasmine entered the conference room. Tyrese, appearing as Silas, Jacques and Asia, appearing as Angus, sat at the table. To anyone paying attention it would appear as Silas having a meeting with his core team minus Hawke and the twins.

"What exactly did they say?" Jasmine asked as soon as they sealed the room.

"General Miller was asked why the Knights were leaving and he told them La Patron gave the men a vacation. That didn't go over well, and they tried to stop the order."

"Stop whose order?" Jasmine asked Jacques.

"La Patron's order giving the Knights time off." He looked at Jasmine.

She nodded for him to continue.

"When threats of courts martialling didn't work and they couldn't physically restrain the men, they reported it to high command. They talked to General Miller and got nowhere."

"So why do they want to talk? Silas gave his men a vacation," she said.

"At the same time?" Tyrese asked.

"Yeah, he can do that. And when you speak with them, that's the attitude you should have."

Tyrese nodded.

Jasmine snapped her fingers. "Jacques, what about that time off clause in the agreement? Silas wanted to make sure the Knights didn't get burned out."

He pulled out a key-board and typed. "They've been on assignments, and most haven't had anywhere near the required 90 days in a calendar year." He smiled when he looked over his shoulder. "Oops, looks like the military overlooked an important rule in our agreement."

"That's the angle you take, Rese. Mention the contractual agreement and that you're pulling all Knights for a mandatory, what?" she looked at Jacques, then Asia and then Tyrese. "Two weeks? A month? How long should we say?"

"Start with a month, they'll want to negotiate," Jacques said. "Two weeks is reasonable."

Jasmine agreed. "Start with a month, and you can consider two weeks. Don't agree, just say you'll get back with them." She thought a few moments. "This may be a smoke screen, they may just want to be sure he's here and not after them." She shook her head to stop second guessing. "No matter." She looked at Tyrese. "Can you give them a hard time like Silas would?"

"I've sat in several meetings when he's talked to them, I can do it. I'll need Angus and Jacques, they're usually with him. Hawke sometimes too."

"We don't have any more chameleons, so we'll make do. This isn't a planned meeting, so it should be fine." She looked around the room, making sure everything was in place before opening the door.

"Have you contacted them, Jacques?" she asked.

"Yes, the Admiral is on stand-by."

She nodded and stepped out the office into the outer office where she placed her hand on a security scanner and entered a small room. Inside she could see and hear what went on in the office.

Silas had created this room for her several years back to sit in on meetings when he didn't want others to know she listened. Afterward, they'd discuss her thoughts and make decisions on how to proceed.

Jacques went through the protocols and finally Admiral Bent and two other high ranking officers were seated at a conference table speaking from a similar secure room. After formal greetings, in which Tyrese did a great job imitating Silas, the Admiral asked why had the Knights been removed from base.

"I've waited to see if anyone in the military would honor our agreement and when that didn't happen, I handled it myself," Silas - Tyrese, said.

"What do you mean? We've honored the agreement." The Admiral looked at the other two who nodded.

"Knights are supposed to have, at a minimum, 90 days off a calendar year. There are six months left in this year and after an audit was completed yesterday, none have had 30 days."

The Admiral opened his mouth and snapped it shut.

"So I pulled them, sent them on a well-deserved vacation."

"For 90 days?" the Admiral sounded apoplectic.

"No, just 30," Tyrese said in a cavalier tone that sounded so much like Silas, Jasmine smiled.

The Admiral's cheeks reddened as he drew himself up. "Thirty days? All of them? Can't you stagger them out, work up a rotation?"

"Why didn't your department do that?" Silas countered.

"I assure you I, we, had no idea this happened. But I will look into it. Can you leave a team for emergencies?"

"No. I've given everyone vacation, they've earned it and I won't go back on my word." Tyrese hardened his voice. "I never should've had to get involved, but if I want to make sure my men are taken care of, seems I'll have to keep a closer eye on them."

"Is there a way to have a team or two return in a few weeks, then start a rotation roster? There are assignments …"

"Use your own men, mine are on vacation. They need a break, as their Alpha, I'm giving them one," Tyrese said mimicking Silas to perfection.

"Please reconsider the 30 days and allow a team or two to return in a few weeks? I'll submit a rotation roster for you, Generals Crall and Miller as well as your handlers here at the Pentagon, that way you'll be able to monitor the vacation status of your Knights."

Tyrese paused in apparent thought. "I'll get back to you within the week on that. Submit the roster to the Generals. Good bye, Gentlemen."

"Good bye, La Patron," the Admiral said in a deflated tone.

Before she left the hidden area, Jasmine reviewed everything that was said in her mind. Tyrese tapped on the door.

She opened it and stepped out. No one spoke.

"What do you think?" Jasmine asked the other three.

Jacques shrugged. "I didn't pick up anything." He looked at the others. "Did you?"

Tyrese released a breath. "Seemed okay, but I'm not sure."

"Who else was in the room with them?" Asia asked.

Jasmine looked at Tyrese. "I didn't see anyone, did you?"

He shook his head slowly. "The camera was tight, just on the three."

"Now that you mention it, we couldn't see who else was there or even what room they were in. Normally we see the crest, the flag, something showing their authority." Jacques sounded puzzled. "I don't recall seeing any of that."

"Me neither," Asia said.

"Which could mean there were others in the room they didn't want Silas to see," Jasmine said, thinking it through.

"Or, they were someplace and didn't want him to know where," Asia said.

"Good point," Jasmine said. "Did the Admiral seem really alarmed when he learned how long the men would be gone?"

"He did," Jacques said. "I don't think they expected La Patron to hit from the contract angle, which was genius by the way."

"What did they have planned for our Knights?" Asia asked sitting on the corner of Silas' sofa in the outer office.

"Something Silas wouldn't agree to. Which means we need to get those four away from them before they decide to keep them for more tests," Jasmine said.

"Have you heard from La Patron?" Jacques asked.

"No. He'll let me know when they reach Central America, or when they arrive in Honduras. In the mean-time, in addition to keeping the Compound safe, we need to make sure everyone believes Silas, Angus and Hawke are here."

"Yes, Ma'am," Tyrese and Asia said.

"Yes, agreed," Jacques said.

CHAPTER SIX

Admiral Bents sat quietly at the conference table as the monitor went dark. He glanced at the other two officers who sat beside him during the call. Silas Knight was an arrogant prick. Son of a bitch found a loop hole in the contract and pulled all his men. How long before they realized four were missing?

"Well, that's done." He looked at the others. "Seems we have to wait for him to get back to us or the month. Reassign what you can, and hold the rest." The two men sitting next to him nodded, pushed back and stood.

"Don't know how we missed not giving them their vacations," one of the men said as he headed toward the door. "Should've been on top of that."

"We'll get it fixed, won't happen again," Bents said wanting them to leave so he and General Lee could talk.

"Is he planning to pull the program?"

That surprised Bents. "I don't think so. What makes you ask that?"

"Seems he's becoming less and less tolerant of mistakes. Our mistakes. To pull everybody at once, he's got to know it's going to cause a problem. There are certain jobs only his people can do."

Bents bit back a caustic remark and nodded. "I'm sure he's aware of that."

"You think he'll change it to two or three weeks?" the hopeful sound in the General's voice irritated Bents. As the most powerful Army in the world, they shouldn't depend on anyone.

"Possibly. I'll send a message to his office in a week to see if he's changed his mind," Bents lied. It wasn't that he hated the dual-natureds, he appreciated what they'd done for the country. And if a war broke out, La Patron and his people would defend this country with their dying breath. They all knew and accepted that.

But the idea that no one could control La Patron or the Wolf Nation, that they operated as a separate Nation within the United States bothered him and a few others. The new President had been fascinated when he learned of the wolves. He'd spent hours watching tapes of their fighting abilities and all but drooled over the prime real estate they owned. Bents had answered every question but realized there would be more.

When the call came, the President asked about offensive measures to protect humans from the wolves, Bents mentioned some ideas he and a few others wanted to pursue. Once he received the green light from the Oval Office, they'd been anxious to start testing.

Most of the members of the Joint Chiefs voted against offensive testing against the Wolf Nation and had no idea of the clandestine research project General Lee headed. Past experience with a pissed off Silas Knight made it imperative to keep the project secret.

Once the door closed, Lee stood and walked to the conference table. "Sir, if I may have a few moments of your time, I'd like to speak with you on a few matters."

Bents nodded and stood. Together they left the conference room and headed to Bents office. Inside, Bents sat at a much smaller table and waved to Lee to join him.

"Well? What did you think?" Bents asked.

"On one hand, I don't like the timing of pulling all the Knights. I don't believe in coincidences. But listening to him, the arrogance of believing he pulled one over on us... it's possible that's all it is. Plus, we've noticed no movement from the Compound. Our people in town near La Patron's Compound haven't heard anything, they haven't locked it down, staff's still coming and going."

"Which means he didn't get the signal you sent begging for help," the Admiral said disappointed. They'd been working on hijacking the pack's internal communications systems for decades without success.

"He didn't hear from his Knights either. So we've learned how to keep them from communicating," Lee said.

Bents snorted. "That only works with them drugged. We can't drug all of them, plus it doesn't work on half-breeds, just full-bloods."

"There's something new," Lee said into the silence. "A researcher named Gent modified some of the Liege's old equipment and developed a patch. He thinks the patch could disrupt the communication signal and give us control over the full-blood for short periods of time."

Bents straightened and met Lee's worried gaze.

"But it's risky."

"What kind of control are you talking about? The kind Silas Knight has over his pack? Or a few hours while they're out in the field on assignment?"

Lee shook his head slowly. "He doesn't know, it hasn't been tested. But he thinks it would be along the lines of Alpha dominance."

That sounded good. To have a group of dual-natureds to use at their discretion was the gold ring.

"What do you think of the research? Is it solid?" Bents asked.

"Yes. Gent's good. High security, excellent credentials. He's been working on this for the past eight years and is excited because this formulation is stabilized. His team feels this will work." He shrugged. "It's the closest we've gotten in all this time, just might work."

"What kind of tests does he need to run?" They had four drugged Knights hidden at a facility in Honduras, not the most peaceful place, but harder to infiltrate because of all the violence.

They planned to release the soldiers today. But with the others away on vacation for a month, who knew when they'd have an opportunity to test this new drug.

"Several and there's no telling how long it would take. But, if we don't release the Knights today, we run the risk of La Patron finding out they're missing."

Bents understood the danger of that. "He'll contact us to ask questions. I can hold him off for a day or so. We can appease him by saying we're looking for the men. That can buy us at least two, three days at the most before he stops talking and starts acting. If testing started immediately, that should be enough time." The more he thought about it, the more he liked the idea of running the tests beneath La Patron's nose.

Lee nodded slowly and pulled out his phone. "I'll contact Gents, have him start right away. They'll need to move the Knights to the research lab near the mountains, I'll have a team accompany them."

"Go there yourself to oversee everything," Bents said. "I have to stay here to deal with La Patron and any fall out. But I want your eyes and ears on-site to make sure we know if it works or not. If the first two tests fail, pull it and get those Knights back here for release. Don't keep them any longer than necessary. Remember, they're our soldiers."

"Yes, Sir."

CHAPTER SEVEN

Silas, Angus, and Hawke, appeared as three old Spanish men walking quietly through the airport after passing through customs. They picked up three rental cars and drove several miles out of town to the house Jacques secured for them late last night. Hawke had been first in their convoy and stopped in front of a black iron gate barring entrance. Once he opened the gate, he waved for Silas and Angus to enter. Silas parked in the carport, Angus beside him and Hawke behind them.

"Just two homes on this street," Silas told the others pleased with the isolated location. The more populated areas were wracked with gang violence. A few years past, the country's murder rate averaged 20 a day which was ridiculous, even for humans. The sad part was nothing much was done about it. Silas didn't want to get caught in the web of treachery during his short visit and made sure they were a distance from the capital, and other major cities.

"Yeah, it's great," Angus said as he grabbed his bag from the trunk. "I'll get set up inside, Hawke you on security?"

Hawke opened a bag and started pulling out equipment. Individually they appeared like clothes hangers and passed through customs without a problem. Once Hawke put them together, they would form a strong scanner and assist in identifying the best places to install security features. "Yes."

Inside the yellow and brown house were four bedrooms and one and a half baths. A large dining room was located off one of the smallest kitchens Silas had seen in years. Grateful they'd been able to secure private lodgings on such short notice, he didn't voice his displeasure at the dingy, broken furniture or cracks in the tile floor. With the Goddess' help, they'd be here less than 48 hours, so he would ignore the unpleasant accommodations.

"*Jasmine,*" Silas said as he entered a bedroom at the end of the hall and dropped his bag on the small bed. He morphed into his modified Silas persona. He preferred not to use anyone else's body unless he absolutely had to. His modified form kept his height, physique, hair color and length. His face was more rounded, his eyes a nondescript brown and he lacked the swagger of La Patron.

"*Silas,* you're there?" she asked sounding relieved reminding him of David's advice.

"*Yes. Took a little longer to get to Texas to catch the flight to Honduras but we made it just under the eight-hour window we gave ourselves. Everything okay?*"

He smiled as she shared having breakfast with the kids. It disappeared when she told him about the meeting with the Joint Chiefs and her suspicions.

"*All in all, we think they bought it. Either you have more breathing room to find the men…*"

"*Or we need to bust our asses before they decide to run more tests on their limited supply.*" He cursed their lying, deceitful asses.

"*Bird in the hand better than five in the bush,*" she said.
"*What? Birds?*"
"*It's an old saying which means I agree with you.*"
"*Okay. As long as they think I'm at the Compound, they'll think they have time. Good thinking by the way. I'm sure Tyrese did a great imitation of me.*"

"*He had you down to that bored scowl you wear just for the Joint Chiefs.*" She laughed. "*I miss you. I couldn't sleep last*" *night. This is the first time we've been separated this long since we mated."*

"Since we had sex the first time," he corrected. *"I never spent a day without you after that, sleeping on the couch doesn't count."*

She chuckled. The sound warmed him. *"We're going into town in a few minutes to find officers to access the base and get a feel for the place. Hawke wants to find someone with a high clearance to connect to their main computer system."*

"Sounds good." She yawned. *"Renée, Rose, Shyla and Asia are coming over later to do some baking. I hope I can stay awake."*

"Get some rest, let them do most of it." He smiled when she laughed.

"No one bakes in my kitchen without me, you know that."

"I do. Get some rest, I'll talk to you later."

"Love you," she said.

"Love you too," he said and disconnected. Pleased that all was well on the home front, Silas strode into the den where Angus set up his equipment.

"Almost ready," Angus said.

Silas nodded and took a seat.

Hawke walked in. *"Security's checked and online. Blockers are up."*

"Good. Let me see the bios of the officers at the base." Hawke handed him the folder. They'd reviewed them during the long flight but hadn't decided who would be the best choice to get the information they needed. Their first choice would be one of the officers who spent a lot of time off base.

Silas told them about the Joint Chiefs contacting him while they were in the air.

Angus grunted and turned on the computer.

Hawke smiled and continued going through the files.

"Military personnel live on base and spend a lot of time in town, that would be the place to find them," Angus said.

"Major Gillian Franz, 53, single, no kids, 5'10, 190 lbs., muscular build, brown hair and eyes. Round face, no tats or

marks," Silas said looking at a page. *"The Commanding Officer for the base is away leaving Franz in charge."*

"On it," Angus said. *"He's been seen off base in the early evenings around four, that may be when his shift's over. We can hit the bars he frequents, might get lucky, otherwise we may need to take a local who works on base and work our way up."* Angus looked at Silas.

"That could get risky, too many bodies," Angus said.

Silas agreed but they were short on time and with military personnel living on base they were short on options.

"Petre Salvador," Hawke said. *"Works communications, high clearance. Weighs 165, stands 5'8, brown hair, brown eyes, round face. Must be a thing here."*

Angus clicked a few keys. *"Good choice. He's single, local. Take him from his home."*

Angus had improved the chameleon so that when they merged with a person, the individual didn't realize they'd been hijacked and would still function if allowed. This improvement allowed Silas and the others to go human deep, and still communicate via their links. Plus, some levels of their wolf abilities, like smell and keen eyesight, continued to work. Afterward, they could leave the person intact with no memory of being taken or having a dual personality. The one downside is the hijack couldn't last longer than five days. After that period, the host started to die.

Hawke nodded slowly. *"Sounds good, I'll take him tonight before he goes in for his shift. I'll need you to drop me off near his home, he rides a bike to work."*

"Where does he live?" Silas asked.

"Two and a half miles from here," Angus said.

Hawke stood and left the living area with his bags.

"Franz is our main target. As an officer, he should know something about the Knights or any odd tests or happenings on post." Silas looked at Angus, who nodded.

"Shouldn't be too hard to find." Franz, twice divorced, had a reputation as a lady's man and frequented the local bars when he was off.

Hawke returned to the living room and did a few stretches. *"Ready?"*

"Just about." Silas stood, stretched and watched Angus as he continued gathering information on pertinent staff.

"Franz's shift is over but he hasn't left the base yet. If we hurry, we might be able to follow him once he leaves," Angus said.

"Sounds good." Silas wanted to know what happened to his pack and who was responsible. The sooner he had answers, the sooner he'd make sure it never happened again.

Angus shut down and locked the system. He took the equipment with him into one of the back rooms. A few moments later he returned. Silas' brow rose as Angus changed his appearance to a woman Silas had never seen before wearing snug fitting jeans and a short top

"Don't ask," Angus said as he adjusted his stacked heel shoes.

Hawke whistled.

Silas chuckled at the finger Angus gave Hawke. Since Angus appeared as a woman to lure Franz, Silas morphed into a large male, hoping he'd blend in as a human tourist.

"You plan to knock on Salvador's door as an old Spanish man?" Silas asked pointing to Hawke's current form.

"I hope we get there early enough for me to check-out his neighbors, see which homes are occupied before I approach his house. I don't want anyone to get suspicious," Hawke said. *"Plus, no one pays attention to stooped, old men."*

Silas nodded as he looked at his watch. *"Let's go."* He and Angus strode toward the cars. Silas drove Hawke's rental since it was parked behind the other car. Angus took his rental and pulled out the driveway.

"I'll meet you there," Angus told Silas.

"Okay," Silas said as Hawke keyed in the address for Salvador into the GPS.

When they reached the end of the street, Silas and Hawke turned right, Angus turned left.

"You'll be the first one on base," Silas said as they turned down a dirt road with several homes, in close proximity to each

other. Every house had bars. Metal bars covered windows, doors and gates. Hawke would need to be really careful.

"Salvador reports to work in a few hours, and works all night. I should be able to tap into the main database to search for our Knights," Hawke said, his voice and commitment solid.

Silas nodded and hoped they could find the men quickly and leave so he could unleash his anger on the Joint Chiefs. They drove past Salvador's home, a small white building behind an iron gate and stone wall.

"I sense one heartbeat," Hawke said. *"He's alone. There are too many people around to jump over his fence, someone lives behind and beside him."*

Silas nodded and pulled over to the side of the road to watch the street activity. A package delivery truck made its way slowly down the street. Silas looked at Hawke. *"That may be your only way inside. Go inside with the driver."*

Hawke opened the door, morphing into a slender muscular man as he did and jogged down the street. When he reached the truck, he shook hands with the driver and stepped inside. When the truck stopped in front of Salvador's home, the delivery man stepped out, rang the bell and waited.

Moments later, Salvador strode outside. Hawke, now dressed similarly to the driver, hopped out, went to the back of the truck and lifted three large boxes. When Salvador tried to read the names on the box, Hawke placed them in the driver's hand and touched Salvador. Anyone looking on would think the three men were having a nice conversation. Salvador opened the gate to allow the two men inside.

Silas watched to see if anyone came outside or watched from their windows but saw no signs of activity. A few moments later the driver returned with the large boxes, placed them in the back of the truck and drove off.

"Everything okay?" Silas asked Hawke.

"Yes, he's an interesting character. Hates his job because he must support so many others and is forced to live in this area. But he has access to the information we need. I'll follow his routine and get inside the base, and search the data to find our men," Hawke said.

"Watch out, this area's congested, neighbors might be watching. I'm headed to the bar to back up Angus. Let me know if you need anything." Silas pulled away from the curb and drove slowly down the road and out of the neighborhood.

"Will do," Hawke said.

With the GPS giving clear directions, Silas made his way to Main Street and headed toward the bar Franz often frequented.

"I'm pulling into the parking lot now," he told Angus after telling him about Hawke's success.

"Franz' car isn't here."

Silas parked in the back of the lot with a good view of the entrance. He did a sweep, searching for full bloods. There were a few in the shopping center nearby and some inside the bar.

"Full-bloods."

A few seconds later Angus spoke. *"We're human deep, they shouldn't pick up anything. Who's the Alpha for this area?"*

Silas shrugged. Protocol dictated him introducing himself to the Alpha and asking permission to seek his Knights while in another's territory. Silas hadn't given it a thought until now. *"Not sure. How long should we wait?"*

"Don't know. The information we have on his social activities is sketchy. I'd say an hour here, if we miss him, then hit the other place..

Time crawled. At the hour mark Silas started the car. *"Looks like a lot of people are leaving."*

"Shift change maybe?" Angus asked.

Unconcerned about human behavior, Silas pulled out of the parking lot.

"Wait," Angus yelled. *"That's him. Franz is pulling in now. Come back."*

Silas drove down the one-way street, turned and headed for the bar. Angus walked into the bar as Silas returned to the parking lot. *"Full-bloods."* He noticed three males head inside.

"I see them," Angus said as he stepped inside. *"Franz is at the bar, I'm going to start a conversation with him. See if I can find out anything."*

"Okay," Silas said taking his time walking into the dim bar. Inhaling, he realized there weren't any humans inside. He took a

seat in the back at a small table and assessed the place. Less than ten people milled around the front. All full-bloods. Someone turned on loud music.

"Do you want something to drink?" the waitress asked.

Silas glanced at her name tag, Raven and nodded. "Gin and tonic."

She looked over her shoulder, leaned forward. Her dark ponytail swayed against her back. Darker, deep set eyes in an ordinary oval face stared at him. "It's getting late, you might want to get something to drink closer to town."

That surprised him. "Where in town?"

Raven bit her lip in consideration before glancing at the others sitting at the table. "The hotel in town's nice, the big one, can't miss it. Safer there at night. You should go there." She turned to leave.

"Thanks. I will, after my gin and tonic."

She nodded and walked off. Slender in jeans and a short-sleeved tee with the name of the bar on the back, he wondered about her age. She looked younger than his girls.

"This is strange," Angus said. *"I'm having a hard time reading him. Shouldn't be like this. I'm skeptical to go deeper."*

"Go deeper, we need information," Silas said leaning forward and clasping his hands together on the table. *"Hawke, how's it going?"*

"I'm getting dressed. I'm leaving Salvador in bed asleep. If anyone comes to check they'll see a naked delivery man. How are things there?"

Angus is touching Franz, lots of full-bloods, and I've been warned to go into town for a drink where it's safer," Silas said.

"Safer? For humans?" Hawke asked.

"I suppose." Silas sensed three full-bloods enter the club before he saw them. Their energy was slightly different. The female stopped and stumped toward the bar. *"We have a situation here."*

"Do you need me?" Hawke asked.

"No. We've got it." Silas disconnected.

"What the hell are you doing letting this bitch touch you?" the full-blood female yelled. Dressed in tight jeans, a short top and black combat boots, the bottle store blond stopped all conversation with her comments. Silas tried to get a better look at her but couldn't.

"Tasha, stop," Franz said holding up his hand, disengaging Angus in the process.

"He has some kind of block, took a minute to get beneath it. He's linked to the wolves in this area. Rogue. The military doesn't know about it. They've got an underground gang going on. He's dirty," Angus said.

"Stop? I come here, on my turf by the way, see my man all cozy with some woman and all you say is stop? I'm kicking ass today," Tasha said. Her chest rose and fell as if she needed more air to speak.

Angus remained on his stool, ignoring the battle brewing next to him.

"Shit," Silas said. *"Blocked? A human?"*

"Yeah, there's nothing that'll get him to share whatever secrets he holds. With more time, I could find out but I'd need to take him completely over, there'd be nothing left," Angus said.

Silas swore. They didn't want to destroy life if they could help it. Especially a human officer.

Franz stood and walked toward the muscular female. "Tasha, not here. You know better." He looked at the other two men who had walked in with her. "I had a late meeting on post, Duke, you got my message?"

One of the men nodded and sat at a nearby table. "That's why we just got here."

Franz looked at Tasha who seemed to have trouble controlling her wolf. He stroked her arm and leaned into her.

"Can you hear what he's telling her?" Silas asked Angus.

"He's calming her beast, telling her to breathe and control it. Someone's coming tonight from D.C., that's why he's late. He's concerned because this person is a high-ranking officer. He's concerned it may affect whatever they've got going on."

"Really? Did you get a name?" Silas asked.

"Major General Robert Lee."

Silas contacted Jacques to run a background check on Lee. The waitress put Silas' drink on the table. He gave her a large bill. "Keep the change."

Her smile widened as she pocketed the money. "Gracias. You should leave after your drink."

"I will, thanks." He stirred the drink as she walked off and pushed it aside.

"How will we handle this new distraction with him and these full-bloods?" Silas asked Angus.

"I don't think he's a good candidate," Angus said sounding disappointed. *"There's something going on with him and this bunch. We don't need this. We'll grab someone else."*

Angus stood and walked toward the exit ignoring Franz and the others. Before she reached the door a large full-blood stepped in front of her. "I'm available, sweetness."

"For?" Angus asked in a hard, feminine voice.

"Whatever you want," he said offering his hand.

Angus took his hand and they walked out. Silas watched the patrons in the bar for a few moments, noticed more full-bloods had entered. Franz, the only human, sat at the table with Tasha and the other two full-bloods who had entered with her as if it was the most natural thing in the world to be in the midst of wolves.

Without taking a sip of the drugged gin and tonic, Silas stood and walked out the bar. Several full-bloods stared at him as he took his time walking down the steps toward his car. Angus stood nearby talking or pretending to talk to the full-blood from inside. He patted him on the cheek and sent him away before sliding into the driver's seat of his vehicle. *"They're dealing all sorts of shit to the human gangs. Their gang runs this section of town. The cops leave them alone as long as the politicians gets their share of money."* He pulled out of the parking lot.

"No big surprise there. We are not getting involved in that BS. Let's go into town, maybe we'll find someone who has to work on base tomorrow." Silas slid into the driver's seat. They left the parking lot and headed into town, fully aware they were being followed.

####

Silas sat at the hotel bar eating a steak while Angus talked to an active duty serviceman. The full bloods who had followed them had sat in the back of the bar watching quietly. Silas had expected questions or some kind of altercation from the wolves but they left an hour after they arrived.

Angus grew more and more frustrated with the soldier's low level of knowledge. *"It won't do any good to use this one either, none of these guys security clearances will get us far. We'd be hopping from body to body to upgrade and that's not good with the down time they need to recover,"* Angus said his frustration lingering in their link.

Silas wasn't opposed to dropping bodies, however, he was opposed to anyone discovering the chameleon bracelets. *"Maybe Hawke will have something for us soon, or he could get us on base as Contractors or something."* U. S. Military personnel were required to live on base, but not additional staff or Contractors who handled a lot of jobs there.

"Hope so," Angus groused as he pretended to listen to the obnoxious soldier.

Thirty minutes later, Angus abruptly and left the table. *"I'm done,"* he told Silas without acknowledging the drunk soldier begging him to return. *"How, forget that, why do women put up with this shit?"*

"Hawke, you got anything?" Silas asked when Angus sat next to him at the bar. *"Angus is about to kick asses in an un-ladylike manner in this place."*

"I believe so. One second let me verify two things."

Silas shared Hawke's message with Angus.

"Thank the Goddess, patch me in to listen when he contacts you," Angus murmured and then took a long pull from his bottle of beer.

Moments later Hawke returned. *"A flight heading to D.C. was canceled earlier yesterday, there was no passenger list which made me suspicious, plus the cancellation happened not long after Rese talked to the Joint Chiefs."*

"Shit," Angus said.

"Tomorrow there's a convoy scheduled to move special cargo from the base to a secure research facility that's shared jointly with the Honduran government and the U.S. near the foot of the mountains. General Lee arrives later and will be in charge of the move and the facility."

"Sounds like they changed their minds to send our men home after realizing you weren't searching for them," Angus said.

Silas grunted. He would make sure they paid for that miscalculation.

Hawke continued. *"Salvador made the assignments for the research facility. I've already picked two single men for you. They're civilian Contractors who live near the capital and work at the lab."*

"Good." Silas and Angus listened as Hawke rattled off more information.

Silas stood, tossed a few bills on the bar and walked out as Hawke gave him the name and address of a contractor who worked at the facility. *"On it,"* Silas said as he strode to his car with Angus following. Moments later they left downtown.

"Have you heard anything from Jacques about General Lee?" Angus asked Silas.

"Not yet. I'll check and then take the contractor." He drove toward the capital, Tegucigalpa.

"Okay, it'll be good to know a little more about him before he arrives," Angus said.

Silas paused. *"Hawke?"*

"Sir?"

"What do you know about Lee?"

"Entered the Air Force through the Reserve Officer Training Corps program in 1986 where he earned a Bachelor's Degree in Political Science from North Carolina State University, Raleigh. He has commanded at the squadron, group, and wing levels. He served as Deputy Director of the Secretary and Chief of Staff of the Air Force Executive Action Group; and as Senior Military Assistant to the Under Secretary of Defense for Intelligence. He was also the Vice Commander and Commander of the 341st Missile Wing, Malmstrom Air Force Base, Montana, and the Commander of the 45th Space Wing and Director of the Eastern

Range, Patrick Air Force Base, Florida. Prior to his current assignment, General Lee served as the Deputy Director of the National Reconnaissance Office, Chantilly, Virginia."

"His current assignment?" Silas asked.

"Hmm, when I cut through the BS, he's on special assignment at the Pentagon," Hawke said.

"Was he assigned to the Knight's program?" Angus asked.

"Nothing in his file regarding that," Hawke said a few moments later.

"Thanks," Silas said.

CHAPTER EIGHT

Hawke sent word the convoy had left the base under guard five hours later. Silas and Angus arrived at the research facility within minutes of each other. Pat Keener, short on stature with a slight limp walked through security thinking of the day and hoping he would secure release for the four Knights enroute to this location. It wasn't that Silas had a problem with Keener's body, which he now shared. Or the extreme orderly way the man kept his home. But the ex-pat from California's borderline fanaticism with porn, weird animalistic porn, twisted Silas' stomach. He pushed down the images that kept surfacing and tried to lock them down without success.

"How the hell did this asshole get a clearance?" Silas asked Angus as he walked down the concrete hall, returning nods and "good mornings".

Angus snorted. *"Puedes, the guy I took over, wasn't much better, but on the opposite end, religious zealot. He had more statutes of saints than I've ever seen. Every room in his house filled with candles and small statutes. Even had an altar in his bedroom. No wonder he's single."*

Silas noticed security guards standing about and wondered if they were because of the General and his cargo or normal protection. A brief search of Keener's memories answered his question. Security had been enhanced. Were they expecting trouble? *"Eyes open, I want my Knights out of here today if possible,"* Silas said. *"Hawke, did you find out anything else about the security in this place?"*

"No much. It's jointly owned with the Honduras government and a private company. They allow the military to use it for tests. The security component is more vague; I'll keep looking but you may have better luck than me."

"I hear cameras everywhere," Angus said.

"What part of the facility are you in?" Silas asked.

"The lab. It's set up like an operating room. Puedes assists doctors in their experiments which may be the reason for the altar. He goes home to get the stench of blood off him," Angus said.

"I'm not that far in, damn it," Silas fumed. *"I'm alone in the pharmacy right now. If someone doesn't come soon, I'm heading to the lounge area to get information."*

"Be careful, we can't get kicked out of here for breaking rules, not yet," Angus cautioned.

Silas exhaled and allowed Keener's personality to surface. The distasteful images rose along with the knowledge of what Silas needed to do to blend in. He picked up the clipboard and verified stock while waiting to hear news regarding the Knights.

"They're here," Angus said 20 minutes later.

"Did you get a visual?" Silas stopped moving and tried to connect with his pack.

"No, but the energy's changed. Puedes' been called to another room for a meeting," Angus said.

"I can't sense them yet," Silas said as he made another attempt at contacting his Knights.

"Stop," Angus said.

"What?" Silas asked.

"Somehow they can sense when someone is trying to reach them. The General's face whitened a few seconds ago as he looked at an electronic pad. He ran into the room where the

Knights are being guarded by soldiers. They're moving from there just that quick," Angus said.

"You saw them?" Silas asked, desperate to know his men were alive.

"A glimpse but it's them."

"Good. How can we take them?"

"That's going to require some planning if you don't want anyone to know you're here or about our ability to change with the chameleon," Angus said slowly.

Silas cursed at the delay and nodded to the person dropping off papers. *"Hawke, they've arrived but have been taken somewhere."* He shared the information regarding the General from Angus. *"Is there a way to block disrupt the pad so I can try to connect with our men?"*

"I'll look into it. Franz is here at the base and he's not happy. Something strange is going on with that guy," Hawke said.

Silas didn't care about Franz.

"He's asking all kinds of questions about the convoy, who was in it, where they went, all kinds of stuff he shouldn't be asking out loud. Insubordination is just one thing they'll bust his ass on," Hawke said. *"I think he plans to come out there. You sure we can't take him?"*

Silas thought about it. *"He's involved with the local pack, they don't know we're here and I'd prefer to keep it that way."*

"Can Angus get a visual of the General's toy?" Hawke asked.

The change in subject took Silas a moment. *"Angus can you get a visual for Hawke of that pad?"*

"I'll try."

"Send it to Hawke when you do, and let me know if you learn anything else about where they moved my men." Silas ran his hand through his hair forgetting how short the muddy brown strands were.

"Will do," Angus said.

Silas turned to fill a few orders when the door opened and General Lee strode inside. Silas immediately allowed Keener's personality to rise. "General, good to see you."

The General smiled, although it never reached his eyes. He wasn't tall, a few inches over Keener's 5'7", with light brown eyes wide set apart in a face that spent a lot of time outdoors. "Keener, how's life been treating you since you moved south of the border?"

"Very good, Sir." He stepped aside and opened two locked drawers. "Here's your shipment. Came in three days ago." Keener lifted three small sealed boxes and handed them to the General.

The General inspected the seals before waving to one of the soldiers who stood nearby to take the boxes. Keener met General Lee's gaze. *"The General is in the pharmacy, stand by to see that pad,"* Silas told Hawke.

"Things okay at the base?" Keener asked although Silas knew the man didn't care one way or the other.

"Yes. Have there been any problems here with the locals?" the General asked and lifted his pad to stare at it before allowing it to drop to his side. In that moment, Silas captured the image and sent it to Hawke.

"Major Franz has been dealing with them. From what I've heard they've come to several agreements but no volunteers have come in yet. We're stocked and ready."

The General rocked back and forth on his heels. "Franz. Hmm, I'll need to talk to him before I leave."

"How long will you be here this time?" Keener asked. "Long enough for a game?" The two men often played poker for hours.

"No, this is a quick trip, I'm afraid. Maybe next time," Lee said as he nodded and walked out the door.

"Did you see his device?" Silas asked Hawke as he snatched control from Keener.

"Yes, I'm running checks now but it may be something customized for one function. They may be further along in their research than we know. I'll work on something to shield your search so it doesn't broadcast," Hawke said.

"Will it stop him from knowing when I'm seeking my men?" Silas asked, needing reassurance.

"Depends on what technology they're using. If they've injected or implanted a device that sends an alert, we may not be

able to get around that. If they've put a collar or something external to block you, the shield will by-pass that. Right now, without knowing more, it's the best I can do," Hawke said.

"Thanks. Let's start with that and move forward." He told Hawke the chemicals the General had picked and wasn't surprised when Hawke whistled. *"Not good, huh?"*

"Not at all. Those are all illegal in the States. I can't imagine what he's planning to do with those."

"I'm positive he's going to use those to test the Knights. We need to find out what he's up to and stop him. Has Franz left the base?" Silas asked.

"I'm not sure, why?"

Silas told him of the conversation with Lee.

"They're negotiating with the local wolves? For what?"

"I don't know. Besides, Franz was dating one of the wolves and may have a separate deal going on. We're working in the dark here. But if I have to use them to get my men out I will," Silas said.

"We're doing another test in an hour," Angus said. *"Doctor Grenwald and Lee are meeting about it right now. Me and two others are setting up the room. Five tables with heavy steel body restraints for the neck, arms, legs and torso have been brought in. I'm getting the impression from my host that this is new."*

"No. Fuck No," Silas gritted as he struggled to keep his wolf at bay. He inhaled, tapped into his beast and searched for his Knights.

"Alpha?" the voice sounded weak but the wolf responded to Silas' wolf.

"Don't speak, just relax," Silas said as he sought connections with the others.

"Silas whatever you're doing is causing Lee to shit bricks," Angus warned. *"He just moved up the tests."*

Silas released the Knights and inhaled. He couldn't allow more tests on his pack, he could not. Moving into the hall, he headed toward the staff lounge, intent on taking another body to get to the Knights. He bumped into someone and was shoved back so hard he slammed into a wall.

"Watch where you're going," Major Franz growled, sounding like a wolf.

Silas reached out and noticed there were full-bloods outside. Blood dripped from his nose as he made his way to the bathroom, made sure it was empty and locked the door. Thankfully there were no cameras. He reached out and pulled every full-blood within a mile radius toward the lab. After unlocking the door, he headed back to the pharmacy and waited.

"Hawke if you have something that can block my transmission I'd like it now, otherwise Lee will be dead and we'll have to answer questions we're not ready to answer," Silas said fighting down his anger over the treatment of his men.

"Yes, Sir. I'm working on it."

Screams from the corridor, a siren and clanging metal meant the wolves had arrived and from the sound of things they were angry. Silas bit back a smile and allowed his host, Keener, to deal with the fallout. The door opened and closed. A thin, white male laid against the door, taking deep breaths.

"It's crazy out there."

"What happened?" Keener asked sounding scared.

"Men, big men, some with huge dogs, just broke through security."

"What? Are you sure? Why?" His host wondered if it were Franz's full-bloods.

"Don't know, but they're pissed. Really pissed." The man shuddered, turned and put his ear against the door. "I think they've passed now. If I were you, I'd stay in here behind the glass." He left the room as quietly as he had entered.

"What's going on, Angus?" Silas took a seat at the desk in the back office and turned on the computer.

"The tests are on hold, there's some kind of problem." Angus paused. *"I sense a lot of full-bloods. Did you call them?"*

"Wolf to wolf, shouldn't have registered on Lee's device," Silas said.

"No, you're right. The device works with something on the Knights. Well, you've bought some time, what next?"

"Hawke's working on something that should work as a dampener of sorts so I can boost their energies and help them

escape. One thing is certain, no tests. Period. We tear the place down first," Silas said.

"It may come down to that, so I'll start working in that direction," Angus said.

"Keener?" A soldier entered the pharmacy.

"Yes?" Silas said confused.

"General Lee wants to see you."

Pleasantly surprised, Silas allowed Keener's personality to rise and kept a tight rein on his beast. He followed the soldiers down a long corridor, turned right and feigned surprise by the large number of full-bloods growling behind the glass door and spilling into the hall.

"Step aside," the soldier in front of him said. "Let us through."

The full-bloods didn't move, both the soldier and Silas brushed against them to reach the door ahead. The soldier knocked and after being told to enter, opened the door. General Lee sat on the corner of a desk and watched as Silas, Keener, shuffled forward.

"You wanted to see me, Sir?" He looked at the three other men in the room and then at the General.

"What happened to your face?" General Lee asked.

Silas' hand flew to his face. "I hit the wall. Thought I cleaned it."

"You did," Lee said. "Did this man knock you into the wall?" He pointed at a scowling Franz who sat in a chair in the corner.

"Yes, Sir." Silas frowned at Franz before looking at Lee. "Is there a problem?"

"Yes, but we'll deal with it. I just needed to verify his story. Put a liquid bandage on that." He pointed toward Keener's face.

Heat flowed up Silas' neck. "Yes, Sir." He turned and headed toward the door.

"Have you noticed anything different this morning?" the General asked.

"Other than people running scared in the hall and those big gorillas outside this door? Nope, not a thing."

General Lee smiled and waved him away.

"I told you I didn't call them here," Franz growled. "I doubt anyone could do that."

"They say you did. I want to know how," the General said in a low voice.

Silas bit back a smile at the exchange as he moved slowly down the hall avoiding the full-bloods. He hadn't thought of the fall out over summoning the full-bloods and understood their anger over a human exercising that kind of control. He'd remember that.

"Where are you going?" a full blood with several tattoos sneered as he grabbed Silas' arm.

"To work," Silas said and tried to move forward.

"Where do you work?" the full-blood peered down, his wolf close to the surface.

Surprised at the level of public aggression, Silas didn't immediately respond. Instead he activated the chameleon to gain information.

"Let him go," a soldier yelled just as Silas was about to answer. "Let him go now." The click of guns ricocheted off the walls as the full-blood released him and stepped back.

Under the watchful eyes of two soldiers sent to escort him back to his office, Silas held back a frustrated sigh of not being able to learn more about the local wolves or search for his Knights.

"The tests are on hold for now," Angus said. *"Franz did something with the local wolves and is in trouble. According to the doc, they may use local wolves for the test, he's not sure. They're waiting for someone from the pack to make a decision."*

"Hawke should be almost done with the block or cloaking device," Silas said, more from the intent on rescuing his men than anything Hawke said.

"How's he going to get it to you? This place is locked down tight after the full-bloods stunt," Angus said.

Silas rubbed his forehead and took a seat in the back office. *"I don't know, but we need to get them out of here and go home."*

"Understood, but we don't want to answer any questions on how we blended in so well on this mission, there are cameras everywhere. Once we take the Knights, the Joint Chiefs will

watch the feed a million times to understand how it was done. We need to cover our tracks," Angus warned.

"Or find scapegoats," Silas said a few seconds later.

"The locals?" Angus asked.

"Seems only fair, they're already working for the government," Silas said.

"Do you know what they're up to?"

"They're expecting Franz to deliver something that will help their beasts be stronger, fight better. Same thing they all want."

"And they believe Franz, or the American government will help them?" Silas understood and agreed with Angus' skepticism.

"I didn't have a lot of time to get more, but that was the crux of it."

"Have they ever reached out to you? Or one of your Alphas?" Angus asked.

"No. I'll have Jacques verify that but nothing I recall."

"When did pack start turning to humans for answers? It makes no sense," Angus huffed. *"They're coming back. Keep me updated on Hawke."* He disconnected.

Silas stared at the monitor for several minutes. The Knights were somewhere in this building locked away. Security had just been doubled because he pulled several local wolves to the location. His Knights were booby rigged in a way that alerted their enemies whenever he attempted to contact them. At least he'd touched their wolves, eased them somewhat. How would he get them out of here and back home?

CHAPTER NINE

"What the hell happened? General Lee asked the two military men he left in charge to watch the Knights.

Frowning, they looked at him and then at the four men lying on the metal gurneys. "Nothing. They've been like this since we arrived, Sir."

Lee knew better but wasn't inclined to share any information with these men. Slowly, he approached the first of the four. Magnificent specimen. The ultimate weapons who always finished their tasks. Pity they weren't completely human and consequently could never be fully trusted.

If there was a way to break their connection to Silas Knight, change their allegiance to the military, then the United States would swiftly rise as the leading military faction in the world. He released a sigh as he touched the metal collar on their neck. The only thing standing between life and death. Death would be a mercy if Silas Knight had any idea what they'd done to these men or what he planned to do.

Dressed in military gear, knowing the history of their service and sacrifice, shamed Lee marginally. As Admiral Bents said, these were their soldiers. He needed to start the tests but first he needed assurance La Patron hadn't attempted to contact them. Uneasy, he looked at the Knights again.

"Move them below," he told the soldiers. "Take them all at once, get help, but never leave them alone and secure them down stairs."

"Yes, Sir."

He brushed pass the soldiers and headed to the office set aside for his use. He made the call.

Minutes later the Admiral contacted him. Lee explained what happened.

"Is it possible the tablet malfunctioned?" the Admiral asked.

"No. I don't believe so. We ran tests before leaving the Pentagon and again at the base. They're still drugged, still out of it but I'm concerned. The alarm ran for several seconds. Long enough for contact to be made. There's no way to tell if he's able to reach them in this condition or not," Lee said.

"What do you expect me to do?" the Admiral asked, clearly annoyed.

"Contact La Patron again, make sure he hasn't left West Virginia or that he's not asking questions. It's not a good idea to start the tests if he's curious. Right now, we can play off them being lost but once we start testing… we lose that excuse."

The Admiral released a long sigh. "No matter what we do, La Patron's going to be angry. It's best to get the tests done now because we'll never have this opportunity again. We may lose the entire program behind this, so let's make it count. We'll need something to appease the others."

Lee knew the Admiral would throw him under the bus with the loss of the Knights. The Joint Chiefs bragged on the excellence of the team who handled the toughest assignments in the military. There would be hell to pay when La Patron pulled the Knights, especially over illegal tests. Admiral Bents and a couple others deliberately broke faith of a binding agreement with the Wolf Nation by performing any type of tests on pack members. He knew the moment he signed on for this program it would eventually mean the end of his career. If he didn't genuinely believe they needed some type of weapon for leverage against the Wolf Nation, he never would've gotten involved.

"Yes, Sir," Lee said.

"I'll contact Knight one last time and let you know."

"Thank you, Sir." Lee disconnected and sat on his desk staring at the tablet. A sliver of cold air from the overhead vent wrapped around him sending chill bumps across his arms and chest. Could Silas Knight find his men in another country, thousands of miles away? Had he contacted them and was sending a rescue team? What impact did these collars have on the men? No one knew. What would happen if Silas Knight knew exactly what was going on?

He shuddered at the possible answer to that question.

CHAPTER TEN

Three hours later, Silas glanced at the clock and then at the door as it opened. "They're allowing us to leave for lunch, you going to the usual?" the same thin man from before asked.

"No. I've got a couple errands to run, see you when I get back." Silas turned his back to cover the diagram Hawke had sent detailing the blocker he'd crafted by reconfiguring a cloaking device he'd stolen on base.

The man nodded and closed the door.

"Hawke, I'm leaving for lunch, are you ready?" Eager to connect with the Knights again, Silas grabbed his keys, and locked everything before heading out the door. In the hall, he nodded greetings to associates as he locked the pharmacy with a sign stating they were closed for an hour.

"Yes. I left Salvador asleep at his place and will bring the device as a delivery to your home. On my way."

Silas moved with purpose toward the staff parking lot, slid into the front seat and drove toward Keener's place. He alerted Angus on his movements and ten minutes later pulled in front of the house, after unlocking the gate he drove into the carport. A neighbor, an elderly Spanish woman, waved as she walked into her gate and locked it behind her. Silas entered the house, checked on Keener who lay asleep in the guest room and waited for Hawke's delivery.

He didn't wait long. Silas wondered where Hawke got the brown van he parked in front of Keener's house. Seconds after ringing the gate buzzer, Silas strode outside to receive the package.

"Put it on your key ring, or necklace."

"I don't have a necklace. Keener doesn't wear them," Silas said as he signed for the package.

"Key ring then. The closer to you the better it'll block. It's not the best but should work. I've got to get back to Salvador, he's working a double, just came home for dinner. I'll keep monitoring flights and let you know of anything that'd impact the mission," Hawke said as he trotted back to the van.

"Find out all we can about the local pack," Silas reminded him.

"On it. They aren't organized, shouldn't be hard to use them as smoke screens," Hawke said as he drove off and Silas returned to the house. Inside he ate leftovers, added the small device to his keyring and sent a prayer for guidance to the Goddess.

"Silas?"

"Jasmine? What's wrong?" He sat at the dining table with his hands clasped together.

"You tell me. The Joint Chiefs wanted to speak to you again. That's twice in two days. When Rese spoke with them, they seemed perplexed and relieved. Here's the thing, they didn't really want anything. We believe they just wanted to make sure you were here. Did something happen?"

He updated her on everything and ended with Hawke's blocker.

"That explains a lot. They probably wanted to see if you were angry or had questions about the Knights. They think they have time to do those tests because you aren't asking questions. We planned to start asking about the Knights tomorrow. They'll put us off, we expect that, so be careful."

"I want to contact my Knights to let them know I will get them out of this." He paused. The anger over what they'd done to those men rose hard and fast. He fought down his beast.

"They know," Jasmine said. *"There's not a person who serves you who doesn't know you'll do whatever is required to save them."*

Silas wasn't so sure. Out of disgust for the Joint Chiefs, Silas had turned over the Knights program to others. After his daughter, Jackie, entered the program he'd been more involved. Had he been too late? Uncertainty robbed him of peace.

"Thank you, Sweet Bitch. I'm headed back into the lion's den for another four hours. Hopefully we'll have a plan to free our men because I cannot allow them to become military experiments."

"You'll think of something, you always do." She disconnected.

He wished he had her confidence as he contacted both Hawke and Angus to fill them in on Jasmine's news.

"They're getting antsy, we're on double shifts tonight. Grenwald's pissed," Angus said. *"I'm going to take him at break, and leave Puedes sleeping on the lounge sofa so it won't be so obvious. When he wakes, he won't remember much of his day. He's such a pious prick, he'll make up something, claiming a visitation from a higher power to cover his confusion. Silas, I need you to grab the body I left at his house when you get off."*

"As the doctor, you'll have better access to the Knights, right?" That would put eyes and ears where he needed them most.

"Yes, plus we'll find out what all of this is about. Grenwald's deep in these tests," Angus said sounding excited. *"He's the one we need to use."*

"Give me Puedes gate code so I can get in and out with the body," Silas said.

Angus gave him the information.

"I just passed through security with the device from Hawke. When's the best time to use it?" Silas asked Angus as he walked down the corridor to the pharmacy.

"Wait until I take the doctor's body and have access to the General to monitor his response. He's still dealing with Franz and the wolf pack."

Silas despised the delay but agreed with Angus' thinking.

"Hey," a large full-blood pointed at Silas. "You work the pharmacy?"

Silas nodded.

"Franz wants to see you," he said waving Silas toward him.

Allowing Keener to rise, Silas watched the action play out. "I've got to open, tell him to come here." He continued toward the door. The full-blood grabbed his arm.

"Stop that," Keener yelled. "Let me go."

Security ran toward them. "Release him."

"Major Franz wants him," the full blood said without releasing his arm. Once again, Silas was surprised by the overt level of aggression displayed by the wolves around humans.

"Release him, I'm not telling you again." The guard pulled his gun and pointed at the full-blood who vibrated with rage. None of it made sense. No full-blood in his pack would behave in this manner, or be at the verge of losing control of his beast for something this trivial. Just as he thought to activate the chameleon bracelet to gain more information, the full-blood released him.

"Come or go, it's between you and the Major," the full-blood said stepping aside. "But if I were you, I'd go see what he wants."

"I have work to do. Have Franz come here." Silas turned his back on the full-blood and entered the door.

"You shouldn't have done that," the full-blood said in a voice too low for humans to hear, before he strode down the hall.

"I wish they'd get rid of all of them," the guard said as he stepped into the pharmacy. "This shit's getting more and more out of hand. First, Franz and his freaks and now the General and that bunch. I hope we get back to the days when we all we did was weapons research." He leaned against the wall and took a deep breath.

"But the money wasn't as good."

The guard chuckled. "True." He paused. "You okay? That asshole didn't hurt you, did he?"

"No. I just returned from lunch, he met me in the hall."

"Be careful. With the General here, Franz is acting like a cornered bitch even though they're both doing the same damn thing. I'll be glad… just be careful." The guard walked out the door.

Did Keener have a gun or weapon for protection? Silas wondered. Franz was trouble and even though Silas wasn't afraid of him, Keener was. The man had been shaking inside as he defied the full-blood. Which brought up another point, what the hell were the full-bloods doing here all this time? He'd expected them to have left but he still sensed their presence.

"*Anything on the local pack?*" Silas asked Hawke.

"*Fractured. A few packs. Not one Alpha. Gangs have turfs in the major areas. They've had several run-ins with humans and are on the cusp of discovery. I'll send you some news articles regarding their violent turf wars.*"

"*Turf wars?*"

"*Yeah, it's a big thing. The area near the base belongs to the Lobo Sups, short for Lobo Superior, they go by the name "Sups."*"

"*Top Wolf.*"

"*They run that area, no outside wolves ever and they clear certain areas of humans after dark,*" Hawke said.

"*We left Franz there after dark,*" Silas said remembering the full-bloods behavior.

"*Guess he's the reason they run that area. Another gang's near the capital, another in Santa Barbara. Human gangs are everywhere. But full-blood gangs, with the exception of the ones I mentioned are just on the outer fringes, that's about it. The dangerous ones are the Sups,*" Hawke said.

"*Those are the ones I pulled into the lab,*" Silas said with a feeling of dread.

"*That's their turf,*" Hawke said diplomatically.

"*We never considered local packs in this equation and it's biting me in the ass. I should've factored them in,*" Silas said in disbelief of the mistake he made.

"*Pulling them in bought time for the Knights and gives Angus cover to take the doctor,*" Hawke reminded him.

Silas rubbed his chin in consideration. "*There's that.*"

The door opened.

Silas didn't turn, he knew it was Major Franz.

"Keener, when I call for you to come, you come, or I'll toss your bony ass out of this facility, is that understood?"

Silas wanted to sigh and snatch the arrogant bastard across the counter but Keener would never do that. "I had to open the pharmacy, you know that." He turned to face the Major. "What can I do for you?"

"What did you give General Lee?"

"I can't tell you that," Keener said in a low voice.

"Did he say not to tell me?" Franz asked.

"He told me anything I ordered for him was classified and not to be shared with anyone," Keener said.

Franz frowned but didn't release Keener's gaze. "If I find out you're lying…"

"Ask the General, he'll tell you." Silas wanted to smile at the dark look on Franz' face. They both knew Franz couldn't, wouldn't ask the General.

"Has my package arrived?" Franz asked.

"Not yet. I told you I'd let you know as soon as it did," Keener said in a moderate tone.

Franz turned and stumbled. He held the wall for a few seconds. His breaths sounded labored. Beads of sweat dotted his forehead. His hair seemed duller, his skin tone, ashy.

"Are you okay?" Keener asked. "Can I get you something?"

"Just let me know when my damn package arrives." Franz pulled open the door and stormed out.

Silas surfed through Keener memories to get an understanding of what was going on with Franz and found nothing, not even the contents of the package.

####

Four hours later, Angus stepped into Dr. Grenwald's office to deliver two classified files. The rest of the staff had gone to supper, leaving the area with a skeleton crew. Angus listened intently for cameras and sensed none.

"Just leave those on the desk," the doctor said as he walked into his private bathroom. Certain there were no cameras in the bathroom, Angus placed the files on the desk and followed the doctor. Minutes later Angus walked out as the good doctor wiping his hands. He turned off the lights, returned to the bathroom, picked up Puedes and placed him on the doctor's sofa to recover from the transfer since it took longer to rejuvenate a returned body.

Angus sifted through Grenwald's memories. *"Silas, we've got problems,"* Angus said as he sat at the desk and turned on a desk lamp.

"You made the exchange?" Silas asked.

"Yes. They want to complete three experiments on the Knights. One is to see how they respond to certain chemicals, Hawke's already said each of those chemicals were bad news. They've made a Compound they think will operate as chemical warfare to stop full-bloods in case of an attack."

"Fuck no," Silas growled.

"Agreed. They've been working on hijacking the pack's internal communications systems. They sent a false signal, and wanted you to respond. They think they failed in hacking the internal communications but succeeded in keeping the Knights from contacting you."

"Wait. The signal I received wasn't from the Knights?"

"I don't know. The doc doesn't know, he was told the results of the tests."

"We need to know."

"I'll look into it. There's more."

"What else?" Silas said, impatience in his tone.

"Damn-it, some Liege equipment resurfaced. Guy named Gent found a way to disrupt the communication signal using some sort of patch. If it works in blocking our links, it could give the military control over full-bloods. The doctor doesn't like or trust Gent and is responsible for Gent not being here."

"The Liege used neck braces before," Silas said.

"True. This one's a patch. It's supposed to be strong enough to allow someone else control," Angus said.

"Is that what they're using on the Knights?"

"No, they have modified collars."

Silas swore.

"I'm going to walk toward where the General's meeting with the full-bloods. When I get near, try to contact the Knights," Angus said.

"Good. I'll be in the parking lot."

"All the better in case he locks down the facility. We need to move that body from Puedes home."

"I know," Silas snapped, irritated at the delays. *"Let me know when I can try to contact them."*

Angus walked down the corridor and nodded to a few people. He marveled at the analytical nature of Grenwald's mind. Hawke would be in heaven. General Lee exited a small conference room with an exasperated expression as he waved Grenwald close.

"Now Silas." Angus said as he moved slowly forward.

The General leaned in to him. "Tomorrow we begin running tests. I finally have an agreement with the locals."

Angus nodded.

"Start the first one at dawn, then prep for the second —" A beeping sound rose. The General spun on his heels and ran.

Angus followed. *"The tablet beeped Silas."*

"I know but I spoke with each of them before the connection died. They know what to do."

The doctor was stopped at the secure door the General entered by a military soldier. He released a long breath, squared his shoulders and turned to walk away. *"Are they okay?"* he asked Silas.

"No. Their beasts… we'll take care of them once we get them out of there." He heard the bristling anger in Silas' voice.

Angus returned to his office wondering what the General used on the Knights that affected their wolves. He turned on the computer and searched for anything pertaining to the make-up of the collars used to subdue the Knights and found nothing. Instead he came across notes for the morning test.

Chemicals.

Angus needed to find a way to invalidate the chemical warfare test results. He'd been studying for an hour when the General tapped on his door and entered. He looked down at a sleeping Puedes.

"Tired?"

"Yes, I've been working him hard, so I let him sleep here." He waited for the General to speak.

"Listen, I know you're more into the research that goes on here and we appreciate all of your work. It's been brilliant, just brilliant." He leaned on the desk. "I've got a patch, a device I need to run tests on. I've finally gotten the locals to agree and would like you to sit in and give your opinion." He looked at his watch. "Shouldn't take more than an hour, two tops."

Angus leaned back in his chair. "A patch? What do you want me to do with this patch?" He opened his link with Silas and Hawke so they could listen.

"This patch can potentially block communications from entering... from controlling a person."

"Full-blood? Half-breed?" Angus asked.

"Just full-blood. But if it works we can develop something to work on them all," the General said.

"I'd like to see the patch," Hawke said. *"Do you have any technical information on it."*

Angus pushed away from the desk. "Whatever you need, General. I'm at your disposal." He turned off the computer and walked behind the General. *"As soon as I get something, Hawke I'll send it your way."*

"To the clouds," Hawke said.

"Right," Angus said as he walked alongside the General down the corridor.

When they reached the door, the General stopped him. "These men," he said hesitantly. "Can be a bit rough, not like the others. Don't pay attention to what they say or how they say things."

Unsure what that meant, Angus nodded and entered the test area. Three full-bloods were chained to metal gurneys with electrodes taped onto their chests. Angus' brow rose but he didn't speak, instead he linked with Silas so his brother could see what he saw.

"Grenwald," Franz called from a door in the back. "In here."

The doctor nodded and headed in that direction. He took a seat next to Franz and looked at the monitor. "Which ones are connected to the patch?" he asked.

"These three." Franz pointed and took his seat.

"Are you sure you want me here for your test?" Angus felt compelled to ask.

Franz' brow rose. "General said you requested to be here."

Angus frowned. "He just asked me to come and watch. I've never sat in on your tests before."

"I know and wondered about that," Franz said in a low whisper. "What's going on?"

Angus shrugged. "He asked me to sit in on this, that's all I know."

Franz nodded slowly and pressed the button. "We're ready."

"Doctor?" the General spoke through the intercom.

"I'm ready." He watched the test patients through the monitor.

Seconds later, screams erupted and chaos followed.

CHAPTER ELEVEN

Night had fallen and Silas lay staring at the ceiling on the bed in the room of the house they rented. Angus had contacted him regarding the experiment with the patches. After three tests in rapid succession, the General stopped everything without bothering to hide his disappointment. The full-bloods were released when their pack mates broke down the door ready to shed blood.

Silas had left Keener at his house an hour before. The subdued voices of the Knights raced around his mind until he wanted to forget protocol, forget their plans and remove his men from the grasp of General Lee right now. But each Knight asked him to secure the threat, to stop the General's plans from ever being used against another wolf. Despite the pain they suffered they wanted him to complete what they considered his mission to destroy the devices and the research against their Nation.

It had been bittersweet communicating with them through their human side for several moments. It wasn't until he checked on their beasts that the alarm triggered.

"Matt? Dr. Passen?" Silas sought the two wolves who directed his lab at the Compound. They hadn't been told he was

no longer in residence but that couldn't be helped now. He needed their assistance.

"Sir?" Matt answered.

"Sir?" Passen responded seconds later.

Silas explained the Knight's condition. *"What's wrong with their beasts?"*

"Listless, slow to recognize you?" Dr. Passen asked.

"Yes. It was as if their beasts were…" he tried to form the right words for what he'd sensed in that brief contact.

"Dying? Changing?" Matt said.

"Could be. Whatever's going on with their beasts, their human side wasn't handling it well. I'm afraid we'll lose them if those collars aren't removed," Silas said his greatest fear.

"Is there a way to find out what the collars are made of?" Dr. Passen asked. *"That would help us determine a way to counter it."*

"Start with your notes regarding the collars from the Liege. Seems everything started from their technology. It's possible they simply ramped things up, increased dosages, that sort of thing," Silas said. He would have Angus and Hawke search records but didn't want to mention it. The less others knew the better.

"Yes, Sir," Dr. Passen said. *"That would be the easiest and most cost effective. In the meantime, we can try to develop something to strengthen their beasts."* He paused. *"I'm not sure how we'd administer it to them."*

"Prepare it for when they return to the Compound," Silas said with grim determination.

"Yes, Sir."

"Timing is critical, Sir," Matt said after a few seconds of silence. *"Beast and human sides cannot be at odds for long periods of time without suffering irreparable damage. At some point they will become feral and need to be put down."*

Silas had been concerned this might happen. *"How much time?"*

"Unfortunately, we don't know how long they've been under the strain of separation. If the experiments are to interrupt our basic form of communications, our links are mental and a part of

who we are. I can't imagine what they're using to interrupt that. Whatever it is, is killing our Knights," Matt said in a sober tone.

"Worse, they probably don't even realize it," Dr. Passen said.

As far as Silas was concerned, those men declared war on the Wolf Nation. He knew it was just a few fanatics but that didn't matter. If blood was shed, if his Knights died, so would the men behind this project and their families.

"That doesn't matter. They broke faith, there was to be no experiments or research against our Nation. We're supposed to be allies, fighting for the same cause on the same damned side. Bastards have no honor." He reigned in his temper. *"Find answers. I want them released tomorrow and on a plane to the Compound for treatment."*

"Yes, Sir," Dr. Passen said and withdrew from their link.

"Sir?" Matt said.

"Yes?"

"Have you considered bringing one of our Generals to the location and having them override whoever is there? It would bring light to what's been done and may be the quickest way to stop the tests and remove the collars."

Silas thought about it for a few moments. *"Will that push their research into a dark room to be brought out later or end it?"*

"With all respect, Sir, nothing will stop them from trying to either be like us, more specifically you. Or trying to discover ways to stop a mythical attack. In their minds, it's a matter of survival and they come out losing in every imaginable narrative no matter what we say or do. I think it's a part of their nature we need to expect and live with," Matt said.

Silas and Jasmine had come to that realization years ago but decided to abide by the contracts as long as the government did the same. *"That's true, it's their nature. Let me know when you have something for the Knights."* Silas dismissed the link and thought of bringing Crall to Honduras for several minutes. He looked at the idea from several angles.

"Lieutenant General Crall," Silas called through their link an hour later.

"*Yes, Sir?*" the General said after a few seconds.

Silas explained what was happening and ignored the man's surprise that he was in Honduras. Crall didn't ask questions but responded to the idea of a surprise visit to the military base. "*It's possible I could get away tonight, I have a dinner party to attend with several high-ranking officials. Between General Miller and myself we could probably pull it off so that they don't realize I've left and be there before the alarm is rung. Timing will be everything.*"

"*They aren't at the base.*" Silas explained where the men were located.

"*I've heard of it,*" Crall said. "*If you want me to be there in the morning, I'll need to fly in on a chartered jet.*"

"*Jacques can handle that. Come through Texas and then to the main airport.*"

"*As an officer, I prefer to go through the base.*"

Silas thought about it. Hawke could handle that. "*Okay. What do you need?*"

"*As long as I get there safe, I'll take care of the rest. Rank has its privileges,*" Crall said.

"*I have men in place at the facility, you won't know who they are but if you need help, it will be available. Getting those men out of there without the collars is the most important thing,*" Silas stressed.

"*Yes, Sir. I will do my best. Will you contact General Miller, or should I?*"

"*I will contact him. Get started on what you need to put in place, he'll contact you soon.*"

"*Yes, Sir.*" Crall disconnected.

Silas contacted General Miller, gave him a brief overview of what he wanted done and told him to contact Crall for specifics. Next, he contacted Jacques, brought him current and had him coordinate Crall's transportation.

"*Today, you received the third invitation from the White House. Each time the person extending it on behalf of the President explains how important it is for you to meet with him. I know you've turned them down in the past but I think Something's going on and you need to accept.*"

85

Silas had no interest in meeting any government officials right now. Their duplicity stank to high heavens and he would make them pay for what they'd done. But he understood his duty to the Nation. His people lived in this country under the American flag and the President was the leader. Despite how distasteful it was to sit at the same table with those who authorized experiments on his men, he would go.

"If Crall gets the men out of here tomorrow, we should be back soon after. Set something up for after that," Silas said and thought about it. *"No. Wait until Crall has them on the plane and then accept the invite."*

"Yes, Sir. Will you tell Jasmine, or should I?"

"She would attend with me," Silas murmured. For a few seconds, he enjoyed the visual of his beautiful wife, elegantly dressed, walking beside him. The idea pleased him. *"I'll tell her."*

He and Jacques spoke for a few more minutes before disconnecting. Silas glanced at the clock. He needed to get across town to pick up the body at Puedes' home before morning. Rolling out of bed, he morphed into a larger human with tattoos and long hair. He grabbed the keys to the rental and headed for the car.

Puedes lived in an area several miles from the outskirt of Tegucigalpa, the capital, on a long dirt road filled with homes similar in style. Understanding the high crime rate of some of these neighborhoods, around four in the morning, Silas drove down the dark road, pleased there were no lights in any of the homes and parked a block away. He sensed no humans or full-bloods on the streets or nearby.

Dressed in all black, he jogged toward the house, entered the security code for the gate and used the key Angus had given him to open the front door. Without turning on lights, Silas made his way to the bedroom, picked up the body and left as quietly as he arrived.

With thoughts on his upcoming conversation with the Knights, he rounded the corner and saw his car. Before he could move out the way a full-blood slammed into him, knocking him and the body he held onto the dirt path.

"What are you doing around here in the dark, carrying a body," a full-blood, dressed in all black with a red wolf on the front of his shirt, asked. Dark eyes, gleaming with mischief peered down at Silas.

"Going home. My friend called for me to pick him up, I'm taking him home," Silas said unsure if they sensed his wolf or they simply attacked humans for being on their turf.

"Not without paying the fee." One of the full-bloods stepped closer, dug into Silas' pocket and pulled out his wallet. He held the money so his partner could see. "Is this all you have?"

Silas nodded, wondering just how far these assholes would take this. The Goddess demanded they keep their dual-natures hidden from humans which kept his people safe for centuries. Attacking humans was a sure way to alert the rest of the world of their existence. Even though he had no jurisdiction here, he wouldn't allow these two to attack humans, period.

"Take him to the ATM, have him pull out more money or we kill his friend," the other said in a heavy accent. He wore a chain with the letters TAG that swung against his chest as they laughed.

Silas was grabbed by the arm, and pulled to his feet.

Tag, the name Silas assigned to the chain wearer, knelt next to the body Silas had dropped, holding a knife near his throat. It wasn't that Angus needed that particular body to transition back into his own, one of the upgrades to the chameleon allowed him to transition with anyone. But they didn't want to damage or destroy any of the bodies they borrowed for this mission.

"Take the money and let us go," Silas said in what he considered a reasonable tone. His beast had grown considerably restless since talking to the Knights and sensing the poor conditions of their beasts. He tamped down his more aggressive impulses of breaking these two in half and focused on finishing the mission without leaving a body trail.

The full-blood holding the knife stood and walked slowly to Silas. "You with the Sups? Talking shit like that get you killed."

He snatched the bottom of Silas' tee shirt and yanked it up. "They didn't mark you?" He took the knife and lightly drew a squiggly line with the tip. "Now you've got their symbol on you which means you broke the rules by coming in to Red Wolf territory.

Silas bit back a sigh at the dramatic drivel the wolf spouted. "I don't know what you're talking about."

"Don't matter, you should always check for information regarding an area before you enter. Tourist or not, you broke the rules, now you must pay." He lifted the knife as if he planned to stab Silas.

"Are you fucking crazy?" Silas snapped as he punched the guy in the face, sending him flying back against the car. Moving quickly, he grabbed the punk's arm, bent it backward, it snagged against the hood. When the full-blood tried to move, his arm broke. "You don't attack humans like this. What the fuck's the matter with you?"

Silas ducked the blow from the other full-blood and smashed him in the face with a back-handed blow. "I can't believe you assholes would try to kill innocents to make a fucking point."

"Who the fuck are you?" the full blood with the broken arm asked while scooting backward trying to fix his arm.

Silas didn't answer. Instead he walked toward the body he had dropped a few minutes ago. Before he reached him, one of the full-bloods slammed into him. The other with the broken arm joined in. They threw punches, several connected with Silas' face and side.

Enough, he thought.

Anger whipped through him as he pushed both men off, stood and grabbed the one with the broken arm by the head. Without thought, Silas snapped Tag's neck and let him fall like a sack of flour to the ground.

The other full-blood tried to run, but Silas caught him, snapped his neck and tossed him aside. He picked up the knife and tossed it blade down into the torso of the full-blood who cut him.

He picked up the body he'd retrieved for Angus, continued to the car, placed him in the back seat and drove to the rental house where he placed the body in Angus' room. Just in case someone had seen the car on the road, or in the area, returned the rental car to the lot to prevent anyone making a connection, and following him to the house . Afterward he walked to Keener's home to wait for Crall to arrive.

CHAPTER TWELVE

The next morning, traffic out of town crawled. When Silas reached the research lab and parked he was surprised by the short line to enter the building. He contacted Angus but released their link when he realized Angus was asleep. Next, he contacted Hawke to remind him of Crall's arrival and to see if anything happened to cause this delay.

"*Gang war escalated overnight,*" Hawke said. "*A couple bodies were found, necks broken. One of the dead was related to a local legend and his family's calling for blood.*"

Silas closed his eyes briefly and released a long breath. Last night, once he arrived back at Keener's place, he and Jasmine started talking. He'd forgotten about the two thugs who tried to rob and kill him which now created another problem.

"*The other gangs are denying they had anything to do with it but since there was retaliation, someone's missing from the Sups, I'm not sure it matters. They're at war, bodies are being discarded. Policia doesn't get involved in full-blood violence, they've got to handle it themselves. Since the Sups were at the lab yesterday, security's tight. It's been locked down again.*"

"Locked down? That won't stop the General from coming to get the Knights, right?" Silas moved forward in the line, praying he hadn't undone their plan with those assholes last night.

"It shouldn't, he's a General after all. Fortunately, the Commander isn't here and neither is Franz so I've coded Crall's arrival as a need to know only basis. He should be here in a couple hours. Hopefully things will have cooled down by then," Hawke said.

"Can you stay on duty until after he arrives? Make sure things go smoothly?" Silas asked as he handed Keener's ID to the security guards, allowed them to search his belongings and then walked through the metal detector.

"Yes, I slept here after my shift last night, so I'll be here all day," Hawke said.

"About those two bodies," Silas said as he opened the pharmacy. He told Hawke what happened.

"Don't blame you. These full bloods are out of control attacking humans. They want the Goddess on their asses?" Hawke said.

"Right. But it started a war that could impede our mission of search and rescue."

"If they'd have stabbed you, your beast would've taken over and the end result would've been the same. Let the locals wage their war, as long as they don't bring it to us," Hawke said in an implacable tone.

None of his team liked the idea of him being in what they considered danger, which was why he'd only shared the altercation with Jasmine until now. Too often they forgot he was a warrior forged by blood and war. His short history with a mate and den dimmed against the long shadow of his life filled with Alpha challenges and bloodshed.

"Let me know when Crall arrives, clear the path for him to get here without alerting Lee," Silas said.

"Yes, Sir. Angus is in a good position to alert us of any changes in the General's behavior," Hawke said.

"You're right, but let's not put him in a position of discovery." Silas disconnected the link and turned as the door opened.

"Good morning, General. Good to see you, what can I do for you this morning?"

The General closed the door, leaving the military soldier outside. He reached inside his pocket, pulled out a piece of paper and handed it to Silas. "Got anything to counter that?"

Silas read the name of the chemical and frowned. Neither he nor Keener were familiar with it. "One second, I'll need to look it up."

The General hesitated and then nodded before leaning on the counter.

Silas read the toxicity report on the chemical and knew this ingredient was killing his Knights. In addition to turning them into zombies, it weakened all their organs and their beasts. It took everything within him not to wrap his fingers around the General's neck.

"Hydration's the only thing," Silas said slowly. "Flush it out, otherwise it'll continue on its course."

The General cursed and held out his hand for the paper.

Silas gave it to him. "Sorry, Sir. There's nothing to counter it," he said to make sure the asshole understood his options.

General Lee nodded and looked at him. "Take that off your computer and forget you ever saw it."

"Yes, Sir." He moved to the keyboard and deleted the search. "Done and done." As soon as the general left, Silas sat at his desk and contacted Dr. Passen to tell him the name of the ingredient. The doctor's reaction mirrored Silas' earlier dismay. But at least they could prepare something to counter it.

Silas updated Hawke on the ingredient and received a confirmation that Crall's flight was estimated to arrive within the hour. So far, no alarms had been raised which was good. According to General Miller, several Admirals imbibed great quantities of alcohol last night at the dinner party and would probably have late starts this morning.

The General stuck his head back into the pharmacy.

Silas stood and walked to the counter holding paperwork he'd considered doing.

"The base is on lock down until further notice. One of the security guards was killed this morning between shifts. We think it's gang related but until we're sure, no one in or out. Eat in the cafeteria or wait for the end of shift." He closed the door behind him, leaving Silas gut-punched.

Would Crall be able to enter and take the Knights? He hoped so. Once Crall arrived, Silas would update him.

Crall arrived at the laboratory with several MP's demanding entrance. He outranked General Lee and was granted access to the facility. Angus had just entered his office and heard the scrambling outside. Crall and the soldiers entered the secure areas without a word and finally took the elevator down to the basement.

Silas, Angus and Hawke waited several minutes to hear what happened. Time crawled. Silas couldn't focus on anything and sat at his desk to wait.

Had Lee moved the men again? Did he hydrate them to remove the poison from their systems?

"*Got them,*" Crall said 15 minutes later. "*Surprised Lee didn't wet himself when I walked in. He tried to double talk, claimed his authority but the Knights belong to us, he knows that. Finally, he stepped aside to let me in the room. They're all hooked up to IV's. I'm waiting for him to remove the collars, he's taking his time but I've mentioned court martialling and a few other things to get him motivated.*"

Silas breathed deeply, placed his fingertips to his forehead and thanked the Goddess for her wisdom, grace and mercy. These men should recover.

"*Neck braces off. They're groggy. If you want to work on their beasts, you can or I can give them a small boost,*" Crall said.

"*Can they shift?*" Silas asked.

"*Yes, all but one. I'll help him,*" Crall said. "*I've had Lee taken into custody. He tried to say he found them and brought them here to work on for transport back to the States. When I asked why I wasn't informed, he stopped talking. There's a Major here, Franz asking questions, he's in charge of the base?*"

"Yes, his CO is away. He's involved with the local wolves. What does he want?" Silas asked.

"He's interested in the collars, asked if he could look at one."

"Take all of those with you for my team at the Compound to research. We need to understand how the drug was administered and the role of those collars," Silas said.

"Will do," Crall said.

"Hawke, I want them out of here as soon as possible," Silas said.

"Yes, Sir. General Crall took a truck with him, once he returns to base he can board his flight."

"Have they gotten the turf wars under control? Can my men travel safely? Right now, they're still weak. The poison isn't completely out of their systems."

"General Crall can order additional soldiers, but the city is still under siege. There's no way to hide the Knights are full-bloods as they travel to the base. It's possible they may be attacked for being in Sup territory," Hawke said.

"Damn-it," Silas said before taking a deep breath and contacting each Knight. They were happy he'd come for them, and prepared to do whatever he needed. When he questioned their strength, each admitted, somewhat sheepishly, they weren't at full speed.

Silas contacted Crall. *"Have the doctor, Grenwald, hook them back up to the IV's to hydrate their systems more. Hopefully they'll be ready to travel in an hour or two."* Silas explained the turf war and the inherent dangers of immediate travel without sharing his role in the uprising.

"Understood, Sir. It's good, really good, to see them. There was a time I didn't think this would ever happen. I don't think they did either, Sir," Crall said passionately.

"We never give up on pack," Silas said simply. *"Get them hydrated so they can defend themselves if necessary on the way out of here."*

"Yes, Sir." Crall disconnected as Silas contacted Angus.

"Hmm?" Angus sounded groggy.

"Up and alert. Crall is here and with our Knights."

94

"What?"

Silas smiled at Angus' surprised voice. *"Arrived an hour ago, I let you sleep a little longer but now I want you to oversee their hydration. It's the only thing to neutralize what they've been given. I want them on a plane back to the Compound as soon as possible."*

"Why can't they go now?" Angus asked.

Silas brought him up to date on the turf war and lock downs surrounding them.

"There's a knock on the door, one second, Silas," Angus said. Several moments later he spoke. *"General Lee is locked up and wants to see me. The messenger from Crall came before Lee's soldier left and ordered me to the Knights. Lee's man nodded as if giving me permission to work on the Knights. Whatever Crall thinks, Lee's not done."* Angus paused. *"The chemicals. We were supposed to test that this morning."*

"Where are the chemicals? Crall can confiscate those as well," Silas said.

"I don't know. Lee has them locked away somewhere. We may need to get those instead of Crall. If he's looking for the Knights there's no way he would know about the chemical warfare or any other tests."

"Unless someone leaked it," Silas said thinking it through.

"But who? The pharmacist? Doctor? Soldiers? None of them would tell Crall. If Crall starts asking Lee will get suspicious and we'll never know his plans. I think we should let Crall take the Knights and the neck braces. I've got a sample of the patch I can send along, but the chemical warfare is something we need to handle," Angus said.

"Lee's asking for you, probably trusts you on some level," Silas said slowly.

"Grenwald's hands are just as dirty as Lee's. Grenwald's the doctor who's been doing the experiments," Angus said.

"Peas in a fucking pod," Silas said growing tired of the treachery and deceit. *"Okay, we'll handle it your way. Just get the Knights well enough to leave, keep Franz away from them. Something tells me our Knights are exactly what he'd love to turn his rag-tag Army into."*

A soldier entered the pharmacy. "General Lee wants to see you."

Silas nodded and walked around the counter. "Give me a second to lock up," he said to the soldier's back to stop the man before he got too far. *"Lee just sent for me, I'll use the chameleon to get information on the chemical tests,"* Silas told Hawke and Angus.

Pharmacy secured, he waved for the soldier to move ahead. Silent they entered the elevator and headed down to the basement level and headed toward the containment cells once they arrived. Silas frowned when he approached Lee's cell. A large sheet of clear, unbreakable plastic separated them. Silas cursed at the inability to touch Lee and activate the bracelet.

"What the hell is going on?" Silas asked injecting the right amount of surprise and disbelief into his voice.

Lee waved down his question and dismissed the soldier. When they were alone, he waved Silas closer to the holes drilled in the plastic wall.

"Are you okay?" Silas asked, sounding concerned while taking in Lee's haggard appearance. The man looked as if he'd aged exponentially in the past hour. If Silas didn't know exactly when Lee had been arrested he would have sworn it had taken place hours ago.

Lee shrugged. "Things will play out the way it's meant to be. Listen, things are going to be crazy in a bit." He glanced at his watch. "Chances are good he knows and are sending in a team right now." Lee took a deep breath. "No telling what he's going to do." He met Silas gaze. "Keener did you destroy all the order invoices?"

Silas frowned and nodded slowly. Keener had destroyed them.

"Think, you gotta be a hundred percent sure, the last thing I want is you dragged into the shit-storm headed our way. Did you destroy all traces of the orders for me?"

"Yes, yes, what shit-storm? What are you talking about?" Silas asked with a smidgen of pride at the scent of fear wafting from Lee. The man knew he was in trouble and not just from his bosses.

"Leave early. Take the rest of the day off, get out of here before La Patron arrives," Lee said.

"La Patron? The head Alpha? He's coming here?"

Lee swallowed hard and nodded. "Him or one of his inner circle, same thing." Lee looked around and then met Silas' gaze. "If I were you, I'd go home."

"Is the lab still shut down?"

Lee shrugged.

"Can I do anything for you?" Silas hoped Lee would tell him to take the chemicals with him.

"Not much can be done for me at this point. Crall's sharp." He hissed. "Knight played us like a fucking fiddle. He knew. Caught us right out, no way to explain this one." Lee walked around the cell with his head down mumbling. Silas wanted to laugh but held out hope Lee would share more.

"I'll go check the computer again but I deleted everything as soon as I pressed order. Then I'll go home." He walked off a few steps, looked over his shoulder and tried to muster concern for the disgusting bastard. "Are you sure I can't do anything for you? This isn't right, you're a General for Christ's sake."

Lee snorted. "Life's about choices, Keener. Go ahead, get out of here while you can."

Silas headed toward the door when Franz entered. He nodded and continued walking even though he wished he could stay and listen. After Angus met with Lee, Silas would have Crall restrict Lee's visitors. Hopefully Lee would tell the good doctor where he hid the chemicals. Otherwise, once the Knights were better and left this place, he would go room by room until he found them.

Knight Rescue

CHAPTER THIRTEEN

Walking back to the pharmacy, Silas wondered what Lee and Franz had to talk about. *"Hawke?"*

"Sir?"

"Can you access the cameras in the containment area of the research lab? Franz and Lee are having a conversation and I'd like to know what they discuss."

A few moments later, Hawke returned. *"No, Sir. It's on a closed loop for that facility only."*

"Thanks," Silas said as he nodded to the security guard standing near the pharmacy drinking coffee. Silas chuckled over Lee's response over La Patron having played the Joint Chiefs. So far, the Admiral and the others had no idea Crall had recovered the Knights but they would soon. He wondered if they would contact him or make it necessary for him to contact them. Either way the Knights program was officially shut down over breach of contract.

"How are my Knights?" Silas asked Crall as he re-entered the pharmacy.

"Coming around, slowly but I see signs of progress. Is Grenwald good? Can we trust him to do the right thing?" Crall asked. Silas debated whether to share Angus' identity but decided

against it. Crall only knew help was nearby but not exactly from who.

"I've been told he was good. Let me know if you have any problems or concerns," Silas said as he walked behind the counter.

"Yes, Sir. I've alerted Miller on the success of my mission, when will you notify the Joint Chiefs?"

Silas explained the chemical warfare tip he received and the importance of retrieving the notes and samples of the chemicals. Angus and Hawke had been searching every data base they could access and came up empty.

Crall whistled.

"That's another mission, yours is to leave as soon as they're able," Silas said.

"Yes, Sir. Another hour tops and they should be strong enough."

"Good. Do you think Lee will share information regarding his plans with anyone there?"

"He doesn't strike me as the type to talk. The look of resignation on his face when I took control said he expected this and accepted his fate. That doesn't mean he wouldn't attempt to continue testing if he could, just that he'd accept his punishment, which is going to be severe."

"Hmm, he'll continue to breathe, so not that severe," Silas said.

"Barely. What he, they, did to the Knights is a big deal and he knows it. I can't imagine how they thought they'd get away with it."

Silas agreed with Crall. *"They wanted to strip our ability to communicate with each other, with our beasts. The only way to do that is to kill us. Maybe they realized that and decided on chemical warfare?"*

"The chemicals would need to kill both sides, including our human part. Which puts all humans who come in contact with the chemicals at risk. We live in cities, and rural areas as well as our private land. There's no way to kill us all without killing themselves." Crall paused. *"They know all of this. Have they found a way to work around it?"*

"That's why we need the notes and not just the chemicals," Silas said frustrated with the delay and new dilemma.

Franz strode into the containment area mulling over how to get Lee's cooperation. If only he'd known the full-bloods in Lee's control group had been turned into super-soldiers he would have acted before now. The Sups, Tasha particularly, were getting restless and pushing him for more drugs to give them an edge. He'd used his meager supply, still they insisted he find more. Franz worried over their increasing lack of control. He hadn't been able to locate Roderick, his former supplier, recently. The man had disappeared. Grenwald thought the idea of researching someone else' work beneath him and refused to analyze the serum.

Lee was the key.

If the man would take the pole out of his ass for a few minutes he might see the benefits of them working together. He stared at the General for several seconds thinking of the best way to gain Lee's interest.

"Sir," Franz said as he moved closer and saluted the fallen General.

Lee glanced at him, nodded and continued staring at the wall.

"The men formally under your care are waking."

The General's head snapped up, his gaze sharpened as he looked at Franz. "You saw them?"

"I followed Grenwald, saw them with General Crall for a few moments before being sent away," Franz said. "I don't think I've ever seen full-bloods so… in such good shape. Soldiers?"

Lee hesitated and then nodded.

Now they were getting somewhere, Franz thought. "Special team? Your team?"

Lee exhaled. "Not mine. Military. Special forces."

That surprised Franz. He had heard rumors of an elite group in the military but didn't know they were full-bloods. He frowned. If those men were a part of the military, what were they doing here? And what about those collars? He recalled hearing something about those years ago. Was Lee and Grenwald doing research on soldiers? That explained Crall's sudden visit and the General's confinement.

"Glad they're on our side," Franz murmured while glancing at the General who would face charges for sure.

"Yeah," Lee said and stared at the wall again.

"Are they enhanced?" Franz decided to get straight to the point. Either Lee would help or not.

General Lee frowned. "Enhanced? With drugs?"

Despite the furrowed brows, there was a light of interest in the General's eyes. "Yes. I've heard there is a serum that increases their capabilities. Are you familiar with it?"

The General nodded slowly. "Heard about it several years ago. What's your interest?"

"The Superiors. They weren't always that way. Over the years I've assisted them in their rise to the top," Franz said watching the General closely. They both knew what he'd done would be frowned upon in the military and was illegal in Honduras.

"You gave them the serum?"

Franz nodded.

"It worked?"

Franz nodded again.

"That explains their erratic behavior, a common side effect of the serum. One of the reasons it cannot be used by soldiers," the General said pointedly. "When they lose control, they disobey orders, create their own paths and disregard the mission, they aren't soldiers."

"What about the collars?" Franz asked.

Lee met his gaze. "What about them?"

"Do they allow you to control them? To bend to your will?" Franz moved closer.

Lee stared at him for several seconds and smiled. "You've lived amongst them, how long?"

Pride stiffened his spine. "Over ten years," Franz said.

"Then you must know there's nothing we can do to bend them to our will. With one word or order from their Alpha, those men will rip this place apart and leave. None of us can stop them."

Franz snorted. "We've got weapons that'll stop anything."

"You take out those four and hundreds will replace them and it'll happen so quick, so smooth you won't be ready or suspect it."

Franz waved down the speech. "In the absence of an Alpha?"

Lee's gaze narrowed. "Alpha's are the strongest in the group and are responsible for the safety, health and well-being of the pack. Unless the full-blood is a loner, there's always a leader, an Alpha," Lee said. "Tell me something, are you the Alpha of the Sups?"

Franz shrugged. "Not really. They listen because I have something they want. Or had something. My supply's gone." He looked at Lee. "How long before the effects wear off?"

"As far as I know the changes are permanent."

Franz stared at him for a few moments. Was it possible? Had the members continued taking the serum when they didn't need too? As much as he hated anyone knowing of his mistake, he needed answers. "If they continued taking the serum, would that ratchet the side effects?"

The General stuffed his hands in his pockets and studied Franz for several seconds. "I don't know, it's possible" he said finally. "It's been years since anyone's discussed the serum or researched it. What I do recall is the change magnifies whatever is already in the person."

"Has it ever been tested on our soldiers?"

"Humans?"

Franz nodded and gave the old man points for not spouting hypocritical outrage over the notion.

"No… that serum has not," Lee said while staring at the wall. "They've had other tests." He looked at Franz. "The idea of a human military fighting force as good as those men has been tested and tried a multitude of ways. But we aren't the same. Can you imagine a team of peace-keepers who speak mind to mind, with great strength, extremely flexible and difficult to destroy?" He waved his hand. "I mean a bullet in the leg, arm or an

extremity won't slow them down. Remarkable, just remarkable."
He shook his head.

"I've never seen or heard of this group, so I'll take your
word." He paused. "Why are they here?"

"Classified."

Franz nodded. "The death last night." He looked at the
General. "The Sups say they didn't kill those two Red-Wolves. Is
it possible your men are guilty?"

"No," Lee said adamant.

"The kills were quick, efficient, missing the sloppiness of the
Sups. It's possible those professional soldiers are responsible,"
Franz said considering.

"One soldier snuck out, went to get the lay of the land, not
understanding the turf wars, wrong place, wrong time. Self-
defense… maybe. He returned, communicated with the team, told
to lay low, wait… could be any of those things. In reality, you
don't know. Because you don't know what's going on inside
them. I'm sure they knew General Crall was on the way."

Lee's face reddened as his jaw tightened. "You're wrong. On
several levels, you're wrong. None of them killed those men."

Confident he had the General's attention, Franz moved so
they'd be face to face. "What makes you so sure I'm wrong, Sir?"

"If they were caught in a turf war there would be no bodies
found. There would be nothing to indicate they'd ever been in
town, nothing. They're ghosts when they work."

"With all due respect —"

The General pointed at him. "I've seen them in action, you
haven't," he yelled and then snapped his mouth tight for several
moments. "The rest of that's possible, although not probable. Not
the deaths, not that."

"Sir, I'll take your word for it. Everyone else… I don't know
how they'll respond. Red Wolves are out for blood and they're
vicious. The government wants to avoid an all-out war even
though they won't get directly involved. They're looking for a
scapegoat."

"What?" The General faced him fully. "They know nothing
of those men. They've been here the whole time."

"The Sups were here yesterday and sensed them, it made them antsy. They accused me of bringing in other full-bloods to help. Then the patch test, that was a fucking disaster, they left here pissed."

"Your problem, had nothing to do with my men," the General said.

"Our problem. Understand, the Sups believe they are the top pack because they're enhanced. They now think you, I or the military have brought enhanced wolves on their turf. They feel threatened. They believe your men killed the Red Wolves to start a war to get rid of them and take their place."

"What? That's ridiculous. Why would the military be concerned about a small local pack?"

Franz shrugged and fought to keep his face neutral. Those assholes in Washington had no idea how to kingdom build one pack at a time. He knew better than most how loyal full-bloods were. They'd saved his ass more times than he wanted to count. He glanced at the clock. A group would arrive at the lab any moment now to ask questions and demand to question those wolves.

"I don't have an answer for that." Franz took a step back. "By the way, I noticed collars in the room with your full-bloods. Did you use them to keep them in line? To make them obey?"

The General glared at him. "No, doesn't work like that."

Franz waited a few seconds to be enlightened but the General didn't speak. "If you need anything, let the soldier on the door know. We take care of our own."

Knight Rescue

CHAPTER FOURTEEN

Intent on continuing his search for General Lee's chemicals, Silas stopped in the middle of the corridor near the pharmacy. A peculiar, guttural sound snaked through the air from outside. A low snarling sound of many voices, rising and blending, as it grew louder and more menacing.

Full-bloods.

Inhaling he smelled them. At least 50, maybe more. Silas shook his head, they didn't need this bullshit. Security and soldiers ran about, fortifying the building and barking orders for people to basically go and hide inside their offices. Which made no sense in Silas' mind. These soldiers had to know they couldn't defeat those wolves.

Someone hurled a something heavy at the building. Yells, demands, and foul language followed. From bits and pieces of what he could hear and make out, the local gangs were united against the outsiders. They claimed the full-bloods inside had killed their two men. Silas snorted over the way they tried to make the decease sound like angels who were mistreated at home.

"Hawke, we have a situation." Silas explained what was happening.

"The lab is under siege?"

"Yes, and my patience is running thin. I want my men out of here as soon as they are able."

"Send the Knights to the base, there might be some bloodshed but they are soldiers, the elite."

Silas thought about it for a few seconds. He straightened and watched as several full-bloods followed soldiers into the corridor. The soldier stopped them, told them to wait. Moments later, Major Franz and General Crall entered the area.

"I'm Major Franz this is General Crall," Franz said.

"Are there full-bloods here?" an older wolf asked. No-one gets to be leader without scars and an embattled soul. Silas suspected this wolf was more a figure head than the one who made the daily rules and ran the pack. He looked at the wolves surrounding the older wolf.

A much younger wolf leaned against the wall a small distance from the others, his face neutral, as if he wasn't particularly interested in the conversation. But the tautness of his body betrayed him, this one was primed and ready to attack. He vibrated in anticipation - anticipation as if something good were about to happen.

"Angus how are the Knights?"

"Much better. Ready to travel I believe. Where's Crall?"

Silas told him about the escalating problem.

"Sir?" Crall called to Silas.

"Yes?"

"We have a situation." Crall explained what was happening in front of Silas.

"The Knights can leave now," Silas said. He watched Crall's face slowly change into a half smile.

"Yes, Sir," Crall said and then he spoke to the older wolf. "I sympathize with you on the loss of your pack mates but the soldiers recovering in this lab had nothing to do with their deaths. They were under medication the entire time they've been here. Ask those who visited the lab yesterday if they ever saw our soldiers walking around, they did not. These men have just been cleared by the doctor to travel."

"They're not going anywhere," the older wolf said. "Not until they answer our questions about Tag and Squire."

Silas was surprised the wolf wore his real name around his neck.

"You've decided to go to war against the U.S.?" Crall asked in a low voice.

"If necessary," the old man snapped. The younger wolf leaning against the wall smiled. With high levels of impunity and low conviction rates in the country, criminals were bolder than most places. Unfortunately, these people never faced a Knight before.

"What proof do you have that our soldiers killed your pack mates," Crall asked.

"Their necks were broken."

Crall's brow rose. "Broken necks? Are you saying full-bloods in this region cannot break necks?"

The older man's jaw tightened and he pointed his finger. "We shoot, use knives, weapons, something we can heal from. No one can heal from a broken neck." The other full-bloods murmured their agreement.

"So, if someone from a rival pack wanted to eliminate an enemy he would simply break his neck to keep the blame from falling on him or her," Crall said. The initial silence was broken by yelling and screaming at Crall. He held up his hand.

"I have told you the soldiers are not guilty of this."

"Where are they?" the old man yelled. Others joined in asking for the Knights. Silas remained in the shadows as the elevator dinged. He smelled them before he saw them. His heart expanded with pride as the four Knights walked out, still in uniform and stood behind Crall.

No one spoke for several seconds. Silas wondered if the crowd had ever seen full-bloods standing over six and a half feet, two were seven feet. They stood in a rest position with their hands clasped in back. Only a fool would think these men weren't deadly and prepared for anything.

General Crall broke the silence. He looked at the old wolf. "These are the Knights. You wanted to ask them a question?"

Silas picked up and understood the pride in the General's voice. Even Franz looked up at the men with an awed expression.

"Are these full-bloods enhanced?" the older man snapped.

"No," General Crall said.

"Why are they so big?" the older man asked.

"Have you ever seen La Patron?" General Crall asked.

Silas smiled at the way the Knights straightened when his name was mentioned.

"No," the older man said sounding uncertain. He cleared his throat and pointed to one of the Knights named Curtis. "Two of our men were killed last night, neck snapped, did you or any of you kill them?" The man's voice lacked the accusatory fire it had before.

"No," Curtis said.

The others with the older wolf continued staring at the Knights. "You're in the military? They let you fight?"

Curtis simply looked down at his uniform, brushed one shoulder and then met the older wolf's gaze. "Yes."

"This is bullshit," the young wolf who had been quietly leaning against the wall yelled. "One of you motherfucking bastards snuck out of this place last night, went into town and killed my hombres. You're gonna pay for that shit." He moved from the wall and pointed at the Knights.

Crall looked at the man. "Do you think if any of these men were in town no one would've noticed or remembered seeing them?"

Silence followed his question. The older wolf exhaled and looked at the younger wolf. "He's right, someone would've seen and definitely remembered seeing one of them."

"Not if they didn't want to be seen," the young wolf said stubbornly. "Just because they're big doesn't mean they can't hide in plain sight. Shit, if that was the case they couldn't go anywhere to fight."

Silas couldn't argue with the punk's reasoning even though it didn't matter. If it wouldn't cause an international incident he'd just confess to defending himself against those two last night and call it a day.

Crall looked at his watch as if the young wolf hadn't spoken. "We need to be on our way." He looked at the older wolf. "Do you have any more questions?"

"If they didn't kill Tag and Squire, who did?"

"That, I cannot answer." General Crall turned looked at the Knights. Two left and entered the elevator. *"Sir?"*

"Yes?" Silas answered.

"We will be leaving the lab momentarily with the collars and the control tablet."

"Excellent."

"We may encounter some resistance outside. What are your instructions?"

"The same as they've always been, get my Knights out of there and back to my Compound. If someone interferes, Knights will defend the mission."

Crall rocked on his heels but Silas could see his eyes were lit with excitement.

"No humans," Silas stressed.

"The Honduran government's position is this is a full-blood issue, they're staying out of it as long as it remains hidden from human eyes and no humans are injured," Crall said.

"Make sure the Knights understand the drill."

"Yes, Sir."

The two Knights returned with three duffel bags. They stood behind the General, waiting for instructions. Crall turned to Franz.

Franz offered a salute.

The General nodded and walked off. The young wolf Silas had been watching waited until the Knights passed him before he made a move. He leapt onto Curtis' back and attempted to get him in a choke-hold. Curtis reached up, pulled the young wolf over his head and tossed him against the wall so hard it left a bloody smear. The Knights never slowed or broke rank.

Silas left the shadows and followed behind them. Outside a much larger group of full-bloods jeered at the Knights, threw rocks, stones, yelled and cursed at them. Security wouldn't allow Silas to go outside so he watched from the entrance as the

Knights walked, head high toward the truck that would transport them to base.

The old man and the full-bloods from inside, exited the building. The older wolf raised his hand to get the crowd to listen but they ignored him. The young wolf who'd jumped on Curtis was carried outside, his clothes bloody. The sight of him inflamed the crowd.

"They aren't going to make it to that truck without a fight," Silas murmured.

"Nope," the security guard standing nearby said. "The others want to fight. Hope it doesn't get too bloody."

"*Do not kill anyone,*" Silas told the Knights just as three full-bloods ran forward to attack. Curtis jumped back, and kicked one full-blood in the ass sending all three forward.

Curtis stopped and looked at the three full-bloods as they stood. The other Knights stopped and looked at the crowd. General Crall moved toward them, extended his hand for the bags and took them toward the truck. "MP's stand down. La Patron's Knights run from no one," the General said. "Neither do US soldiers, if you attack they will kick you asses." With that warning, the General headed to the truck.

The three full-bloods attacked again, this time each was picked up and thrown across the field by three Knights. Curtis' gaze roved over the crowd with a clear warning and ironically, an invitation. Silas understood the pent-up fury each man felt. They'd been betrayed by those they served, their beasts drugged, their energies drained. A good fight would go a long way in making them feel better.

A yell erupted from the back of the crowd and several pack members rushed the Knights. For a few seconds, it looked like the full-bloods had the advantage. Then the Knights exploded into action, moving so fast Silas doubted the human soldiers could track them. Full-bloods were tossed, kicked and punched so hard Silas heard the impacts inside.

"*What's going on?*" Angus asked as he approached and stood next to Silas. "*Why didn't you call me?*"

"We need the chemical warfare information," Silas said as one of the Knights jerked back from a punch that landed on their cheek.

"Lee gave that to me when I went to talk to him, I've been working on it with Hawke so we can send it to Passen."

Silas glanced at him. *"We go home tonight."*

Angus nodded while watching the fight. *"The cops really aren't going to break this up?"*

"Crall instructed the soldiers to stand down. Security's inside, no human cops," Silas said as the Knights thinned the crowd. Several full-blood lay bloody on the ground, holding their ribs or limping off to go shift for healing. Thank the Goddess they knew better than to shift in public. The old wolf walked off shaking his head and muttering about arrogant fools.

When no one else challenged them, the Knights clapped each on the shoulder with wide smiles. The fight was just the medicine their beasts needed. They walked toward the truck and headed toward the base to go home.

"They're on their way," Silas said. *"Now to deal with the Joint Chiefs."*

CHAPTER FIFTEEN

"Pablo, are you sure this is the right house?" the Red Wolf gang member asked while hefting the bag with weapons and a couple explosives they bought on the black market, on his shoulder. They moved steadily towards the large house with an iron gate.

"Fuck yeah. Gaffe works at the car rental place where the bastard returned his car. Gaffe took it be cleaned and found some of his hair and black material with Tag's scent snagged in the hood. He called me and we tracked the other scents from the car to this place." Pablo looked at the other two gang members. "Gaffe's our best tracker and he says the man who drove the car that killed Tag and Squire are staying in that house." He pointed to the home at the end of the road. "They're from out of town. Americanos. Too bad he couldn't get their credit card information, we could've really fucked them up over and over."

"Yeah, would've been good."

Pablo stared at the house a few moments and then spit in its direction. "Tight security, Gaffe said they'd know if we went inside. Silent alarm. Didn't want to let them know we found them, they might've run away. That's why we're here to repay them for Tag and Squire."

"Una vida para una vida."

"Si. A life for a life. Human or wolf, makes no difference." They moved forward watching the road. If the foreigners returned before they finished, they would use their automatic weapons to gun them down. But that was too quick, too easy. These assholes needed to suffer for the injustice of what they did.

"We're near Sup turf."

"Yes. There's a temporary truce until we find the killers," Pablo said looking around. Sup's were mean and unpredictable. They could've easily snapped Tag's neck last night. Except everyone knew they would've owned up to it.

"That's just til sundown," the other said while testing the locked gate.

"We'll be done in time." Pablo looked at the house and grounds. "After we set things up, we can wait over there." He pointed to a well-known neutral area. "I want to see this motherfucker blow."

The other two nodded and jumped over the fence. "Place it so they can't see it when they drive in, maybe the back wall, near the porch."

"Neighbors?"

"Fuck them," Pablo said walking behind his pack mate. With his expertise handling explosives, he placed the putty-like material in the middle of the back of the house, and inserted the detonator.

Pablo tested the back door and backed off when a security camera light flicked on. He cursed and moved further out of range. He seethed with impotent rage that a human killed his full-blood brothers. It hadn't seemed possible but Tag's scent on the car was irrefutable proof and the car had been left at the rental lot not long after Tag's death. When he and Gaffe came by the house earlier, they only scented humans.

Both had suspected Sup's involvement until that moment.

With one last look at the house, they moved to wait in safety. An hour and a half later two vehicles, one with two human males, the other with one, drove slowly down the road and stopped to open the gate. Silently the cars entered the yard, the driver of the second car closed the gate behind them.

Pablo watched with merciless anticipation as they grabbed bags of food from their cars and headed to the house. They wouldn't be eating anything tonight, he thought. He waited a few minutes and sent the signal to detonate.

The shot rang out.

The building exploded.

Fire consumed the house as all manner of debris rained down. The car in the garage caught fire and eventually exploded. The burning house was a blazing light for miles around. The house would burn to the ground before any life support services would make it out here. If the house was on their turf they'd have a party for Tag and Squire around the remains of their enemies.

Pablo wished he could do more, but the heat from the flames discouraged him from taking a closer look. No one could survive that explosion, he made peace with avenging his brothers' murders.

Concerned the Sups would come to investigate, Pablo and the other red wolf members, gave each other fist bumps as they loped down the hill toward their vehicles.

"Take that motherfucker. Payback from Tag and Squire."

####

"Silas!" Jasmine yelled. One moment she and Silas were teasing each other with sexual promises, the next their link went silent. Her heart raced as she searched for him through their connection. He wasn't dead, she would know if he were. Something had happened. What? Eyes closed she went deep, seeking his heartbeat. When that didn't work, she sought his beast.

"Silas," she moaned as intense pain radiated from his beast. Without thinking she sent healing energy through their link while praying to the Goddess for help to save him.

"Mistress?" Asia called several minutes later. *"Hawke has been hurt. A bomb went off, he's regenerating slowly, the metal in his arms and legs won't burn but the re knitting of that much skin is debilitating. Angus is not responding and he can't find La Patron."*

"A bomb?" Jasmine's mind was stuck on that word. Why? Who? No one knew who they were. Why would they bomb the house?

"Yes, Ma'am. The house is far out, no sirens, no one's come to offer help. The place is on fire. Hawke's going to move Angus out as soon as his legs flesh out more around the metal. Have you heard from La Patron?"

Heard from Silas after a bomb? Jasmine shook her head to dispel the disbelief. It happened. She had to deal with that new reality. Her mate had been blown up.

She gasped and bent over holding her stomach as nausea rolled through her. Silas, her heart cried out. Her man, hurt thousands of miles away.

Bombed? She couldn't believe it. *"No, he's hurt. I'm sending energy to his... to his beast. Does Hawke need anything?"*

"If we could send energy it would help him heal faster to get them out of there so they could start searching for La Patron," Asia said.

Jasmine wiped the tears from her face. *"Right. Right. I should've thought of that. Ready?"*

"Yes, Ma'am."

Carefully, Jasmine pulled energy from her base of women through-out the Nation and sent it to Asia. Asia sent it through her link to Hawke. *"We'll need to get Shyla to help Angus."*

"Yes," Asia said. *"You may need to talk to the twins and the pups. They may need to help."*

Unsure how her kids could help Silas, Jasmine didn't respond. Instead she sent more healing energy to Silas' beast, trusting him to keep all of her mate alive and whole.

Jacques knocked on the door of her private quarters. "Jasmine? A couple Alphas have contacted me, they can't reach Silas."

She released a long breath, closed her eyes for a few seconds and stood to open the door. "Come in." She walked slowly to the kitchen for a glass of water and realized she couldn't drink anything. "Have the twins, David and Renée come here." She never hated her inability to mind-speak with her family more than right now.

"Okay," Jacques said softly.

Jasmine appreciated he didn't push. He must have sensed something was terribly wrong. She remained in the kitchen staring at the granite counter top without moving. The light tap on the outer door, footfalls and then silence.

"Mama?" David said walking closer.

She sensed Renée on the other side. Turning, Jasmine looked into the concerned eyes of Tyrese and Tyrone. She exhaled and told them what she knew about the situation.

Renée gasped and grabbed Jasmine's hand. Jasmine placed one arm around her, holding tight as Tyrese picked up her other hand. No one spoke for several seconds.

"I'll contact Grandfather, we may have kin in that country," David said.

Jasmine nodded and accepted the kiss he placed on her cheek. "Daddy's strong, he'll catch his wind and be in contact," David said with a level of confidence Jasmine envied.

She nodded.

"Hawke's moving around," Tyrese said. "He says Angus isn't moving. We need to send energy to him as well." He looked at Tyrone. "Let's do it." Tyrone nodded.

Jacques moved into the spot Tyrese vacated and looked at her. "This wasn't the military."

Jasmine blinked. "What?"

"I just wanted you to know this wasn't the military. The Knights are airborne, on the way here. Silas made sure no one knew who he was at the research facility. The Joint Chiefs think he's here, angry and refusing to speak with them."

She nodded slowly recalling Silas' comments regarding starting a war. "Okay." She wouldn't make any promises yet, if it hadn't been for the Joint Chiefs her man wouldn't have been in Honduras. Knowing Silas was regenerating kept her sane, and hopeful.

"Right now, I don't care who did this, I want Silas found and brought home along with the others. What's the best way to make that happen?" She looked into the face of her children and then Jacques.

"Hawke's got Angus out of the building and into the woods. No one's come to help yet. We'll keep sending Angus' beast energy so he can shift. Hawke's looking for dad," Tyrese said.

"He had just stepped outside when the bomb went off," Tyrone said. "Hawke thinks he went airborne."

Jasmine closed her eyes. He had mentioned stepping outside when they'd been talking.

"Cameron's here, he's got questions," Jacques said. "He has no idea Silas and the others left."

"What do you want me to tell Adam?" David asked. "He woke sensing something's wrong. Jackie probably will too."

Jasmine met the concerned gazes of her family and shook her head. "Give me a minute." She left the kitchen, headed for the bedroom, and closed the door behind her. She ran into the bathroom, leaned against the closed door, her knees buckled in agony as she cried on the floor.

CHAPTER SIXTEEN

Lucian Saldivar loved running alone at night through the forest after work or when he had free time. Here he was free to think and dream. No one yelled or called him "Runt" a name he'd long outgrown but his Uncle enjoyed reminding him of the time he wanted to forget. He stopped and looked at the darkening sky.

Rain.

Possibly thunderstorms he thought as he changed directions and started for the cozy home he shared with his sister. Raven worried when he came home late which made him smile. She worked in a full-blood bar with a violent gang as customers and she worried about him.

Their Uncle Rick was a hard, unforgiving task-master with his hands in too many pies. He insisted Raven work at the bar to keep an eye on her. Lucian believed the man wanted at least one honest employee he didn't have to pay much.

Once their Uncle realized he and Raven wouldn't do anything illegal, he'd tried expel them from the Sup's. Several pack members vetoed the idea because of Lucian's loyalty to the pack. Several pack members wanted an Alpha challenge which the older wolf didn't want.

Lucian believed that scare pushed his Uncle into an alliance with a military guy named Franz. They spent a lot of time together working on improving full-bloods. His litter-mates Tasha and Duke were deep into the experiments, and taking drugs. Tasha barely had control of her beast and Duke seemed high most of the time. Lucian worried one day one or both of them would die because of that poison they took. Not that they'd listen to him, he warned them against messing with their beasts until they begged him to leave them alone.

So he did. He and Raven moved away from the main house to a smaller house at the edge of pack lands.

Lucian tripped over a log and fell to his knees, coming face to face with a dead human. Shifting to human, he shuddered as cold droplets of rain pelted his skin. He sniffed.

Not human. Wolf. No. Human.

Frowning he looked at the black-haired man who appeared asleep. Wolf or human? Lucian was unsure. The first drop of rain slid down his forehead onto the face of the man.

Uncertainty plagued him. They were forbidden to have dealings with humans, although few heeded that warning. He looked around hoping to hear someone calling in the distance, but heard nothing but the whistle of the elements. Could he leave this one here to die in the storm?

Thunder boomed in the distance. Lightning split the sky. Standing, he picked up the man and took off running.

Lucian walked out the shower with a towel around his waist. Raven stood over the man lying on the sofa in their front room.

"I've seen him," she said slowly, looking over her shoulder at her brother. "He's the human 1 told to leave the bar, the one who gave me the 100-dollar bill." She faced Lucian. "Where did you find him?"

"In the woods, a few miles west of here." He looked at the man again. "So, he's human then?"

She clicked her tongue at him. "Of course, what else?"

"Not sure, for a second back there… it was nothing." He walked to his room in the back to get dressed.

"Another one of your feelings? Are you having those dreams again, the big black wolf dreams?" she asked following him.

"Yes and no."

She snorted. "Don't let Tasha or Duke know. Tasha swears by your feelings and Duke will just press you to get more involved in pack business. He swears you'd be a natural, rise to the top."

Lucian had heard it all before. "Not interested in going to prison."

"Hardly likely. No one gets arrested here," she said. "Uncle owns the Policia and the politicians. Money is god." She headed into the kitchen. "Come eat and tell me what you plan to do with the human."

Lucian glanced at his house-guest again and sat at the table. "I have no plans for him. There's a storm outside, I couldn't leave him lying on the ground. Plus, he gave you a nice tip."

She placed a plate of food in front of him. "Security might scent him and stop by. Be ready to explain his presence I doubt the tip excuse will work. We don't need to give them any reason to kick us out."

"Us?" He eyed her. "Not you. I did this. I couldn't leave him —"

"Neither would I," she snapped. "It's both of us. I didn't see any blood or bruises, hopefully he'll wake soon and leave. Or we can take him back to his hotel, somebody's probably looking for him."

He nodded and ate in silence. Had he sensed a wolf earlier? Lucian was certain he had. It was as if it flipped back and forth between human and wolf, which made no sense. He must have gotten it wrong. Then why does it feel that he was right?

"Stop thinking so hard," Raven said.

He smiled and took another bite. "Should I leave him on the couch or put him in my room?"

She looked in the direction of the living room. "I'd leave him in case something's wrong that we can't see." She frowned. "He doesn't smell sick."

Lucian paused. "No, he doesn't smell much at all."

She met his gaze with a puzzled frown. "You're right, he doesn't. Strange for a human. Maybe it's because he's unconscious."

"Seriously?"

She chuckled. "You got a better explanation?"

He thought for a moment and shook his head. "No. No I don't." Moments later he finished eating, cleared his plate and went to clean the kitchen.

Raven stopped him. "I'll do this. Go ahead, get settled, this may be a long night if he wakes. You'll need to take him to town or wherever he's staying."

Tired, Lucian rubbed his neck and nodded. "Good point. I'd hate to drive all the way near the bar, but if that's where you saw him, he might be staying near there. Thanks, I'll get some sleep." He headed to the back while she went into the kitchen. Exhaustion hit him hard. As soon as his head hit the mattress he was asleep.

He dreamed.

He dreamed of a big black wolf.

"Hello, Grandfather."

"Hello, Lucian."

CHAPTER SEVENTEEN

Jasmine watched the sun rise with a burning hope in her chest that Silas would heal soon and speak or whisper or sigh or give any response at all. This silence weighed heavily on her shoulders. She never fully realized how much she depended on his constant presence until now. Over the past several hours she'd known loss in a way she'd never experienced. David and Renée shadowed her, both in hopes that she would hear from Silas and to make sure she wasn't alone. There was a chance David didn't want her anger to spike but she wouldn't think about that.

"Breakfast, Mom?" Renée called from the kitchen.

Even though she had no appetite, she would need energy to make it through the day. So far, they'd put the Alphas off but the longer Silas was off-line, the more likely they would know something was wrong and would seek answers. Jasmine and Jacques hoped Silas would regain consciousness, which would at least reconnect him with the pack. She wasn't ready to think of the alternative.

"Yes, be there in a minute." She wiped the trail of tears from her cheeks while wondering when she would stop crying. "Not anytime soon," she muttered. The idea of Silas being in an explosion and sent flying through the air sent chills down her spine each time she thought of it. Tears were never far behind.

She went into the bathroom, washed her face and put on a clean tee-shirt with a pair of jogging pants. "Something smells good," she said entering the living area.

David smiled as he leaned close and kissed her cheek. "Renée did most of it. I think she's ready to do the homemaker thing." He winked at his sister who snorted.

"Boy, please. I just want the wedding not the rest of it. Not now anyway." She placed a tall glass of sweet tea in front of Jasmine and pushed the plate of pancakes close. "Bring the bacon and sausage."

"Yes, Ma'am," David said mocking her.

Jasmine laughed at their antics and it felt good. Almost normal. Silas would enjoy this. Her throat tightened at the thought of him alone in the woods, fighting to live.

"Mom. Mom, it's okay." Renée wrapped her arms around Jasmine and held tight. "Jackie and Quinn are on their way. Adam and Bella will be here later today. We'll get through this. Whatever you and Daddy need, I promise we will get through this."

Jasmine sniffed and tried to smile as she patted Renée's arm. "Thank you, baby. Now let's eat, we're going to have a long day ahead of us."

Renée leaned back and met Jasmine's gaze. "Alright. But you don't have to do anything you don't want to do. That's one of the perks of being in charge."

Jasmine chuckled. "Being in charge means doing things I don't always want to do. But I understand what you mean."

David took a couple pancakes and meat. "I spoke to Grandfather, he promised to help. Have you talked to the Goddess?"

"I've prayed, She's aware of what's going on. He's regenerating, based on what Hawke explained, Silas took a big hit being outside near the explosive and Angus was standing almost in front of it inside. He's still not responding well." She took a long sip of tea and winked at Renée. "Perfect."

Renée grinned and took a bite of sausage.

"The rain didn't help," David muttered.

Jasmine reined in her exasperation over the weather. "By the time Hawke's legs and arms were healed enough to move about, he had to work on Angus. Rese and Rone spent a couple hours helping to get Angus' wolf to the point it could begin healing his human side." She paused at the memory. "There were times we thought we lost him. He stopped breathing. I can't imagine…"

David covered her hand. "He pulled through. His wolf is healing his human side which takes longer but he will heal. Just like Daddy's wolf is healing him. They will both heal and come home."

Jasmine nodded and squeezed his hand. "I know you're right. My head tells me that all the time, but my heart… I need to hear him, touch him if only with words. My soul needs to touch his again."

"You will, Mama. You will," David said as he rose and hugged her close.

She inhaled the scent of her children and thanked the Goddess for them. They kept her grounded when her natural inclination was to fly off in a rage, to punish someone for what happened to Silas. The hugs, kisses, encouraging words were balms against her beleaguered spirit.

"I know, baby."

"Mistress?" Asia reached out to her through their link.

"Yes? How's Hawke?" Jasmine prayed he didn't have a relapse, he was Silas and Angus' main shot of leaving that place. Late last night he found an old house tucked away in the mountainside and took Angus there to heal in case their enemies returned.

"He's almost at 80%. Angus is still at 50% and angry over the delay. He wants to hunt for La Patron right now even though he's in wolf form. Hawke's having a hard time keeping him confined. Is there any way for you to speak to Angus, to calm him? Hawke can't leave him like this, the storm is over but it's wet and muddy. Not ideal for a wolf at 50% of his strength."

Jasmine thought about it for a few seconds. *"I can piggyback with Shyla, I've done that before. I'll have her come here, or I'll go to their quarters and speak to him."* She paused. *"Does*

Hawke have any idea which direction Silas went?" Jasmine didn't want to push the search, after all someone did try to kill them and may try again.

"He's ruled out the directions La Patron couldn't have gone and plans to start searching as soon as Angus calms down."

Jasmine pushed back from the table, startling her kids. "I need to talk to Angus, he's stopping Hawke from going out to search." She stood and headed toward the door. *"Call Shyla, let her know I'm on my way."*

Jasmine inhaled deeply, tucked her hair behind her ear, took one last glance in the mirror and walked out the door. In the living room, Jackie, her mate Quinn, Renée, David, Tyrone, his mate Rose, Tyrese and his mate Danielle sat talking softly. They looked at her as she entered.

"Ready?" Jasmine asked, as her gaze lit on each of them.

"Yes," they said or either nodded.

"Good let's go. Jacques has everything set up, so there's seats for everyone." Her gaze lingered on Quinn who volunteered to remain behind in Jackie's room during the meeting.

He smiled as he nodded.

Jasmine headed toward the door. David moved quickly, wrapped his arm around her shoulder and whispered in her ear. "You look gorgeous, and powerful. I'm so proud you're my mama." He kissed her cheek and stepped back to walk behind her. Jasmine looked over her shoulder at them as they lined up behind her. She understood the gesture of their support and nodded because she couldn't speak around the lump in her throat. Instead she straightened her spine, and walked toward the elevator to head to the conference room.

Inside the conference room the large monitor flickered on. Several Alphas were checking in, she heard echoes of their comments as they searched for the connection to Silas. Her children sat along the wall as she and Jacques sat at the table.

As each Alpha checked in, Jasmine tightened her link to them, surprising many. Once the last voice stated present, the room fell silent and they looked at her. When Jacques suggested she have this meeting with the Alphas, initially she refused. In her mind Silas would be fine within the hour and on his way home.

That was six hours ago. Six hours with no verbal response from her mate had been torturous. Jacques explained the Alphas were also feeling the loss and were concerned. It was better to address the issue rather than allow uncertainty to foster and grow.

"Hello Alphas."

"La Patroness." A few responded with various manners of address but all stared in anticipation.

"Silas was on an expedition, yesterday the house he was staying in exploded. He, Angus and Hawke were inside." She held up her hands as the Alphas yelled outrage, battle bulked to fight, and asked questions. "Gentlemen, refrain from interrupting me." She spoke the words in a moderate tone but they heard the steel beneath. One by one they settled and met her gaze.

"Hawke is one of the best hunters in the Nation and is searching for Silas. Once Angus has recovered he will join Hawke."

"Where is he?" an Alpha shouted. "We will bring our Alpha home."

Jasmine leaned forward, clasped her hands on the table and stared at the Alpha who spoke. "Alpha Stone from the great state of California, right?"

He straightened in his seat. "Yes, Mistress. I am honored you remember me."

Jasmine smiled. "Of course, I remember all those who serve my mate and I." She paused to allow her words to settle. "But let me make this clear. No one is going anywhere until I deem it's safe. There are matters involved in La Patron's expedition that you don't know about, it's a highly sensitive situation." She thought of the bracelet and the havoc it would cause if it fell into the wrong hands. She held up her hand to stop his response. "We know every one of you would give your life to find Silas... we know that and appreciate it more than you know. I'm telling you now is not the time. I will not allow anyone to jeopardize Silas' original mission or his return home. Is that clear?" her voice sharpened at the end.

They were slow to agree. Her eyes itched, she knew they changed colors. She slapped the table and pointed at them. "I will say this once more," she growled low in her throat. "Is that clear?"

"Yes, Mistress."

"Yes, Ma'am."

"Yes, La Patroness." The responses came faster and she listened to make sure each person agreed. "If you have a problem with what I've just said, save your complaints for when Silas sits in this chair, in the meantime listen to what I'm going to share with you and keep it to yourselves."

This time they agreed immediately.

Jasmine shared what happened with the Knights and the Joint Chief's role and their calls to make things right. "They don't know Silas is not here. Staff don't know either and we will keep it that way as long as possible."

"Who did it if not the government?" an Alpha asked.

"We don't know. Hawke thinks it was a case of mistaken identity, there were no triggers that someone had been on the property or inside the house." She refused to replay the explosion in her mind, now wasn't the time to get weepy, she needed to get through this meeting and check in with Angus and Hawke.

The Alphas discussed the possibility of who attacked Silas and Hawke's perspective for several minutes giving her a mental break.

"How is Angus. A blast like that could have killed him," Alpha Theron asked concerned.

Jasmine inhaled and met his sympathetic gaze. "Almost did. The twins worked on him with Hawke for a while, until his beast stabilized. His human side is still broken and healing."

Alpha Theron nodded. "Thank the Goddess."

"That's what's going on with Alpha. His beast is strong, he's healing. Wherever he is, his beast is working to heal him," Alpha Lyle said with confidence. The others nodded, the mood shifted. They appeared more confident that Silas would survive whatever befell him and that was a good thing.

"Plus, Mistress has been feeding his beast energy constantly. My bitch sensed a pull yesterday but had no idea why," Alpha Jayden said nodding slowly. "Great idea, get his beast healed so Alpha can eventually shift and finish healing."

"My bitch mentioned the same thing," Alpha William said looking at Jasmine as if seeing her for the first time. "You've been working on Alpha the whole time."

She didn't respond, instead she cleared her throat. "Does anyone else have questions regarding what I expect you to do until Silas returns?"

"I sensed you linked to me the same as Alpha, does that mean I report to you?" Alpha Paxon from Arizona asked.

"Yes. Until Silas returns the structure is the same. Asia is on the KnightForce desk, Jacques has Administration, Tyrone has Half-breed Issues and Concerns, that hasn't changed. If you have an issue you'd like Silas' input on, contact me." She thought about everything that was said and unsaid. "Let me be clear, my mate will return soon. He's not dead, it's already been said - he's healing. When he returns home, he'll release me from this position when he's ready, not a moment before. Until that time, we will continue as if he were on the other side of the door, with excellence and honor." She took her time and met each gaze on the monitor, accepting their agreement.

When they'd all agreed, she nodded. "Be well Alphas, look after the Goddess' people." She inhaled deeply once the monitor disconnected. "One down." She looked at Jacques. "Are the Generals ready?"

General Crall did not arrive at the Compound with the four Knights. As soon as the plane landed on American soil, he had been called to Washington immediately. The Knights arrived earlier that day and were undergoing tests and treatments with Dr. Passen.

"Yes, Cain and Abel as well."

She looked over her shoulder at her kids. They returned her gaze with smiles, thumbs ups, and a couple winks.

"My Shero," Jackie said.

"I know, right," Renée said meeting Jasmine's gaze. "I wanna be like you when I grow up."

"Me too," Tyrone said.

Rose bumped against his shoulder. "I know that's right."

Danielle laughed and leaned against Tyrese. "Mom rocks. Did you feel the temperature drop in this room when they took too long to agree?"

"Brrrr, it did get cold, didn't it?" Tyrese said. "Now you know where I get that from."

"Get what?" Danielle asked, watching her mate.

"My tough machismo." Tyrese said with a straight face.

Jasmine laughed. It was wonderful having the kids here. Tension rolled off her back and shoulders.

"Are you ready, Jasmine?" Jacques asked from the controls.

"Yes, thanks Jacques. I'm dressed and here, time to get it over with." She inhaled, straightened in her seat and watched the monitor. This time Generals Crall and Miller's faces filled the screen first. Next, Cain and Abel joined them.

Since they knew about the Knights, but not that Silas had gone after the team personally, Jasmine danced around the facts differently. She didn't mention the explosion, it was too easy for the generals to connect the dots in Honduras, she made it seem as if he were in Canada, without saying it directly, to check on expansion in that area and would be out of touch. Cain and Abel seemed skeptical but didn't question her. The Generals thought it was a good idea. The meeting lasted less than 15 minutes which suited her fine.

"Mistress, I heard from Hawke. He found the area where La Patron landed, but he was moved."

Jasmine couldn't have heard right. Surely, Asia meant Silas walked, crawled or scooted away. *"Moved?"*

"Yes. Hawke picked up another scent at the same place where he located La Patron's scent. Someone moved him."

CHAPTER EIGHTEEN

"Wake up now, Lucian." Grandfather's voice snapped loud in his ear. He jerked awake confused by the darkness of his bedroom.

"Stop, leave him alone," Raven yelled.

Lucian rolled out of bed and ran barefooted to the living room. Raven's face held a red palm print, tears rolled down her cheeks. Lucian took in her disheveled appearance in a glance and leapt forward. He slammed into the first full-blood security patrol, punched him in the jaw, knocking him sideways and ducked the blow from the second guard. The body that had been on the sofa was now on the floor.

Lucian picked up the second guard and body slammed him on the hardwood floor. Chest heaving, he looked at the two fallen guards and pointed. "Which of you touched my sister?" He zeroed in on the bigger wolf, leaned forward and dragged him to his feet. Before the guard could speak, Lucian punched him three times in the face and then slapped him, leaving a similar mark.

"Lucian," his sister called as she picked their guest up from the floor and replaced him on the sofa.

He glanced at her, grabbed the second guard and shook him. "Who hit my sister? You?"

"No, Lucian," the guard said blocking his face. "Honest I didn't hit her. You know me better than that."

Chest heaving, Lucian stared at Berto, an old friend a few seconds long and released him. "Who is he?" he pointed to the guard lying on the ground.

"New to the pack. Rick and that guy Franz, brought him in a few days ago. He's learning the ropes, today's his first day on security. Might be his last too." Berto scowled at the fallen guard. "He picked up the human's scent, ran in this direction before I could reel him in. Raven didn't want him inside, he hit her while explaining she broke pack law." He rubbed his chest. "You still packing a mean punch, did you have to hit me so hard?"

Lucian took a step back and exhaled. "Berto, you know I don't play with Raven's security. He pointed to the other guard. "If you ever touch my sister again, I'll kill you. Are we clear?"

The guard glared at him as he tried to stand, stumbled and held onto the wall for a few seconds. "You're hiding a human on pack land."

Lucian stepped closer. "Touch her again, ever, and I will kill you. Do you understand or do I need to kill you now? Make your decision."

No one spoke. Lucian's muscles coiled in preparation to strike. He would break the fucker's neck and toss him outside with the trash.

"Fine, I won't touch her, but I'm calling this in." He strode toward the front door and stepped outside.

Berto groaned.

"What?" Everyone knew his Uncle didn't bother with him or Raven. Chances are he'd ignore the guard or curse at him for disturbing his sleep.

"That military dude is with Alpha Rick. Whenever that guy's around Rick acts all tough and by the book with rules," Berto said leaning against the wall. "Something's wrong with that Army dude, he's on some kind of drug, makes him…weird and shit. Nobody messes with him, no matter where he goes, reds, blues, giants, all the gangs give that motherfucker a pass, treat him like a real threat and it's not because of the military either."

Lucian didn't care about his Uncle or his friends. Something… no not something, someone, woke him. They told him something he needed to remember but couldn't. "Raven." He extended his hand to her.

She took it.

"You okay?" He placed his fingers beneath her chin and turned her face. The bruise was disappearing but he'd seen it and that was enough. This country was hard on women, offering them very little protection and not much in the way of legal recourse. He couldn't protect every woman, but he'd die protecting his litter mates Raven and Tasha. Everyone knew they were off limits.

"I'm fine, he caught me off guard, that's all." She glanced toward the door where the guard stood outside, no doubt speaking to Rick.

"Sorry this happened to you." He squeezed her shoulder and looked at Berto who wore a pained expression. She followed his gaze and then looked up at him. They both knew nothing good was going to happen when Berto pushed off the wall and took a couple steps toward them.

He sighed and met Lucian's gaze. "Alpha wants us to bring the human to him. He's got something going on and feels this man could be the answer."

Lucian's gaze narrowed on Berto. Normally it wouldn't bother him what happened to any human, so why did the idea of his Uncle taking this one send a streak of cold dread down his spine. He glanced at the man lying on the sofa and wondered why he couldn't simply abandon him to his fate.

Berto stepped closer. "Look, don't fight him on this. He just needs to throw some meat at one of the gangs to seal a deal. You don't know this guy, do you?"

Lucian shook his head slowly. "No but I have this strange feeling I'm not supposed to let anything happen to him." He stared at Berto. "Why do I have these inconvenient, weird ass feelings?"

Berto chuckled. "Don't know, you've always had them since you were a cub. Pick him up, bring him with us so you can protect him. You know better than to ignore your feelings."

"I'll get my jacket," Raven said running to the back.

"She's going?" Berto asked craning his neck to see down the hall.

"Looks like it." Lucian picked up the sleeping human, and held him in his arms while waiting for Raven. Lucian stared at the stranger for several seconds trying to recall the voice from his dream. Had it been Grandfather? He couldn't remember. Who are you? Why is your life important? He wondered.

Raven returned. "Uncle Rick doesn't want me to come. He's afraid Duke will kill the guard if he sees my face."

"Or Tasha, she's meaner than Duke, tougher too," Berto said. No one mentioned his Uncle's response in Lucian accompanying the human, they all knew he would go regardless and they'd have to convince him to release the human instead of trying to take him, or there would be problems.

"Lock the door behind us. I'll let you know what happens," Lucian told her as he stepped outside. Three additional guards stood off in the distance. Reinforcements he guessed, although if he were really angry, he'd shift to his two-footed beast and no one could bring him down in that form. Being the only one in the pack, or any pack in the region, with that ability was both a blessing and a curse. His Uncle wanted to use him as extra muscle in his illegal business deals. Disgruntled pack members wanted him to challenge his Uncle for the Alpha of the pack.

He took off running.

When he neared the mansion, without breaking stride, he held onto the human tighter, jumped and cleared the high railed balcony. His sister, Tasha, sat on a smaller sofa with Franz. Duke and a few other Sup's stood further in the room. His Uncle stood in the middle of the room in front of the fireplace.

"Franz have you met my litter mate's son? As a pup, I called him runt. You can see he's far from that now." His Uncle smirked.

Franz stood and walked toward Lucian. "Who is he?" he pointed to the man in Lucian's arms.

"A friend." The words surprised Lucian as much as Franz and his Uncle. He had wondered how he'd help the human and hadn't come up with a plan. Saving a friend was definitely in line with his character and something that his Uncle would believe.

"You know this man?" his Uncle asked incredulously. "Is he someone from the hotel?"

Lucian managed both hotels the pack owned. He looked at his Uncle and noted the cunning gaze, twisted lips and pinched nose as if he smelled something foul. Since that was the way he always responded to Lucian's presence, he didn't take offense. "Why?"

That one word challenged his Uncle's authority, something Lucian was careful not to do. He had no desire to become Alpha of a group of wolves chasing after power, selling drugs and weapons. But he had to make it known he was serious in offering the human protection. The silence lengthened as his Uncle stared at him.

"I'm curious why he was in your… your parents' home. Is he friends of the departed?" his Uncle asked.

Lucian sensed Duke's unease over his Uncle bringing their sire and mam into the conversation and decided to bring it to an end. "Not that I'm aware of… Uncle." He turned slightly and looked down at Franz. "Why are you standing so close? Do you plan to stick me with that needle in your palm?"

Franz looked up and met his gaze. "No. Not this time. I've been told not to do anything to you against your will which leaves us with a particular problem." He walked back to the chair and sat next to Tasha. She placed her hand on Franz' thigh and looked up at him with a silent plea. *Don't hurt him, please.*

"You can do better," he told her.

"Probably but I want him," she said. *"He's useful. Understands and spoils me."*

"Okay."

"This one isn't interested in pack problems or dilemmas," his Uncle said smoothly re-inserting himself. "Over the years we've all tried to get him more involved."

Duke groaned. "Don't do this."

"Do what?" his Uncle said holding out his arms in an innocent gesture.

"Explain the problem, Franz," Tasha said, her gaze flitting between Lucian and Franz.

Franz looked at Rick who nodded as he walked back to the fireplace.

Lucian glanced behind him and walked toward a long sofa. "Can you move please so I can lay him down?" he asked the three men sitting there.

They nodded and stood.

Lucian gently lay the human down and covered him with the brown chenille blanket that had been draped across the back of the sofa. He sat at the head of the stranger and looked at Franz in expectation.

Duke watched, took a deep breath and shook his head.

Franz cleared his throat. "There was a death, two Red Wolves were murdered. The gangs have been looking for whoever did it because if you can snap the neck of two wolves and get away with it, what's to stop you from taking out four or seven or ten?" He looked at Rick and then at Lucian.

"We need the Red Wolf to get something really important for a special project we're working on, they won't do that unless we help find the man or men responsible for Tag and Squire's death," his Uncle said.

"Okay," Lucian said and looked at each man, waiting for them to continue.

"Some people think it was a human who did it," his Uncle said.

Lucian laughed. "A human snapped Tag's neck and then took on Squire? How? Drugged them?"

"No drugs were in their system," Duke said frowning.

"Explain how a human could snap the neck of any full-blood, let alone two," Lucian said.

Several members frowned as they thought it through.

"You may be right, nephew," his Uncle said slowly. "But you could, couldn't you?" He pursed his lips. "You could snap Tag's neck, right?"

"I don't know. I've never tried to snap a neck like you have, Uncle." Lucian met his Uncle's hard gaze with silence.

"I was at a dinner party when those two died... you?" his Uncle said softly.

"Not sure when they died, but after work I went home and went to sleep, like always." He waved down his Uncle's next comments. "Can anyone in here still smell a lie?" he looked at the full-bloods scattered around the room. Several raised their hands.

"Good. I did not kill Tag or Squire or anyone else. Not yet." He stared at the guard who hit Raven. The man moved to the back of the room. There was a smattering of laughter around the room.

"He's telling the truth," a couple of pack members said as they nodded to him.

"Now that we know you didn't kill them, can you vouch for your new friend?" Franz asked.

"No, I can't. When he wakes he will answer for himself," Lucian said with a note of finality.

"Red Wolves are searching for some humans who escaped a burning fire. Seems they blew up a house and can't find the remains," his Uncle said.

Lucian looked down at the human and then at his Uncle. "He wasn't in a fire." Several pack members looked at the human and nodded their agreement. "What's really going on?" He grew tired of the back and forth, it was time to go home.

"Do you really want to know?" his Uncle snapped.

"I asked." Lucian held his gaze for several seconds and only looked away because he didn't want anyone to think he wanted to challenge his Uncle.

"Follow me." His Uncle looked around the room. "Franz, Tasha, Duke, you come too."

Lucian watched his Uncle leave the room with trepidation. When he called Lucian's litter-mates as well, his gut clenched. Something was wrong with Tasha or Duke, possibly both given they'd been taking drugs lately. Tasha and Franz remained seated until he rose, turned and picked up the human.

Something told him this wasn't going to be good.

CHAPTER NINETEEN

Silas gasped as he opened his eyes. The sun blazed brightly in the cerulean blue sky. Water trickled nearby in a stream. A cool, comfortable breeze caressed his skin. Soft grass, green and vibrant covered the valley and hilltop.

He frowned. Valley? Hilltop? "Where am I?" he tried to move but couldn't, not even the simple act of turning his head. He reached out to Jasmine and received static. Concerned he reached out to Angus, Hawke, Jacques, the twins, David, even a few Alphas. Nothing but static.

What happened? The Knights! He went to save his Knights. They boarded the plane… he frowned in concentration. They left with the General for West Virginia to his Compound.

That's right, they're safe. The tension eased and then coiled around him again. "Where am I?" he asked again, hoping he'd remember something that would clue him into what happened.

Still nothing. He sought his beast and was surprised at the amount of energy it used. Where was the energy coming from and why? No matter how hard he tried he had no memory of anything after the Knights boarded their flight.

No idea where he was.

No idea what kept his beast so busy.

No idea how to get home, especially since he couldn't move.

In the distance, he heard the soft footfalls of a wolf and resigned himself to whatever the Goddess allowed, he belonged to her.

"So, you're awake."

Silas stiffened. He'd heard that voice before when the Shershone tried to split his connection with his mate. "Black wolf?"

The wolf moved slowly and stopped so that Silas could see him. "I've been called that." He sat and watched Silas. "Questions?"

Silas snorted. "Where am I?"

"You are here."

"Obviously, where is here and why am I here?" Silas was in no mood to be played with.

"Goddess didn't want you in the darkness of pain and had me bring you to my world until you are ready to leave."

Silas frowned. "Darkness of pain?"

The black wolf blew on him.

Back buckling, horrific pain assaulted him from every pore. Even his eyeballs hurt. His mouth opened to scream but no sound emitted. As soon as it started, it stopped. "She wanted you to avoid suffering through the pain as your body regenerates." He shook his head. "You took quite a hit from the blast. What the bomb didn't tear apart, the fall broke in pieces. Couldn't kill you, your connection to the Goddess prevents that, but for all that, your human side died and had to be repaired. It's extensive and intensive, your bitch supplied your beast with the energy to get it done but it's going to take time."

"Bomb? There was a bomb?" He tried to remember but couldn't. "When? Where?"

Black wolf explained the car rental connection and what happened at the house.

"They blew up the house?" That made no sense.

"To avenge the death of their pack mates. The two you killed."

"They were about to kill me," Silas shot back as the memories assailed him.

"The first yes, the second tried to run and you killed him."

Silas released a breath. "You're right. I could've spared him." He couldn't wrap his mind around what happened.

"Why didn't you?"

"I thought it would start a war, seems it did anyway." He couldn't believe they blew up the house. They were crazy out of control. If Jasmine sent healing energy to his beast that meant she knew he was alive. Still, she had to be worried, he hoped she didn't start a war over this.

"Yeah and you're right. Those packs, they've broken so many rules I think the Goddess or Shershone will cut them off." He sighed. "They're conspiring with humans, selling pack members blood and urine for experiments, they don't remain hidden and have stained the ground with innocent human blood for decades. The ones you terminated had many offenses of killing innocents."

Silas' mind went into overload mode as he sifted through information. "Where is here?"

"A realm of rest for weary souls." He paused. "This is the place David and others came to play when he was a pup."

Silas suspected the wolf was Grandfather, now he knew for sure. "He has good memories of this place."

"Yes. He asked me to find help for you." Grandfather morphed to his human form. Tall, muscular with long, white hair and close-cropped beard, dressed in a green robe that matched his eyes.

"Help?" Silas met the calm green gaze of his ancestor.

"Yes, the explosion sent you flying off into the distance, lost, alone, unconscious in the woods, there was a terrible storm. A good Samaritan found and moved you out of the elements. Hawke is searching for you."

Silas frowned. Something was off about that statement but he couldn't put his finger on it.

"That country's pack is in turmoil. It's ripe for a Lot moment," Grandfather said with sadness.

"What? Who's Lot?" Silas had no idea where this conversation was going. One moment Hawke's searching for him the next is about someone named Lot.

"Lot's account in the Bible. Old Testament."

Silas continued staring at the old man. He knew of Noah and the Ark, but nothing about this Lot person.

"You don't know it, do you?"

"No." Silas refused to feel embarrassed over his lack of knowledge of Christianity.

"To keep it simple, I'll give the brief version. Lot was chosen by God to lead the faithful out of a wicked area because He planned to destroy it. Lot and the few righteous escaped punishment."

"You're saying Honduras will have a moment like that?" Silas asked confused.

"No. Just the full-bloods for now. Many operate as corrupt gangs with impunity…they will have that moment for sure. They think they don't need to follow the rules regarding how we must live. They are wrong. Just because nothing has happened doesn't mean it won't."

Silas wondered what that had to do with him but remained silent.

"I wonder how all of this will end?" Grandfather said a few moments later.

"End?" Once again Silas was at a loss. His thoughts bounced from the explosion, to having a conversation with Grandfather, to his beast healing his body.

"Eventually you'll heal, be found and return home."

If Silas could have nodded he would have. He didn't see a problem with that statement.

"Mission accomplished, hmm?" Grandfather said.

"Yes." The Knights were rescued and probably at the Compound. His pack was safe and that was important to him.

Grandfather released a long sigh. Silas wasn't sure what the old man wanted from him.

"I wondered why She agreed for you to come here," Grandfather said.

"Jasmine?" His mate agreed with him regarding this mission.

Grandfather chuckled. "No. The Goddess."

Silas stilled. Bringing the Goddess into this conversation changed the tenor and flavor. As his benefactress, anything She

142

did with him was important. Had he missed something? He recalled her question to him.

"You are wise to be concerned. There is darkness afoot. Alpha Wolf do you sense a trap?"

The problem with dealing with higher beings is they spoke in code. Seldom did their words hold one meaning. *"Your desire to know the location of the missing wolves is granted. Remember, pack cares for pack, find our wolves and bring them home."*

The Goddess hadn't said for him to go find the Knights, but as Grandfather said, She allowed it. The choice in all of this was his. Had it been a trap? The darkness She referred to, was it the General's experiments or something happening with the Honduran full-bloods? Yesterday he would've said the experiments, now he wasn't so sure. To bomb humans… that was over the top.

"While you did not know what was happening with the full-bloods in that place, she did. She knew their violent nature, utter disregard for rules and penchant for killing innocents."

Silas remained silent. His thoughts raced through the planning of this mission, his initial reaction to the bars on the homes, shock when the waitress told him to leave the bar, as a human he should've been safe from full-bloods. Especially when all he did was order a drink. Plus, they drugged the alcohol, why? If they hadn't been there to get information —

He jerked. "Angus? Where's my brother?" Fear gripped and locked onto his chest. Grandfather mentioned Hawke searching for him but not Angus. That's what was so odd about that statement.

"He sustained significant damage."

Silas tried to swallow and couldn't. Not Angus.

"Currently his beast is doing the same thing to him, yours is doing for you. Although I understand he has opened his eyes and is able to communicate."

A roll of relief washed over Silas. The idea of Angus' death over this could not be borne.

"I'm sure you're feeling guilt over your decision for this mission. Yes, you could have sent others but you missed the thrill of the chase I suppose. Now you're stuck in it. Not just you but those most loyal to you as well."

"What?" Shock raced through Silas. "I feel no guilt overseeing the mission to rescue pack members. As Alpha, it's my responsibility to ensure the well-being of the pack. The Knights were betrayed by the U.S. military. We had an agreement. They lied and cheated. Our men could've died," Silas yelled. His nostrils flared at the idea he was somehow at fault for securing the release of his men.

"Are you saying no one else could've rescued the Knights?"

"It's possible. But the decisions to engage, or not engage required instant responses which couldn't have been done remotely. I changed plans on the spot because I saw the situation, it wasn't relayed to me which aided in the success of the rescue."

"Perhaps you're right. But your involvement created a larger problem. The full-bloods seek vengeance against those who killed their pack-mates. The situation in that area was already volatile. Now it's downright explosive. Soon the world will know, dual-natured beings exists. Some tourist will record the gangs fighting in the streets, taking mortal blows and walking away. Once it hits the internet it will go viral. Researchers will descend on that small country like vultures trying to get answers. Which is code for the Liege all over again."

Silas' jaw tightened over the implication that he started the demise of a regional pack. "If they kill each other all the time, why blow up a house over the death of those two?"

"Good question. Something has changed and I don't know what it is. Using explosives, even in a sparsely populated area, is crazy. And if they're using explosives to fight, where will that leave the country in a year or two?"

Silas didn't want to think about that country. It didn't fall under his jurisdiction.

"No comment, eh? Don't blame you. It's a lot to take in. Plus, you've got North America. Central America's not your problem, eh?"

Central America? "What do you want me to say?" Silas couldn't leave or tune out the old man and that chafed his ass.

"Say? I'm just chatting, passing the time. We can talk about anything you'd like or I'll leave you alone to the silence if you prefer."

"No. It's just… I can't move. My body is useless. I'm having a hard time holding onto my thoughts and I get the feeling you want a commitment from me for something. Now's not the best time for me to deal with the world's problems." Silas met Grandfather's gaze. "I don't want to agree to something now that I'd have to honor later, that's all."

"The thing is, we're all interconnected. Once the world discovers dual-natureds in Honduras, and they're on a course to make that happen soon. How will that impact your pack? Or Barticus' in Europe? You can't think they'll stop with that small country, do you? They'll spread through Central America, each of those countries have pack problems."

Silas had been trying not to think about it at all. Now he had to give the matter consideration. "What about the Shershone, they had no problem coming down hard on me. Why haven't they dealt with these packs?"

"Believe me when I say nobody wants them to police our world. They see things in black and white, like humans and wolves mating is wrong, remember? They don't understand the human element of choice or quirks. But… if the matter isn't handled, they will get involved."

"Hmm," Silas said remembering the cold calculation of the entity when it passed judgment on him and Jasmine. His mate threatened to pull the entire pack's energy to fight the Shershone if they didn't release him. "It's obvious you have something in mind, what is it? A coup?"

"Coup? Nothing that drastic." Grandfather paused. "The human criminals are running drugs, and all manner of vice through that place like it's their backyard. The government is ineffective, which seems to be the norm in the area, or continent. Instead of remaining in the background as the Goddess dictates, the full-bloods emulate humans with gangs, open warfare, criminal enterprises and shedding innocent blood. It will not be tolerated."

"If it just the gangs causing problems, get rid of them. Don't punish everyone for a few."

Grandfather sighed. "Why does anyone join a gang? Hmm? For a sense of family, belonging, protection and survival. Sounds like pack, right?"

"Yes, very similar. But packs have leaders whose job is to make sure those needs are met."

"Indeed. How does a pack leader ensure there's enough food, clothing and shelter for his pack?" Grandfather sighed again. "Gangs originated because packs failed them."

Silas thought about his early challenges of meeting the needs of his people. It hadn't been easy that first winter over 300 years ago. "Hard work, everyone pulling together to make sure there's enough to go around. Become a solid community, staying together to share."

"Yes, but what if that's not enough? Do you become an infamous Robin Hood Alpha for your pack?"

"I would do whatever necessary to see the survival of my pack," Silas said honestly. "But I would teach them how things were supposed to be done and prepare for lean times."

Grandfather nodded. "You're an Alpha with a heart for pack. Which is why you're here, or in Honduras more precisely. If you open your eyes, see the condition of this nation's pack, you could offer assistance. Help them survive. You're their Lot, if they listen they will survive. If not, they will not be allowed to continue."

"What? Wait, I'm not here as La Patron. No one knows I've left the States. I can't just show up and start giving orders or tell them how to live."

"Sure you can. Every full blood in the world knows of you and how America prospers beneath your hand. They know you're a fair and honorable Alpha who cares for his pack. Chances are you're the only one they'll listen to at this point. Not all, but most. For their sakes, I hope they'll make changes and punish those who would cause their destruction."

Stunned, Silas met Grandfather's serious gaze. "I don't interfere in other countries." *Pack cares for pack,* the Goddess' words replayed in his mind.

"Which is shameful. You were given the North American continent yet Mexico and Canada are left to fend for themselves. But that is a conversation for another day."

"I'm responsible for 50 states and over 30 million pack members, that takes a lot —"

"Which you've handled admirably. I doubt anyone would've done it better. But you have trained Alphas with no territory, why aren't they in Mexico or Canada? You have KnightForce and the Knights to assist them, yet you remain safely within your borders while the rest of your mission remains incomplete," Grandfather said with a bite to his tone.

Confused, Silas continued staring at the black wolf. "Why are you angry? Have I done something to you?"

"Yes. You've been given a great gift and commissioned to do great things, yet you're sitting safely on the sidelines as life passes you by. How many sons and daughters do you have?"

"Six," Silas said slowly wondering where this was going.

"How many are Alphas?"

"Six, Jackie and Renée are born leaders as well as my sons."

"What assignments have they received? Are they training as Alphas to lead one day?"

"Yes, they've received training. When the time is right, they'll have assignments. Right now, they're enjoying being young pups in their 20's and 30's," Silas said with heat. He and Jasmine both agreed the pups should have time to explore life, within reason, until they were ready for more responsibility to the pack.

"That's understandable and commendable," Grandfather said in a more moderate tone. "Do you deny you have a surplus of trained Alphas?"

Silas gave the matter some thought. "No, I don't deny it."

"Then why haven't you fulfilled your original quest?"

"I thought that was a discussion for another day," Silas hedged.

"By the Goddess we're having it now," Grandfather yelled as he pointed his finger. "To whom much is given, much is required."

Cornered, Silas shut down. He didn't want to have this conversation. He didn't have a good reason for not expanding into Mexico or Canada. He just hadn't.

"Nothing to say, eh? Didn't think so," Grandfather muttered.

Silas refused to be led into a trap of agreeing to expand. That was something he and Jasmine would need to discuss and prepare for. Off the top of his head he could think of a dozen trained Alphas he could send to organize packs for the Goddess in either Mexico or Canada. Why hadn't he done so? He simply hadn't thought of it.

"Once Angus is healed, he and Hawke will be at your side as you re-enter Honduras. This time the full-bloods will know you're coming and why," Grandfather said in an implacable tone. "There are too many good wolves to die because of those who prostitute themselves for money and power. As the Goddess' emissary you will remind them of what it means to be pack and challenge any who refuse to submit to Her authority. When you leave that place, there should be a pack similar to what you've established in your pack."

Goddess' Emissary struck a nerve within Silas. He was her voice to the pack, he couldn't refuse this assignment.

"And if they say no?" Silas hated not having a choice in the matter.

"Some will, that's a given. I think the majority want peace and long for the days when pack afforded safety and provisions. Unity means something. The Goddess will have a person in that area to help the other countries. Plus, once they return to the Goddess, their gifts will be restored."

"Gifts?"

"Some can use mental links to communicate but not all, some can shift to two legs, that will still be monitored and given to a few, some can decipher truth. The further they moved away from Her, the less they functioned as a pack and lack the abilities to do so."

That sucked and explained a few things he'd noticed about the full-bloods he'd met. Silas gave the matter some thought. He wanted to go home, make love to his mate and see his pups.

Goddess' Emissary.

"As long as I'm not expected to govern, or assign an Alpha from my pack, once we're healed we'll return to this place to make the corrections the Goddess requires."

Grandfather chuckled. "I see why you're Her favorite. Her interests become your interests, well, with the exception of the other American countries."

"Stop with that," Silas said, tired of the harping. "Jasmine and I will discuss the matter on my return."

"About that." Grandfather took a deep breath. "Goddess has extended the life of the bodies you used to enter the country by five days. Instead of returning them within the next two, you now have seven. Which means you won't be returning to the States. Instead, you'll meet with Angus and Hawke soon to explain the mission. You'll leave the mountains as La Patron. Rumors of your arrival are circulating as we speak, started right after the explosion."

"You're kidding, right?" The serious gleam in the old man's eyes said no.

"This is a matter of life and death for this nation's pack. You will need every second to persuade them and deal with all the Alpha challenges. Fortunately, the country's not that big, four maybe five territorial Alphas and one Alpha over them should work."

"You can't expect to get all of that done in seven days." Silas was sure the man had lost his mind. Changing into a National pack took time. Finding a worthy Alpha, the challenges, accepting fealty, all of that took time and diplomacy.

"No. Just set the framework in place. Afterward send the twins of thunder, Abel and Cain, maybe a couple others to work with the regional Alphas." He paused. "You'll probably need to mentor the Alpha for a while."

Silas released a sigh. "Mentor? That takes a long time."

"Exactly. As I said, this matter is serious, you're doing a good thing by assisting them to survive. You'll be waking soon, make sure you explain everything to Jasmine, she's getting worried. Adam and his mate are arriving at the Compound later today. In fact, all of your pups returned once you went missing."

Silas' heart squeezed. He wanted to see them.

"Make sure none of them fly down to meet you. Things will be extremely dangerous initially. People hate change and full-bloods are no exception. The Goddess hasn't extended protection to anyone other than your small team to do this job."

"She is most gracious, I will be sure everyone knows of the importance of this mission." He hoped the pups extended their visits until he returned home.

"Alpha Silas, blood of my blood, the time has come for you to wake and complete this mission."

Silas opened his eyes. Heat flooded his body, then cooled. Thankful he felt something other than debilitating pain he exhaled.

"Thank goodness, you're awake," a woman said.

CHAPTER TWENTY

Jasmine sat at the dining table with the kids and grandkids enjoying an early dinner. Shyla and the boys were there as well as Asia and her teen-aged sons. It was a melancholy event, the whole strength in numbers thing made sense. At any rate, she laughed at Jackie and Renée 's antics regarding a wedding and commiserated with Quinn who only wanted Jackie happy. It was obvious he hated being in the middle of the funny debate.

"Jasmine." Her hand flew to her chest. She closed her eyes in gratitude.

"Silas, baby it's good to hear your voice. How are you feeling? I've missed you so much. Where are you? When are you coming home?" Tears rolled down her cheeks, impatient for answers she swiped at them and stood.

"Mom?*"* Jackie called to her back.

"Your father's alert," Asia whispered. "He contacted Hawke. Angus is awake as well."

Jasmine stopped and leaned against the wall. *"Silas?"*

"I had an interruption, it seems the good Samaritan has left me in the care of the waitress from the bar, they're litter mates. He's negotiating with someone who was using me as bait or a hook to get him to go along with whatever."

"What?" Jasmine had no idea what he was talking about.

"I'll explain everything and there's a lot to explain. Grandfather held me captive for a while."

"David's Grandfather?" Her son had mentioned asking the wolf for assistance in locating Silas.

"Actually, you and I are mixed up in his line, but yes, David's Grandfather. One second, the waitress has questions."

"What waitress?"

Moments later Silas returned. *"Her brother saved and moved me out of the storm, seems he brought me to their home on pack lands where humans are not allowed. He's in some sort of trouble behind it. She had a few questions to ask. I miss you too. I'm healing well, the pain is manageable and I plan to leave this place soon to find Hawke and Angus."*

"Strange how both of you woke and were healed around the same time," Jasmine said wondering if Grandfather delayed their healing for some reason.

"Not so strange when you understand what's going on." He told her about the attack and how he killed the two wolves, the bombing, and everything Grandfather said. He asked her to keep it to herself for a while until he spoke to Hawke and Angus. By the time he finished explaining and answering her questions an hour and a half had passed. The kids sat around the living room watching her and waiting for answers. Asia and Shyla had both left.

"You're staying in that place to save the full-bloods in that country? Is that what you're telling me?"

He released a long sigh. *"Remember what the Goddess said when we sought direction from Her?"*

"Remind me," Jasmine snapped, not liking the direction of the conversation.

"She said there is darkness afoot, asked me if I sensed a trap and said pack cares for pack."

Jasmine cursed. *"I'm getting tired of all this double-talk, Silas."*

"Sweet Bitch, we have seven days before the bodies we borrowed die to accomplish this task for the Goddess. I can't do this without you. Tell me your thoughts."

Several nasty, cruel ideas of what the Goddess could do with this task flew through her mind. Why didn't the Goddess mention this when they spoke last time? Why be so underhanded? What if Silas hadn't gone to retrieve the Knights? Would She have sent him to that place anyway? Questions with no answers rolled through her mind. She didn't have the same level of faith in the Goddess Silas had, which made accepting this dangerous assignment harder to accept.

"You don't want to know my thoughts, believe me they won't help you do any of this."

"Jasmine."

"I'm not feeling this, not one bit. Not the way you're being roped into it or the magnitude of shaping a pack you won't be a part of. What happens if they do what you say while you're there and then revert next year or the year after? Will they be killed then? Or what if the other countries… Guatemala, Belize, who else? Nicaragua, El Salvador and any others in that region, what if they retaliate in fear that you'll step in to make changes with them? What right do you have to do that?"

"The same I had when I went to the untamed colonies over 300 years ago. Instructions from the Goddess to do a certain job. That drove me then and it drives me now. If She intends to tame this continent, She will. How She does it, I don't know. Only that Honduras is to be saved and I'm the instrument to get it done." He paused. *"I cannot do this without you. We are one. I need your support to effectively do this."*

"Even if I don't agree?" She hated asking but needed to know where she stood when it came to her and the Goddess.

"If you do not want me to do this, I will not. I'll return home and tender my resignation as La Patron. You are first, my mate, my heart. I cannot live without my heart."

His words ripped her apart and healed at the same time. Love for him welled in her breast so strong she couldn't speak for several moments. Instead, she opened their link wider so he could experience her feelings.

"Sweet Bitch," he said on a breathy sigh. *"How could you ever consider anyone coming before you? I'd give my life for you in a second. You're with me always. No matter where I am."* He

paused. *"I will return home, they will search for another champion."*

"No." Jasmine turned and wiped her face with the back of her hand. *"You're my champion. Champion for the Goddess, for pack, for decency and honor. I'm so proud of you, that you're the one She chose. I won't apologize for being selfish, for wanting to hold you close, place kisses all over you and inhale your scent. I miss you like I've never missed anything in my life. So, no apology for wanting you here with me. None."*

"Okay."

"You're Alpha and that means sometimes sacrifices have to be made... by everyone. Right now, knowing you were in an...an explosion... it hurts that I can't touch you, to see for myself that you're alright. Know that I hate that more than anything."

"I know."

"The timing sucks. Well, maybe not since you're already there. The fact that full-bloods used explosives to kill humans says how out of control they are." She sniffed. *"I can't wrap my head around that. Never would've guessed that at all. It's overkill. Don't they have guns? Knives? What happened to hand to hand fighting? How'd they go to explosives? It's crazy."*

"I agree."

"Which is evidence that Grandfather's concerns are valid I suppose. But to use Lot? That's Old Testament, harsh days for sure." She sighed and glanced over her shoulder at the kids. She shared what they'd been doing, Adam and Bella's imminent arrival, how good it was to have everyone home and she promised they would wait until he returned.

"I love you more than life," she whispered and poured her feelings into their link. *"You say I'm your heart, well you're mine."*

"I know, Sweet Bitch. We are well mated. My love for you grows stronger with each sunrise."

"Be very sure of this Silas. I'm on the edge, with the Joint Chiefs blowing up the phone trying to get you to talk, the President's invited us to dinner at the White House, and now you're in danger again."

He reminded her of the Goddess' protection and the reason no one else could venture over there now.

"I know all that, but it doesn't change how I feel."

"We'll use my presence here to stop Washington from bothering you."

"Once they know you're there, that will stop them from trying to speak to you here. They may send someone there," she said.

"Possibly, but it won't stop what I'm doing here. The human government can't or won't get involved in pack affairs, and since they have no organized pack like in the States, I have to deal with factions." He paused. *"There will be bloodshed. This will be violent. I want you to know that."*

"That's why I'm afraid. Those assholes used bombs, Silas."

"But they've never used anything like that on other packs. Although I suspect it's just a matter of time. The Red Wolves who bombed the house must be made an example of to discourage that behavior ever again," he said.

"You think?" She wished she knew who they were, she'd hang them high and whip their asses until they repeated the Lord's prayer in several languages.

"Have the Knights made it home?" he asked.

"Yes. They arrived earlier. They've been with Dr. Passen. He and Matt have been running tests. From what I've been told whatever was given to them is running its course and they shouldn't have any lasting effects once it's been eliminated. Matt seemed excited about something. I cut him off because of the meeting with the Alphas." She told him about the meeting and what was discussed.

"Maybe you should greet them, ease their minds," she suggested.

"You handled it."

"Yes, but if they know you're okay, it would make life easier for everyone."

"I'll let them know I'm okay but to still deal with you while I'm on this mission, is that alright? I don't want any distractions."

"Okay. I'll tell the kids what's going on. The rest of the pack will no doubt hear about it in the news..."

"You're right. I'll tell the Alphas and trust them to handle rumors and damage control. Anything else?"

"Just finish this job and come home. We'll discuss kingdom building in Canada and Mexico at a later date."

"Yes, Ma'am. Love you."

CHAPTER TWENTY-ONE

Silas kept his eyes closed for a few more seconds and listened intently for the waitress or her brother. Both started asking him questions while he spoke to Jasmine earlier and he went human deep to become unresponsive. Otherwise he would never have any peace. Slowly, he rose to the surface to listen for heartbeats.

Two. Those weren't bad odds. But he didn't want to hurt anyone. He scanned further out and sensed others, some close, others a good distance away.

Hmm, how to play this? He heard a low murmur of voices.

"I'm telling you don't do this. Uncle Rick's using your loyalty to Duke and Tasha to open a Pandora's box. They never should've dabbled in those drugs, you warned them, Lucian."

Silas recognized Raven's voice.

"Don't you think I know that? Even so, knowing the two of them will suffer if they don't receive help, another drug," he spat. "I can't not help, can I?"

"To rob the Red Wolves? That's insane. Haven't you heard they used a bomb on humans. They've gone loco," she said.

"And no one's going to do a damn thing, are they? No one. They'll do it again, and again. All of this, one pack trying to outdo the other, using drugs, weapons and now bombs." He sounded tired. "It's got to stop."

"Have you heard?" she asked softly.

"What?"

"La Patron is coming from the States. I heard them discussing it in town. He may already be here. There's going to be a meeting. Some say the Goddess has sent him to deal with the bombers, others say he's coming to help our packs maybe take over. There's a lot of talk right now."

Lucian scoffed. "I'll believe it when I see it. It'll take a lot more than La Patron to fix our packs. He'll be lucky to survive the trip. No doubt one of the gangs have a big welcome prepared for him already."

"Maybe. But it'll be good to see a real Alpha again. Someone who puts the needs of the pack first and follows the Goddess. I miss those days," she said.

"Those days are gone for good. Alphas like Rick will never relinquish the realms of leadership. The other Alphas are no better, it's no wonder pack members are scattered all over hiding from those who should protect them," Lucian said.

Silas closed his eyes and shook his head. This might be harder than he thought. Who set up a meeting? He contacted Hawke. *"Do you have a cell phone?"*

"No. It was destroyed in the fire."

"Can you get one quickly?"

"In an hour or so."

Silas wanted to be gone before that. *"I need to leave here. I figured I'd call you to pick me up in Comayagua, or I'll have someone drop me off there, blend in with the crowd, ditch whoever follows me and head into the mountains to meet you and Angus."*

"I'll need to get transportation as well."

"Not yet. I'll have Jacques make reservations for lodging. We've got a long road ahead of us and not a lot of time. Start with the phone. I'll take care of the rest. Let me know when you're ready. Make sure you have food, I'm hungry."

"Yes, Sir."

Silas contacted a happy Jacques and filled him in on what they needed. Jacques would use a South American contact to pick them up, take them over the border and fly them back into Honduras with luggage, credit cards and Id's. Since Jacques vouched for the person, Silas agreed to the impromptu plan.

Now to get his rescuer to drive him into town without answering a lot of questions.

"If he has a meeting I want to go," Raven said.

Silas smiled at the stubbornness in her tone. She reminded him of his princesses, Renée and Jackie.

"Okay, if it's in town away from any pack lands I'll take you. But don't get your hopes up. This isn't the States with decent government and police."

"What if the Goddess has sent him? That means something, yes?" she persisted.

"Maybe, maybe not. Why now? Where have they been all these years? Things have gotten worse but they've been bad a long, long time," he said.

"Never have we taken drugs to change ourselves, maybe that's what's happened," she said.

Silas became more alert. What drugs? The Liege used drugs and technology to change full-bloods years ago. Or did this have something to do with what General Lee had been doing? Silas wasn't sure.

"Even that's been going on for years, it's just worse now." He sounded defeated.

"Still you can't do what Rick wants, not only is it wrong but it may not help Tasha or Duke. All of this is a guessing game, more experiments which got them into this mess in the first place," Raven said.

A door opened.

Silas counted heartbeats and footsteps. Two full-bloods entered the house.

"It may not help me, Raven, but if I don't get more I'll die. Is that what you want?" the female argued.

"Back off her Tasha," Lucian barked.

"She's so self-righteous it's disgusting," Tasha said.

"Nobody told you to start taking those drugs now you want Lucian to risk his life to save yours when you do nothing to help anyone else," Raven said, her voice trembling.

"Don't touch her, Tasha, last warning," Lucian said in a hard voice.

"You always did take up for her against me," Tasha said.

"Cut the drama, Tasha, Lucian would do the same if Raven tried to attack you."

Silas frowned. The voice sounded familiar but he couldn't place it.

"Right, Duke. How could I forget how often my saintly brother defends me?" Tasha said dryly.

"It's late, what are you two doing here?" Raven asked.

"Came to make sure the human hadn't slit your throat in your sleep," Tasha said and then laughed. "Where is he?"

"In there," Lucian said. "He woke earlier."

"Yeah? What did he say?" Duke asked.

"Nothing, went back out," Raven said.

"Are you going to work today? You didn't get much sleep last night," Tasha said.

"I'm good," Lucian said.

Silas looked around the small room for a window. None. Was it morning? He wasn't sure. If Lucian went to work, Silas could ride into town with him.

"Want me to babysit for you?" Tasha asked. "Promise not to hurt him… much."

"No," Raven said.

"Wasn't talking to you, Chica," Tasha snapped.

"Stop. No more arguing. I'm tired of it," Lucian said. Moments passed. "Tasha, I plan to take the human into town with me, I'm sure he has friends, someone looking for him."

"Okay, just being helpful." She paused. "Have you given any thought of what Franz said?"

"Yeah, I have. I don't see why Rick can't just ask the Red Wolves for it, go into a joint venture or something. Stealing from them… that's asking for trouble. They have noses in their pack who never lost the ability to scent shit from miles away."

"Except whoever broke Tag and Squire's neck," Duke muttered.

"Good point," Lucian said.

"So, you aren't going to do it?" Tasha snapped.

"Whoa, stop, Tasha," Duke said. "If he doesn't do it, I'll do it or you can. Don't put pressure on him to do something we both know goes against what he believes in. We knew that when we made the decision to sample that shit."

Silas listened a few more seconds to the back and forth bickering and wished they'd just leave. It'd be easier to deal with Lucian and Raven than the druggies.

What seemed like an hour was in reality around 25 minutes later, the four were eating breakfast in the other room. No one had come to check on him. His stomach growled and he wondered when was the last time he'd eaten anything.

"I have a phone," Hawke said and rattled off the number.

"Thanks. I'll see about getting that ride into town, the markets should be opening. By the time we reach Comayagua, the streets should be busy." Silas recalled all the stalls and open shops lining streets in the former Honduras capital. Renée would love the colonial architecture and beautiful churches located throughout. He sat up, stretched and mumbled loud enough to be heard in the other room.

Footsteps moved toward the door. A click in the lock and the door opened. Silas blinked against the light and placed his hand on his forehead to provide relief. He waited for someone to speak.

"Who are you?" Tasha barked.

"How are you feeling?" Raven asked.

"Would you like some water?" Lucian asked.

Silas looked up with relief. He could answer those questions easily. "Tyrone, friends call me, Ty. I feel like I've been hit over the head with a bat." He touched the back of his head and looked at his hand. "Yes, I'd like some water, please. Thank you." He didn't look at the three who remained in the doorway while

Raven left to get him something to drink. Instead he focused on his plan to meet the others and re-enter the country as Silas.

"Ty, Si?"

Silas nodded and accepted the bottle of water. He drank the entire bottle without pause. The cool liquid eased his parched throat.

"Thank you." He handed the bottle to Raven.

She took it and leaned against the wall watching him.

"What were you doing in the forest?" Tasha asked.

"I was in the forest?" He looked at her for the first time. She was dressed similarly to the first time he saw her in the bar with Franz. Tight jeans and shirt, combat boots. Her eyes were a lighter shade of brown. Dark hair with blond tips in a short, almost military buzz cut. That was new.

"My brother found you lying on the ground." She tipped her head toward Lucian. "The one who looks like Jude Law on steroids."

"You brought me here?" Silas looked at the tall, muscular, wolf with light brown, wavy hair brushing against his face and cleft chin.

Lucian nodded.

"Thank you, man. Thanks a bunch, I appreciate it." He looked around. "I don't see my wallet or anything, but once I get back I can give you something for your trouble."

"How much?" Duke asked.

Lucian straightened. "No trouble helping someone in need." He looked at Duke. "Pass it on to someone else one day."

Duke turned and walked off.

Tasha glanced at Silas and followed her brother. The outer door closed.

"Would you like something to eat? I can fix you something," Raven asked.

As much as he would enjoy a meal, Silas wanted to see Hawke and Angus to make sure they healed properly. He had a lot to explain regarding their assignment. "I'd better not. The water's holding but I don't want to push it."

"Two men were killed a few days ago, necks broken, did you have anything to do with that?"

Silas went human deep and lied. "What? No." He sounded appalled.

Lucian nodded. "I didn't think so but I gave my word I'd ask." He looked at Raven. "Tell Uncle Rick what he said and that you were a witness."

She nodded.

"I'm going to work in another hour. I can give you a ride as far as Comayagua. You can get a cab or transportation wherever you need to go from there," Lucian said.

"Thank you, I appreciate it. Do you have a phone? I'll call my buddy, tell him where to meet me."

"Signal's weak this far out, once we get closer to town you can call," Lucian said.

Silas wondered how far were they from town but didn't ask.

"I'm going to shower, and get dressed, be back in a bit," Lucian said and walked off. Raven entered the room and sat on the edge of the bed.

"I remembered you from the bar, the tip you left, I appreciated it."

Silas smiled as he nodded.

"You are American?"

"Yes."

"Texas?"

He chuckled. "No, north east coast."

"Ah, yes, of course. New York then?" She had a nice smile and eyes full of curiosity.

"New York is a nice place to visit, have you been there before?"

Her smile faded. "No, I've never left home. I'd love to travel one day." She looked at him with large wistful eyes.

"Maybe your brother will take you, it's good to see different things in the world, broadens your perspective."

"You are married?"

"Yes, I am," he said without hesitation.

"I thought so. You are too nice to be a single man." She smiled as she stood. "I am sorry you were hurt during your visit. Not all parts of our country are… painful. Visit the waterfalls in the National Park, or Lake Yojoa if you like water-sports. Our beaches are beautiful and you will have a lot of fun." She walked toward the door and stopped. "If you will be here much longer, another place you will enjoy is Río Plátano Biosphere Reserve. It is one of the most spectacular places in the world, I visit once a month and always see something new."

Silas had heard of the Reserve from Dr. Patten who'd been full of ecstatic praise for the various plants, wildlife and birds living in there. But he wouldn't be traveling that far north. "Thank you, I'll see if I can put it on my to-do list."

She nodded and left the room.

Silas inhaled deeply and stood. Physically, he felt and looked okay. Nothing seemed out of order, he probably had Grandfather and the Goddess to thank for that. Eyes closed, he offered a prayer of thanksgiving for his healing and the healing of Angus and Hawke as well.

Leaving the small room, he walked into a brightly painted living room. A large sofa sat in the middle of the room facing a flat panel screen TV. A kitchen and dining area was to his left and a hall to the right. Raven sat on a soft, cushy chair next to the sofa with her legs beneath her.

"Have a seat, Lucian will be ready soon." She yawned as he moved to take a seat. "I'm going to bed once I lock up after Lucian leaves. I got off work late."

Silas nodded but didn't say anything.

Neither spoke for several moments. She was nodding off when Lucian strode down the hall dressed in black pants and a neatly pressed beige short sleeve shirt with a company logo above the pocket. "Go to bed, Raven," Lucian said as he walked to the door and nodded for Silas to follow him.

"Okay, just wanted to lock up." She looked at Silas. "Take care of yourself, no more getting hurt in the mountains."

Silas smiled and nodded. "I won't." He followed Lucian to a dark blue truck with a crew cab and short flat bed. It was unusual to see such an expensive vehicle in this part of the region. Lucian slid in behind the driver's seat and waited for Silas to enter. After buckling up, they pulled out and headed down a long dirt road.

Silas glanced at the large mansion in the distance. "Nice place."

Lucian didn't say anything. They drove in silence several miles. Once they reached the paved road, Lucian stopped, put the truck in neutral and looked at Silas.

"What were you doing in the mountains?"

"I don't remember going to the mountains, I planned to ask my friend what happened." He wondered if Lucian would toss him out the truck.

"You wake with no aches, pains or anything after being unconscious for hours. How's that possible?"

"Unconscious?" Silas' brow rose. "I don't know." He shrugged. "I don't know."

Lucian continued looking at him. "I hope you're not planning anything that will come back to bite me in the ass. I won't like that, Ty. Not at all."

"I promise you won't see me again. I'm leaving as soon as I can find my buddies." Silas said with feeling.

"Good." Lucian started the truck and pulled onto the highway. "Go see a doctor when you get home, what happened is not normal."

Silas looked out the window and murmured his agreement.

CHAPTER TWENTY-TWO

Silas thanked Lucian for the ride into Comayagua, refused to take money for a cab and walked briskly down the street toward the market. Inhaling he scented a few full-bloods and headed toward Central Square. Hands stuffed in his pocket, he walked briskly down side-streets, avoiding merchants and their colorful wares. The smell of food caused his stomach to grumble, he quickened his pace while scenting the air for full-bloods.

Once he made it toward Central Square, and passed the fountain, he breathed easier at the sight of the Immaculate Conception Cathedral, a landmark in the city and one of the oldest cathedrals in Central America. Inside, a few early morning believers sat in wooden pews with bowed heads. Most importantly, there were no full-bloods. Silas walked to the side, avoiding the main area and headed toward a small area void of heartbeats and electronic devices. He morphed into the older Spanish man he'd been when entering the country a few days ago. He took a deep breath, turned and left the Cathedral.

Appearing as an older male, he returned friendly greetings, waved to those who waved but never stopped his trek out of town to meet Angus and Hawke in the mountains.

"I'm clear of the town," Silas told Hawke as he trudged up a dirt road.

"We can meet you and head out," Hawke said.

Silas agreed and kept walking close to the road trusting his men to find him. The hot sun beat down unbearably, causing sweat to drench his shirt. He stopped once beneath a tree for relief from the heat and took in the natural beauty of the country. It would be terrible to allow a few to ruin life for everyone else in the pack. He'd walked about seven miles when Hawke and Angus picked him up.

"Where too?" Hawke asked as Angus handed Silas a bag with a plate of food.

"We have a new assignment, for now we'll head to the pickup point and I'll explain."

"New assignment?" Angus asked leaning back in the rear seat. *"What about these bodies? They have expiration dates? The bracelet only holds them for five days."*

"Goddess extended them five more days, total of seven." Silas dug into the rice and beans.

"Goddess?" Angus said.

Silas nodded and took another bite. *"Turn here, drive another six miles up this road. There's a house where we can talk and plan."* He had no idea what kind of meat he ate and didn't care. No one spoke as they drove over bumpy terrain into the forest.

"Any other time I'd really appreciate all this," Angus said looking out the window. "Be nice to go for a run."

"Don't have time," Silas said. "We're cutting it close as it is." He shoved everything back into the bag and pulled out a plastic covered bowl of sliced mangoes.

"You took a direct hit, you okay?" Angus asked.

In the middle of eating as many slices of fruit as he could, Silas nodded. "Goddess and Jasmine fixed."

"Good, I was worried when I didn't see you, couldn't contact you." Angus frowned and then turned to stare out the window.

Finished scoffing down his food, Silas upended the first bottle of water, wiped his mouth, and then drank the second. "Ah, so much better. Thanks." He returned everything to the bag and placed it next to his foot. Silas went over the instructions he received from Jacque's contact, they were almost there. He searched the area for full-bloods, found none and spoke.

"Shift to your normal form." He flowed into Silas Knight. Angus appeared confused as he shifted. Hawke tapped the brakes, the car stopped. He shifted and pressed the gas pedal. Silas shared his conversation with Grandfather and explained their mission. By the time they pulled up to the small house tucked neatly into the mountainside, Angus and Hawke were throwing out ideas how to accomplish what they considered borderline impossible.

"Someone set up a public meeting for you? Do you know who?" Angus asked.

"No. We'll find out after we check into the hotel I suppose," Silas said. *"No dual-natureds up here, good. Let's go inside, either he's here or will be here soon."* They exited the car, Silas entered the code on the door and walked inside. Cool air brushed against his skin, a wonderful welcome after so much time in the sun. Wood panel covered the walls in the foyer, colorful blue and yellow tiles, some with paisley designs covered the floor. More care had been given to the living room. The furniture was more modern, better quality.

"La Patron, welcome. I am Umi, for your service." The tall, brown, slender man, bowed. "Would you care for refreshments? A bath? Change of clothes? Or would you prefer to leave at once?"

Silas wanted to leave immediately but appearances meant everything. "Clothes? Luggage?"

Umi nodded. "There are new clothes for all of you inside your luggage."

"We'll shower, change and eat something on our way to the plane." He glanced at Hawke and then Angus. "You guys go first, I'll eat a little more and then shower."

Hawke nodded and looked at Umi. "Which way?"

"This way, Sir." He walked down the hall, Hawke and Angus followed.

Silas inhaled and found the kitchen not far from where Umi greeted them. His mouth salivated at the fresh fruits, rolls, and meats. He took a plate, loaded several pieces of meat and ate standing at the table.

"Can I get you anything to drink, Sir?" Umi asked.

Silas eyed him. Umi was some sort of breed, yet he didn't register when Silas searched for full-bloods. "Water is fine, thank you." He played with the idea of asking Umi about his lineage but realized he didn't care. *"Jacques?"*

Seconds later, his administrator responded. *"Sir?"*

Standing in the middle of the semi-modern kitchen, Silas accepted the bottled water from Umi and told Jacques about their host. Jacques told Silas about a tattoo on Umi's right, upper back with the numbers 5-10-2 in small roman numerals. Silas waved Umi over, twirled his fingers, signifying the man should turn. Silas lifted his shirt and rubbed his thumb against the tattoo.

Nothing smeared. Good. He released the shirt and shook Umi's hand. "Thank you."

Umi smiled brightly. His dark eyes sparkled and creased at the corners. "La Patron is most welcome." He bowed again.

"When I get home, tell me what those numbers mean," Silas told Jacques as he headed toward the room to look at the Id's, credit cards and clothing Jacques sent.

"He's a servant, that's the number from his Master. He's on loan to me for this job."

Silas wasn't sure what to say about that, but Umi appeared healthy and happy. *"We'll be leaving for re-entry within the hour."* Angus must have showered first. He walked out in a nice black suit with a crisp beige shirt and spit-shined black shoes. He placed a pair of sunglasses up his nose and shook droplet of water from his hair.

"Thanks, Umi. Everything fit perfectly," Angus said stroking his goatee.

"Your Mistress, La Patroness was very specific in how she wanted you to appear. I merely picked up her orders from the shops." Umi bowed and returned to the kitchen.

"Wonder what Jasmine chose for you to wear, Boss," Angus said as Silas walked toward the back. There was only one bedroom. On the bed, one suitcase was opened. Next to it, another suitcase, closed with a piece of paper with "La Patron" written on top.

"One way to find out." He opened it, pulled out a black suit and laid it on the bed. She sent several dress shirts. The one that caught his eyes was white with Kelly-green pin stripes. He set that aside, along with black shoes, a belt. He held up a pair of boxers and looked at Angus.

"She expects me to wear these while I'm here?"

"Sent me some too," Angus said. "Sister wants it covered up."

Silas didn't think he owned a pair of underwear, he never wore them. For Jasmine to send these… she was making a statement. He put them aside and looked at the other things for their stay.

"The cologne was nice, not strong at all," Angus said.

"Hmm, I don't wear it," Silas said replacing clothing and opening the packet with his Id, passport and credit cards. Everything looked legitimate. He looked at Angus. "You checked yours?" He lifted the packet.

"Yes, it's all good, put most of it in my new wallet." He patted his back pocket. "She's good, thought of everything."

Silas nodded and sat on the edge of the bed. "At the airport, Umi gets a car for travel. We check for explosives, be prepared for any and everything. Treat this as a hostile trip. Not everyone's happy about this."

Angus nodded. "Wish we had some of our security stuff from the house before it blew, it'd make things easier."

"Rely on your beast, me and Hawke to watch your back. This will be old school for sure. It's been years since I've had to prove myself like this." He smiled at Angus. "I'm looking forward to the challenge, you?"

"Kind of. I don't like the disrespect for pack ways I've seen here. Still can't get over them using explosives to kill humans, that's crazy." He shook his head. "What if it hadn't been us? Plus, did they really think humans could snap the necks of full-bloods?"

"I plan to address that." Silas would make sure they never did anything like that again.

"Good. They give full-bloods a bad name," Angus said.

Hawke walked into the room dressed in boxers. He moved to his suitcase and started to dress. Silas stood, and headed to the bathroom.

"Silas," Angus called.

Silas looked over his shoulder and caught the black boxers with one hand.

"Don't forget your chastity belt," Angus said, and then laughed when Silas gave him the finger.

Umi landed the private jet at the airport smoothly and waved good bye to Silas and his entourage as they exited the plane and headed toward customs. He would meet them out front later.

Word of Silas' arrival spread, or the sight of three, dark-haired, well-dressed men, each standing either at six and a half feet or taller, striding through the concourse stopped people in their tracks to stare or ogle. Silas inhaled the scents of several full-bloods and met their gazes directly until they turned away or lowered their gazes. They were ushered through customs as if they were celebrities.

Some full-bloods smiled and nodded greetings, others looked from a distance with worried expressions, others frowned. None approached, which was as it should be. They picked up their luggage, noted the plastic wrap that Umi used had been torn in places but not removed. He looked at his watch. Umi should be bringing the car around soon.

Silas had no idea how Umi completed all his tasks with the level of excellence he displayed but was grateful for his service. Moments later a dark car pulled in front of the airport. Umi stepped out and opened the back door. Silas strode out and handed Umi his suitcase. Umi popped the trunk, placed the luggage in back and closed the door behind Silas as Hawke and Angus stored their luggage in the trunk and closed it. Angus sat next to Silas while Hawke sat up front next to Umi.

"I trust all is well, Sir?" Umi said.

"Everything's fine," Silas said.

"Did you notice anything unusual at the airport?" Silas asked Angus and Hawke.

"Lots of full-bloods. I don't recall that many when we arrived the first time," Hawke said. *"Mostly curious though. I didn't see anything hostile."*

"Me neither," Angus said. *"Did you scan the car?"* He looked at Silas.

"Yeah, twice."

"So did I," Hawke said.

"Are we going to Téguz while we're here?" Angus asked.

Silas didn't want to take this battle to the country's capital and preferred to remain in the outer regions at least initially. Unfortunately, the capital, Santa Barbara and the more densely populated areas were hit with gang turfs for humans and full-bloods. He'd need to convince the packs to give up gang warfare, and develop a better way of life separate from humans. Quite frankly he didn't think it'd work, not in the seven days the Goddess allotted them. All he could do was try and he was willing to do that.

"I'm not sure," Silas answered and looked out the window. Several people watched as they drove by. Word of his arrival spread fast. Grandfather had been burning the midnight oil to pull this off. When Umi pulled into the portico of the hotel. The doorman opened Silas' door with a large smile. "Welcome to the Palisades. I'm sure you'll enjoy your visit."

Silas nodded, buttoned his jacket as he inhaled and identified the full-bloods watching. He met their curious gazes and held them until they turned or bowed their heads. The doorman took the luggage inside, Hawke entered the foyer first, then Silas, followed by Angus. They'd decided the optics of his arrival were critical and he agreed with the grandstanding. Hawke checked them in while Silas scanned the area and met more curious gazes. Once Hawke had keys for their rooms, Silas led the way to the elevator, an older female full-blood was cleaning a mirror while watching them. She'd rubbed the same spot for a few minutes.

Silas stopped and smiled at her. "Buenos Dias," he said, using his limited Spanish.

Her face reddened as she beamed. "Ah, La Patron, it is a good day when you arrive here. Buenos Dias, Sir."

He patted her hand and nodded before entering the elevator to head to the third floor. Jacques had rented the entire floor for their use.

Hawke tipped the porter and locked the door behind him before scanning the room for bugs, bombs or electronics. No one was surprised when he found a few listening devices and cameras. Perhaps they thought Silas didn't use his mental link to communicate because they couldn't. He sat on the sofa and looked out the window for a few minutes. Did the Goddess give him the ability to compel the wolves here like in the States? Not the small episode he'd done at the lab the other day which was limited to the immediate area and was a simple tug to bring them inside the building. If he could control the wolves here, it would make his job easier. He would know one way or the other soon enough.

There was a knock on the door. Angus looked at his watch. "That was fast, not here ten minutes." He looked out the peephole and then over his shoulder at Silas. *"It's the old full-blood who challenged Crall at the lab the other day."*

Intrigued, Silas removed his coat, laid it over the sofa and unbuttoned his sleeves. *"Let's hear what he has to say."*

Angus opened the door and scanned the man. He stepped aside.

Silas threw a protective bubble over the floor. No one in or out until he released it.

"La Patron welcome to Honduras." The older man bowed his head and looked at Hawke who stood in the doorway of a bedroom. "I'm Jorge Fajardo, an elder of the Red wolf pack, near the mountains."

Silas pursed his lips. "Is that a pack or a gang of rebellious youth who disobey the rules set down by the Goddess?" He decided to get to the point, no sugar-coating, they only had seven days.

Jorge's face tightened. "You have no doubt heard rumors of our pack, most are untrue, founded on jealousy and mutual distrust."

"You have no idea what I've been told, or who sent me, or the purpose of my visit," Silas said in a hard tone. "Don't presume to second guess me, Jorge. I assure you I have not traveled this distance because I don't have affairs at home that need my attention."

Jorge nodded. "My apologies, La Patron. Word of your arrival spread after an incident in which members of my pack have been unfairly blamed. It was my intention to discuss the matter with you before your views were tainted with gossip and misinformation." He sounded like a petulant child.

"Tainted? The Goddess does not taint. Members from your pack used plastic explosives to kill humans… did you hear me? They went there to kill humans because they assumed a human broke the necks of two full-bloods." Silas crossed his arms. "Tell me, Jorge. How likely is that to happen?"

Jorge swallowed hard. "Not likely, Sir."

"Yet these men, three of them, used explosives to take innocent lives, which could impact our way of life on every continent. Did you think the Goddess would allow this type of behavior to continue?"

The older man seemed to shrink within himself. "I… I guess not."

"Why are you really here?" Silas asked after a few moments. "Not to plead for the lives of the guilty, so why?"

"To find out if it's true? Are you here to take over our country as Alpha?"

"No," Silas said without hesitation.

Jorge frowned. "Then why?"

"Think, Jorge. Think," Silas said softly as he moved closer to the old man and placed his hand on his shoulder. Within seconds he had the names of the three gang members who used the explosives. He passed those names onto Angus and Hawke to keep a watch.

"For justice? To destroy our pack?"

"No. I'm commissioned by the Goddess. She's giving the packs here, in this country a chance to change, follow the rules and live."

Jorge's eyes widened. "You'll destroy us?"

"No. I can't do that." Silas paused and removed his hand. "The Goddess will take care of that detail."

"What do we need to do?" Jorge asked in a tremulous tone.

Silas waved to the sofa. "Please, have a seat." He sat next to his guest, crossed his leg over his knee and met Jorge's frightened gaze. "How difficult would it be to return to the ways the Goddess set forth decades ago?"

The old man shook his head. Sorrow leaked from his pores. "We're doomed, they will not change their ways, they've been doing it too long."

"If you had to designate someone for Alpha, who would you choose?" Silas ignored the gloom talk and zeroed in for a list of candidates.

"Alpha? For Red Wolves?"

Silas waved. "No for the country?"

Jorge's eyes bulged. "Honduras Alpha? No... cannot be done. Packs will not serve. We are different here, La Patron. Too many go their own way. Too—"

"But if you had to think of someone, who would you choose?"

Jorge frowned and looked up at Silas. "One Alpha?" He looked at Hawke and back at Silas.

"One Alpha in charge of other Alphas who serve the pack in their areas," Silas clarified.

"Like in the States?" Jorge said slowly.

Silas nodded and waited.

"There are a few, but they may not want the headache." He glanced at Hawke again. "You will help these Alphas? There will be trouble."

Silas grinned slowly as he looked at Angus who also smiled. "How would I get the word out that I'm looking for Alphas to step up to help save Honduras? We'll have some challenges, some meetings and choose some Alphas," Silas asked. He wanted to get started as soon as possible.

"I... I don't know for sure. This is not, we thought you... I must think, maybe ask others, when do you wish to start?" He rubbed his palms against his pant legs.

"We have started. Get the word out what I'm looking for and why, bring a list back this evening. The Goddess didn't give me a lot of time to get things done so you'll need to move fast," Silas said.

"Will you mention this at the meeting tonight?" Jorge asked.

"What time is the meeting?" Silas glanced at Angus.

"Seven this evening in the parque, many people are planning to come," Jorge said.

"*We need security,*" Silas told Hawke.

"*Not sure what I can rig up that fast with no equipment,*" Hawke said.

Silas nodded.

"Bless the Goddess, you mind-speak," Jorge said, his gaze flitting from Silas to Angus to Hawke. "I've lost the ability, so have many others but a few still can and we depend on them to get the word out about things. Can we get that back?"

"You'll need to petition the Goddess, it's Her gift to give," Silas said.

"Yes, Si, Si, of course. So, you will do to my country what has been done in yours? Is that why you're here?" Jorge asked.

Silas leaned forward and met Jorge's curious gaze. "I'm going to be honest with you, the packs in this country have a choice, change and follow the Goddess' rules or cease to exist. Your sloppiness endangers full-bloods all over the world, including me and my pack. We can't allow the humans to know about us, that's the number one rule, which your packs, all of them, are breaking. No way it will continue."

"Cease? To exist?" Jorge stuttered as his brows rose and hands shook.

Silas glanced at Angus and then at Jorge. "Have you heard the Old Testament story of Lot?"

CHAPTER TWENTY-THREE

Silas, Angus and Hawke walked the three miles to the park which was simply an open clearing in the woods near the mountain about half the size of a high school football field. When they arrived, Silas walked a circle and place Angus in one spot and Hawke in another across from Angus. He then placed a secure bubble around the circle, instructing Angus and Hawke to scan and only allow full-bloods to enter. Everyone had to enter by Hawke or Angus's hand opening a door in the bubble. Silas stepped out the bubble and announced how he expected everyone to enter, the safety precautions he put in place and warned violence wouldn't be tolerated. After his announcement, he walked inside the bubble and waited as full-bloods entered. Many didn't think the bubble would hold and tried to walk through the invisible wall without success.

Once they realized Silas was serious about safety more entered and sat on the ground or on blankets they'd brought. Franz and another human tried to enter and was turned away. He stood outside with his hands stuffed in his pockets watching Silas greet people. When it was time to start, Silas had Angus and Hawke step inside and sealed the bubble. Late comers were not allowed inside and were disappointed that they could not hear anything being said in the meeting.

Hawke stepped outside twice to speak to a few who tried to force their way inside. One threw a punch, it made contact on Hawke's belly. He didn't flinch. He picked the two full-bloods up and tossed them screaming across the park before he re-entered the meeting.

Silas didn't mince words. He explained the Goddess' position, laid out their sins and the only acceptable resolution. He opened the floor for questions and possible debate. For the next two hours, the 100 or so people who arrived on time despaired over their fate, tossed around names of possible candidates, even though they wanted what the Goddess offered they didn't trust Her to make it happen. By the end of the meeting Silas was ready to leave them to their fate. It had been centuries since he'd listened to full-bloods with no hope or fight for their way of life. They acted like sheep instead of wolves.

"I'd like to start the challenges as soon as possible. I prefer the Alphas come from your homeland, but if the Goddess allows, they can come from Nicaragua, Guatemala, El Salvador… anywhere in Central America. Send me challengers before outsiders come to lead."

The idea of outsiders leading them energized the people at the meeting. Silas looked at the large number of people standing outside the bubble. "We'll meet here again tomorrow evening, same time, on time."

Those inside looked at the ones outside and nodded.

Silas released the bubble and the noises from the crowd expanded. People were amazed they couldn't enter the meeting and asked questions of those who attended. Several looked at Silas with respect and envy. He wondered if the future Honduran Alpha was in the crowd as he walked about greeting pack members.

A large stone was thrown toward Silas who stood next to a full-blood and his mate listening to their concerns. Silas erected a shield in front of them, the stone hit with a loud bang scaring those nearby, and dropped to the ground. Angus flew forward with blurring speed. Shouts came from the distance as Angus walked toward him with his hand around the neck of a young, full-blood dragging him forward.

Everybody stopped and watched.

Silas looked at the couple standing next to him. "What's your name?"

The male looked nervous from the surrounding attention. "Renaldo, Sir. My mate, Sophia." He pointed to the woman standing closely next to him.

Silas glanced at the struggling male in Angus' grip. "You owe this couple an apology. That stone would've hit his mate and then he'd have to kill you. You can also thank me for saving your life."

Those closest, gasped and whispered fiercely.

The youngster spit at Silas' feet.

Silas sought the pup's wolf, and squeezed its neck, which stopped the pup from shifting. Instantly, the pup fell and writhed in pain on the ground. Soon he was crying. Then he begged Silas to stop. People moved closer to see what was happening since Silas wasn't touching the pup.

"Are you ready to apologize to Renaldo and Sophia for interrupting our conversation?" Silas asked matter-of-factly.

"Si…Si. Please stop."

Silas released him. The young man gasped, taking in air as if he'd been close to suffocating. He said some words in Spanish.

"Again, so I can understand," Silas demanded.

"Please forgive me, Senor, Senora."

"Si, no worries," Renaldo said taking his wife's hand and moving aside.

Silas stopped them. "If you have any problems because of this, I will find out and take care of it, even if you do not tell me. I will not have pack terrorize pack." He said the last loud so they could all hear and pass the word along.

Renaldo's gaze flitted over the others as he nodded. "Thank you, La Patron." He and his mate walked off. Silas bent and pulled the young pup to his feet and activated his bracelet. His heart wept for the crimes this one committed at the young age of 24. Silas thought of his pups at home and wondered if Solo, the pup's name, would've had a sire and mam who cared for him as a pup, if his life would be different. Still, the blame lies at the feet of the pack for not training pups correctly if the parents weren't around. Who was his Alpha? He found no answer to that question in Solo's memories.

Silas bent close Solo's ear and repeated the many crimes the pup had committed, and warned him the Goddess would give him one last chance to straighten up.

Solo's eyes widened with shock and fear as if he'd seen a ghost. He backed away and ran off into the night. Silas hoped the pup would correct his life before too late.

"La Patron, my name is Raven, and I'm so glad you're here."

Silas looked down at the waitress and smiled. She was dressed in jeans and a tee-shirt with the name of the bar where she worked. Her dark hair was pulled back in a pony-tail making her look like a high school student.

"Did you hear the discussion?" He couldn't recall seeing her earlier.

"No, I got off from work late and by the time we got here the doors were closed." She giggled. "Not doors, but we couldn't get in. I'll be here tomorrow early."

"That's nice, Raven." Silas searched for her brother but didn't sense him.

"About the Alpha, can anyone volunteer? Even women like my sister?"

"Yes. As long as they pass the challenges anyone can compete. In the end, the Goddess places a seal on Her chosen and empowers that person to lead."

"Like what you did with that thing, keeping people out, keeping those inside safe. That was really cool. We couldn't hear anything."

"Yes, things like that." He smiled and watched Hawke speak to a group of full-bloods while Angus watched a few gang members on the fringes of the park. "Will you be safe returning to work or home?"

"Si. My brother's here somewhere, probably at the car waiting. No one will bother me," she said with confidence.

"Good. It was nice meeting you, Raven." He stepped aside and headed toward the back of the park where Angus stood.

When he reached Angus they both walked toward the four young pups sitting on the hood of a car and standing around. Solo stood at the back smoking a cigarette and staring at the ground.

"So much talent going to waste," Silas said to Angus. *"Think the next Alpha's in this motley crew?"*

"Could be, can I challenge one to see?" He smiled at Silas.

"No. But I'll ask if anyone wants to be Alpha." Silas stepped closer to the car, bent forward and lifted the front of the car and shook it up and down.

Two pups dressed in black tees, jeans hanging off their hips, and crew cuts stood with guns pointed at Silas. Solo stepped away from the car but didn't move forward. A fourth member yelled, calling Silas all kinds of names in Spanish as he moved to stand next to the two holding weapons.

Silas smiled and placed a bubble around him and Angus.

"Incoming," Silas said as he and Angus stepped back. Hawke flew through the air and landed behind the car. The ground shook on impact. He jumped up, flipped and landed behind Silas.

Gunshots were fired.

Silas moved so quickly, the pup firing the gun didn't realize he'd been disarmed until he lay on the ground bleeding. Silas slapped two others across their cheeks as they went for their weapons. When they tried to run, he grabbed their wolves and held them close.

Solo stood apart, watching and shaking.

Angus and Hawke hadn't moved.

Silas erected a bubble around himself and the gang. Then he released them.

"Stand up," he demanded.

Slowly, they stood. One had vomited when he grabbed their beasts, another pissed on himself, the third rubbed his stomach with watery eyes.

"What the hell are you doing with your lives?" he asked and looked at Solo who interpreted what he asked.

They looked puzzled.

"You cannot shoot guns in public like this. We're full-bloods, humans aren't supposed to know we exist, that's the Goddess' first rule. We're supposed to be invisible around them."

"Fuck that. No invisible," one of them said.

Silas slapped him across the face so hard he spun around, hit the bubble and fell to the ground. "You won't live to the end of the week with that attitude." He pointed at the pup. "Say something like that again and I'll be on your ass so hard you'll pray to be invisible."

The pup rubbed his cheek, extended his hand backward and touched the clear wall.

"Now that's invisible, soundproof too, so let's have a talk."

Solo repeated his words.

"This country needs Alphas." He waited to gauge their response. They looked confused. "Let me rephrase that, there will be Alphas running this country or the full-bloods who follow the Goddess will be moved and leave the rest of you to die."

Solo's eyes widened but he relayed the message causing the others to make mocking noises.

"I feel like Noah sometimes," Silas told Angus and Hawke. *"The one in the Bible."*

"I know who Noah is," Angus said. *"Knew the story of Lot too."* He grinned.

Silas shook his head and glared at the gang members.

"Laugh if you want but the Goddess sent me here, I can grab your wolves, hold you hostage, take you into the mountains and put you places you'll never be found. And that's just me, Her servant. Imagine what she'll do."

Solo side eyed him and told them what he said. The mocking stopped as they stared at him.

"We need Alphas. These full-bloods will be challenged physically and emotionally and mentally. In the end, the Goddess will choose the Alpha for this country and restore gifts to the packs. If any of you want to be Alpha, be here tomorrow same time, on time. If you know anyone you think will be good, tell them to come. Spread the word. And as long as I'm here, do nothing to alert humans about dual-natureds. Is that clear?"

"Si, La Patron," some muttered. Others nodded.

Silas released the bubble and walked toward the road.

"How many gangs are there?" he asked.

"One is too many," Angus said as they left the park and walked back to the hotel.

CHAPTER TWENTY-FOUR

Later that night, Silas and the others had just finished a late-night meal and discussing their first meeting as well as strategies going forward, when a call came from the front desk. Angus answered.

"Jorge is downstairs with a few Alphas. They want to talk to you. Seems they tried to exit the elevator on our floor but couldn't. He's asking permission for an audience. Something he should've done first," Angus said.

"Tell them to come up," Silas said and looked at Hawke. "We'll meet with them in the room at the end of the hall. Go ahead and prepare it."

Hawke nodded and left.

Silas stood, released the protective shield. "When they arrive, scan each one. No devices of any kind will be allowed in the room," he told Angus.

Angus nodded and left. Silas stretched and headed to the bathroom for a quick shower and change of clothes. He'd been in business clothes most of the day and wanted to get comfortable.

He met their guest 15 minutes later dressed in a pair of black jogging pants and black short sleeved polo shirt that stretched tight across his chest. Wearing a pair of black leather sandals, he stood in the middle of the room and sealed it.

Jorge stood when he entered.

"Hello, I'm La Patron. Apologies for the slight delay but I was not expecting you." He looked at Jorge and smiled. "It's good to see you again so soon."

Jorge spine straightened. "Yes, La Patron, I have spoken to many people regarding your mission. These Alphas had questions I could not answer. I brought them to ask you in person if that is alright."

"You are here and I've granted your request for an audience. In the future call and make an appointment to be sure I'm available. Usually I'm not." He smiled to take the sting from his words.

Jorge's cheeks reddened. "Si. Of course. Many apologies. I know you want this done quickly. I did not think. It will not happen again."

Silas waved down his apology and clamped his hand down on his shoulder as if they were old friends. "No worries. As I said, I've granted you this opportunity."

"Gracias. Gracias." Jorge said as he turned to introduce the five men who sat on the sofa and chairs in the room behind him. "La Patron this is Alpha Hector Amata, his pack is to the west of the Reserve to the Nicaraguan border." Hector stood and came closer to Silas.

Silas had heard great things about the Reserve. It was a high tourist area, he hoped Hector kept his pack in line. He shook the Alpha's hand, activated his bracelet and placed his hand on his shoulder while searching his gaze. "I look forward to working with you Alpha Hector."

Hector nodded, blinked and cleared his throat. "Ours is an agricultural pack, I hope we can work together La Patron." Silas released him and looked at Jorge.

"Alpha Pedro Zelaya." The tall, slender, dark haired Alpha stood and met Silas' gaze. "His pack is south of the capital, around Choluteca, down to the water…ocean." He looked at Alpha Pedro who nodded.

Silas extended his hand. Pedro shook it but released quickly. Silas held his gaze and touched Pedro's wolf as a reminder that the Alpha was in the presence of a much stronger Alpha. Pedro's eyes widened.

"It is an honor to meet you, La Patron," Alpha Pedro said bowing his head.

"The honor is mine," Silas said graciously knowing he'd just scared the Alpha. Pedro returned to his seat and a tall, muscular full-blood stood. His dark gaze, swarthy complexion and shoulder length hair seemed familiar.

"This is Alpha Ricardo Saldivar; his pack is near Comayagua and the surrounding mountains."

Silas recalled Lucian and Raven speaking of their Uncle Rick in less than glowing terms. This was the Alpha of the Sups, the one dealing with Franz and the drugs.

Alpha Rick smiled wide and extended his hand. Silas took it and activated the bracelet immediately. He placed his hand on Rick's shoulder as he returned the smile.

"It's an honor to meet you, Sir," Rick said trying to break free of Silas' grasp.

"The honor's mine," Silas said as he released his hand. He petted Rick's wolf and was surprised at how weak the beast was.

"What are you doing?" Rick demanded stepping back.

"I'm introducing myself to your wolf, it's proper to greet both your natures," Silas spoke as if the Alpha should know that.

"My apologies," Alpha Rick stuttered. "No one has ever… it's a weird feeling." His cheeks flushed as he returned to his seat.

Jorge cleared his throat, drawing attention to the last two Alphas in the room. "Sir, this is Alpha Jose Angulo and Alpha Tonio Angulo, litter mates with packs from San Pedro to the Guatemalan and Nicaraguan borders." The two men stood and approached Silas. They weren't identical but it was obvious they were related. Both slender, average height, with dark eyes, dark hair and thick mustaches.

Silas greeted Tonio first, and was pleased with the health of his beast. Greeted his brother Jose who was solid Alpha material with a healthy wolf. Either of these men could become the Alpha.

"It is nice to meet all of you," Silas said as he took a seat and waved for Angus and Hawke to do the same. "What questions do you have?" He looked at the men and waited.

"You have come to set one of us as the Alpha of Honduras?" Pedro asked.

"No." Silas' answer was swift and definite. He explained his assignment was based on the current problems in the country, and that he was sent to set the matter right. "The Goddess can choose anyone to be Alpha in this country."

"Already we have challenges from Guatemala packs," Tonio complained.

"And Nicaragua," his brother added. "For one of them to become Alpha…" he shook his head. "I cannot see it."

"In that case, answer the call to be Alpha yourself." Silas looked at the men. "All of you should accept the challenge for the position."

"What happens after the Alpha is installed?" Hector asked. "Will Honduras be broken into areas as in the States?"

Silas nodded. "Yes. It's the easiest way to manage and ensure all pack needs are being met. I cannot personally make sure every member of my pack has food, water, jobs, an education. I depend on Alphas in each state to delegate responsibilities to make sure those things get done." He paused. "Who is the Alpha for the capital? Santa Barbara?" he looked at the men.

"Those areas are run by gangs, as far as I know they don't have Alphas," Jorge said without looking at Ricky.

"Gangs? Like the ones I spoke with tonight?" He looked at Angus.

"They would have been to the meeting," Jorge said.

"Those are pups with no direction, they need pack structure more than most," Silas said.

"They are very violent," Hector said moments later. "Uninterested in the way things are done, no respect for our ways."

"I spoke to them," Silas said. "I don't think they were ever taught pack rules. Who would be responsible for that?" No one answered. "That's the problem the Goddess has with this area. No one is accountable for the condition of the country. Are you aware a pup, used explosives to kill humans?" He watched them. Jose and Tonio were the only two who were surprised.

"The day after that happened I was sent here. That's how bad it's gotten." He paused to let it sink in. "Who's responsible? The three pups after vengeance for the death of their pack mates? Or the pack who allowed them to run wild, with no discipline or guidance, until they got to that point?"

No one answered.

"Now you see the dilemma. Someone must be responsible. All packs have Alphas. That's how we operate, how we survive, flourish. Pack looks after pack, we care for each other. When one has, we all have." Silas met each of their gazes. "There are over 30 million people in my pack. Right now, I can call every Alpha to this country and within 24 hours we can pull a coup, and install new Alphas who answer to me." He watched the various expressions on the faces of the Alphas and smiled.

"Here's the thing. I've got my hands full. This is an assignment that will be completed quickly." He met each person's gaze. "Either one of you, or someone else will become the Goddess' Alpha, not me." He pointed to Angus and Hawke. "Or any of mine. Now if you don't want Her to choose someone from a neighboring country, get your asses in gear and petition to become the Alpha. Yes, you'll have to fight for the position, that's the way it's always been done. The winner will interview with the Goddess or me, whichever She chooses. But in the end, the choice will be Hers, not mine."

Silence filled the room. Silas could hear the men thinking.

"I've never fought an Alpha challenge," Hector said. "Could you tell me more about it?"

Silas spent the next 30 minutes explaining how they would fight each other in different rounds, and go on to the next rounds until one person won. There would be no cheating, he would monitor each man to make sure the fights were fair.

As for the interview, he spoke simply. "Being Alpha is a heart issue. You must genuinely care for pack above all. Want the best for them and be willing to intercede on their behalf. If I ever used the gifts and abilities the Goddess gave me to harm my pack, I believe I'd be destroyed. She's never said that, but I believe it. For one, it would rip me apart to hurt those I love, and second to know I've disappointed the one I serve would kill whatever is left." He eyed the men. "Alpha is an all-consuming position, no question about it."

"How does your mate handle it?" Tonio asked. "My bitch already complains when I travel out of town for pack matters."

Thinking of Jasmine made him smile. He waved toward Angus and Hawke. "We're all mated. The best thing I've ever done was made my mate my Beta."

The Alphas frowned and murmured their dissent. Silas held up his hand. "First off if you're Alpha, you can share your energy with your mate to handle problems. She can and will see things from a different perspective which will help you lead the pack better. My mate has spoken directly to and received praise from the Goddess for her wisdom." Silas shook his head. "She's your mate, the two of you are one. Use her to help and that will solve most of your problems."

"I have never thought…" Tonio said. "She does see things differently." He looked at his brother and nodded.

"Does your mate command your 50 Alphas?" Rick asked.

"Of course. She's in charge while I'm here. To disrespect or disobey her is the same as doing it to me and the penalty is the same. She has never had a problem." He paused thinking of the time with Jacques and Cameron. "She's earned the respect of those who serve her. They'd rip your heart from your chest if they thought you were disrespectful, but that's if she didn't beat them to it. And of course, I back her up in every way." He looked at the men who seemed surprised. "So, I strongly suggest you empower your mates to help with your packs, it will make it stronger."

"It is something to consider," Tonio said.

"What will you do about the gang problem?" Hector asked, again not looking at Ricardo.

"Good question," Silas said. "Ricardo, what should I do about the gangs?" He looked at the Alpha of the Sups.

Ricardo froze and remained silent for a few seconds. "I don't know what can be done about them. They're strong and unmanageable."

Silas looked at Jorge. "Why didn't you bring the leader of the Red Wolves?"

"I asked, he refused." Jorge shrugged.

"Thanks, I appreciate your effort. I'm going to ask you to leave, there are some sensitive matters I want to discuss with these Alphas."

Jorge looked surprised but stood. Hawke walked him to the door. It wouldn't open.

"Sir?" Hawke said.

Silas looked over his shoulder and waved. The door opened. Hawke stood in the doorway until the elevator dinged. He returned to the room and Silas sealed it again.

"Why wouldn't the door open?" Ricardo asked.

"I sealed the room, the whole floor as well. This is a private conversation and I don't want to be disturbed." He faced Ricardo. "I'll ask again, what should I do about the gangs?"

Ricardo flushed. Opened his mouth and snapped it shut. All the Alphas watched him in silence. Finally, he released a sigh. "Honestly, other than kill them, I don't know. I'm over the Sups in name only. I never fought for the position, it fell into my lap when my brother and his mate died years ago. He was more into true pack structure, worshiped the Goddess and kept the old ways. I... I never really got into it that much. Ours is a poor country, there never is enough to go around. So, I stopped trying, stopped looking out for others." He dropped his gaze. "I really don't know what to do about our problems. But I don't want someone from the outside coming in." He pointed to the other Alphas. "Any one of you would be better than an outsider."

"Tell us about the drugs," Silas said.

Ricardo froze and met his gaze. For the first time Silas saw and then smelled fear. "Drugs?"

"Yes, your pack's been experimenting with drugs. It's causing problems, serious problems. Tell us," he waved to the other Alphas. "About the drugs. We need to know so we can work together to fix the problem."

Ricardo swallowed hard and looked at his hands. "I don't know what you're talking about."

"I smell a lie," Hector said in a hard voice.

"Talk to us, we're pack," Pedro said.

"No one will mention anything that's said in this room from this moment on," Silas said looking at each Alpha. "But you'll tell us about the drugs on your own. I prefer you share rather than tell what I know."

Ricardo swallowed hard and spoke slowly. Franz had been taking a drug that altered his human abilities. The man was super strong, had excellent hearing and vision. Initially, Ricardo assumed Franz thought he was human and played with the idea of selling drugs to humans to make more money. But he later discovered Franz knew about full-bloods and offered them drugs that would enhance their abilities as well. Unfortunately, the side effects caused them to lose control over their beasts, they became irrational and dependent on the drug. It had been a horrible mistake he admitted and wished he'd never started taking the drug.

"Can you quit?" Pedro asked softly.

"Yes and no," Ricardo said. "Supposedly there's a cure, something that breaks the grip of the drug but the main ingredient is in a cave that's on Red Wolf's turf. Franz wants us to get it so he can fix the problem. Otherwise I must take it every other day."

Silas looked at Hawke. "Do you have any of the drug?"

Ricardo looked surprised and then nodded. He pulled a small yellow packet from his pocket and showed it to Silas.

Hawke walked over, took and smelled it. He called out a few ingredients Silas didn't recognize. *This smells familiar, something from the Liege days. I can probably make something to counteract it once I get back to the lab.*

"I'll send Umi to the States…Theron in Texas, in the morning with the sample, Passen can have it picked up from there. Work with him to get this done ASAP," Silas said.

"Sounds good, I'll brief the Doc on my suspicions," Hawke said.

"Can we keep a sample of this to send to the lab so they can create an antidote? I promise we will fix this and send it to you for your pack. Breaking that addiction is the first order of business as their Alpha."

Ricardo stared at him with a shocked expression. "Yes, Sir. You'll let me remain their Alpha? After everything I've said and done?"

"It's not my job to make changes on that level. As long as your pack wants you and pledge fealty to the national Alpha it's good."

"Fealty?" Hector asked. "What does that mean?"

"Every full-blood in this country will pledge loyalty, and obedience to the Goddess' Alpha. He'll have the ability to make sure they do or suffer the consequences. Understand once the Alpha is chosen, his abilities will be amplified. He will be able to call the pack together from all over, mind speak to everyone or just his Alphas and heal those who are sick."

"We've never been able to do that," Jose said.

"You will," Silas said. He created mental links to each Alpha and then added Angus and Hawke to the connections. *"Can you hear me?"* Silas asked.

Ricardo's brow rose as a slow smile spread across his face. *"Si...Si."*

Pedro smiled as he nodded. Hector, Jose and Tonio all nodded as they answered, *"Si."*

Hawke and Angus nodded but remained silent.

Next, Silas interconnected the Alphas with each other. Jose and Tonio, the brothers already shared mind links. They looked at Hector, then Pedro and Ricardo as they tested their links. Silas remained silent in the background as the five Alphas greeted each other via this more personal method of communication.

Minutes later Silas called their attention. "This is the first step in unifying this country. You're one pack. If one Alpha has a need for his people, he should be reach out to another Alpha for help. We don't turn to humans, not to help pack."

The conversation turned to problems within the country and how to correct them. Silas, Angus and Hawke listened and offered advice sparingly, allowing the Alphas to make decisions regarding change and implementation within their packs.

With the help of the Alphas, Silas had split the country into five regions, leaving most of the Alphas in charge of their current areas with increased acreage and the understanding that the future

Alpha could change everything. Hours later, the Alphas left in an upbeat frame of mind and acceptance of the Goddess' plan for their country.

CHAPTER TWENTY-FIVE

The next evening, Silas allowed Umi to drive them to the park. The man had made the trip to Texas at the break of dawn and returned eager to work. Angus and Hawke had been downstairs dealing with full-bloods with questions regarding the competition tonight. The response had been overwhelmingly positive. Hawke and Angus spent a couple hours using the applications to set up the fights for tonight. There would be three at a time with the winner resting until much later for another elimination round. If they remained on schedule they'd finish with the first set of eliminations by midnight. Tomorrow, they'd have final rounds and hopefully choose an Alpha and regional Alphas. Then the Goddess could empower the new Alpha to bring the country together.

He and Jasmine dealt with issues back home most of the day. There were issues she wanted to discuss with him and they briefly touched on which country, Mexico or Canada, should they review for expansion first. Jasmine wasn't excited over the prospect but understood it was a part of his job that needed to be done. She voted for Canada because the trained Alphas, Knights and KnightForce agents, predominantly spoke English. They could send the other Alphas to school to learn Spanish while they worked on Canada.

Sound reasons made it easy to agree and have her review the list of candidates for them to make decisions on later. Also, he'd send the Knights to Canada to assist in the transition. Jasmine suggested they announce their intentions to the Canadian pack, but Silas wasn't sure and wanted time to review the situation first.

Alphas from Guatemala, Nicaragua, Belize, Costa Rico, Panama and El Salvador arrived at the hotel during lunch and asked to meet with him. He met with them an hour later to answer their questions and concerns. Their primary concern centered around an Alpha for Central America which Silas had no knowledge of and couldn't address. Next, they wondered if the Goddess would place an Alpha in each of their countries. They agreed Silas and Barticus had been successful and wanted the same. Silas encouraged them to seek the Goddess for answers and directions on establishing a National Alpha. He warned the Alpha would need Her support otherwise it wouldn't work. At the end of the two-hour meeting, several decided to participate in the Honduran challenge since their pack lands bordered on Honduras.

Between consulting with Jasmine, meeting with the Central American Alphas, refusing to meet with any U.S. officers requesting an audience as well as reassuring the Honduran President his mission would benefit their country and accepting their promise to not interfere, Silas was ready to be done with this assignment.

A large crowd greeted them on arrival. Silas waved and spoke to those closest as he made his way to the edge of the park. Umi followed with a large bag holding orange cones, poles and yellow caution tape. Working quickly while Angus and Hawke dealt with the challengers, Silas and Umi ran the tape the length of the general area where the competition would take place. A few volunteers approached offering assistance.

Silas supervised the placing of poles and yellow caution tape five feet behind the first row of tape. Everyone would need to stand between the tape because he would close the bubble behind it.

Next, he separated the three areas for the fights to occur with cones and tape. Once he finished, he enclosed the area, those on the opposite side of the yellow tape ran to the front to get inside. Silas waited for Angus and Hawke to finish before allowing anyone else to enter.

"Ready," Angus said as he walked to toward Silas. *"I'm bringing in the challengers, Hawke's got the door."*

"I'll help at the door," Silas said and opened another area for entrance. He stopped several humans who tried to enter.

Franz and a few other humans stood in the distance watching. Silas had refused a personal meeting with him earlier. He would have to do something about Franz, the man was bent on enslaving wolves. Ricardo mentioned the blood samples Franz constantly collected, and promised not to be involved with the man any longer. Silas wasn't sure how long that would last, Hawke spoke to Matt regarding the drug and hoped they could get something soon.

Silas was pleased to see Solo and two of the gang members from the night before. The crowd was much larger tonight which wasn't a surprise. Wolves loved watching fights as much as fighting. Silas allowed those who were in line to enter even though it was a few minutes after the start time. Late comers were running toward the event when he closed it. Silas dimmed the bubble on the outside to prevent anyone from seeing the challenges.

Angus set up the first round of fights in each ring. Hawke oversaw the ring to Silas' left, and Angus watched the one on the right. Silas' first contestants had to be two high school students. Once the fight began the two fought in earnest, but nowhere near what was needed as Alphas. It was difficult to choose a winner, they were both bad, neither had been knocked out. Silas choose one and gave his name on the roster for another elimination round.

And so the night went on. Angus stopped a contestant from shifting early by grabbing him by his neck and shaking him hard. Hawke and Silas had no real problems with the first rounds. The crowd grew more excited and in the enclosed area tempers flared. When the second fight broke out in the crowd, Silas shifted to his two-footed beast and yelled. "Stop this shit."

Either everyone was shocked to see him in this form or the noise in such close quarters hurt their ears to the point they covered them. Bottom line, they stopped shoving and fighting for the rest of the eliminations.

Solo surprised Silas by winning against another pup in the elimination round. He had heart and fought with skill. At the end of the elimination rounds, Silas made an announcement.

"Tomorrow, should be the next elimination rounds. Well done to all of you who've made it to the next level. Alphas Hector, Pedro, Ricardo, Jose, Tonio and several others will be joining us tomorrow as challengers." Groans, cheers and whoops filled the air. Silas waved down the noise.

"Honduras requires a strong Alpha, and you will have one. He will be gifted to fill the position. Some of you are thinking when I leave and a new Alpha is in place things will return to normal. I've even heard some of you fear for my life and that of any Alpha placed in a position of power." Silence filled the space as everyone watched him. "Let me be clear, the Alpha position may start with these challenges, that's for you. But the Alpha is chosen by the Goddess. She empowers me, and will empower your Alpha to do the job of keeping the pack safe, keeping our secrets safe, and give him or her the wisdom to carry out her dictates. Don't worry about your Alpha, save that for your enemies."

The crowd cheered and clapped.

"Go home. Tomorrow we start the challenges in the afternoon." He dismissed the crowd and watched for trouble. Angus and Hawke spoke to the winners from tonight while Silas listened to the pack as they left. Umi pulled up the poles and took down the tape with the help of a couple volunteers.

In the distance, he sensed Franz and the bitch, Raven's sister Tasha, watching. "*We need to eliminate Franz, he's a problem,*" Silas said to Angus and Hawke.

"*Ricardo didn't check in today,*" Angus said without looking up.

"Franz wanted a one on one with you, wonder what he wants?" Hawke said while sending a challenger off with instructions.

He didn't care what Franz wanted, the idea that this man used drugs on pack angered Silas.

"What about the three Red Wolf guys who used explosives, what do you want to do about them?" Angus asked.

"Let the new Alpha handle them," Silas said while scanning the area for trouble.

"A bloody start might not be a good idea," Angus said. *"We could make them disappear, save him the headache."*

Silas didn't respond. He followed Umi to the car and scanned it before the servant reached it. "Wait Umi."

"Check it Hawke," Silas said when Umi stopped and looked at him.

Hawke moved through the crowd and walked around the car. *"Some asshole placed an explosive device under the car. You'll need to surround it, before I can move it."*

"We'll wait until the park's almost empty before we move it," Silas said as he scanned the car again, located the device and wrapped it in layers of protective energy. Then he and the others leaned against the car and discussed the fights as his anger simmered.

There were innocents in the clearing, children and adults. For someone to attack him was one thing, to do something to harm pack in an open setting like this another. He stooped and pulled the device from the undercarriage. It was barely visible, he'd wrapped it so tight.

"What should we do with it?" He looked at Hawke.

"If you can contain the explosion, detonation would work best, save time too," Hawke said. *"Or I could try to defuse it."*

"Get something to put it in, a box or bottle, something I can enclose." Silas looked around the car.

"Sir, La Patron, there's something wrong with Ricardo," Alpha Hector said. *"He called to me in the last hour but has not responded to me. I'm on the way there with Pedro. Can you meet us there?"*

Silas placed the energy wrapped device in a small brown corrugated box Umi found in a trash bin and enclosed it in a tight bubble. He pulled energy from a few of his Alphas to make sure the explosion was contained.

"We will meet you there, Hector." Silas looked at Hawke. *"Now what? How does it detonate?"*

Hawke took the box, shook it and tossed it across the park. It went off in mid-air, like a fire-cracker. The sides of the box expanded but didn't break.

Silas slapped the back of the car. "Umi, head back to the hotel, we've got some things to take care of and will see you later." Umi's room on their floor was automatically shielded against anyone entering except him.

"Yes, Sir," Umi said as he slid in behind the wheel.

"Let's go," Silas said and took off running toward the mountains. Angus and Hawke followed without questions. Once they reached the forest, Silas shifted into his wolf and they headed toward Ricardo's home.

###

Security was lax when Silas arrived at Ricardo's. He sensed a large concentration of full-bloods near the mansion and headed in that direction.

"Ricardo, this is La Patron, I'm on the way. Hang on, I'll help you."

"Si, Gracias," came the weak reply.

Minutes later Silas leaped onto the balcony and walked into a large room. Pack members gasped and pointed as the three of them padded across the floor to Ricardo who lay limp and sweating on a sofa.

"He's in distress from the drugs," Hawke said.

Silas morphed to human and stood over Ricardo. He touched his stomach, and sent healing energy through the Alpha. The other Alphas arrived causing a stir with the Sups.

"How are you my friend?" Pedro asked Ricardo.

"Feeling better by the second," Ricardo looked at Silas with wonder in his gaze. Drops of sweat loaded with the poison exited Ricardo's body and hit the floor

Pack members watched amazed as Ricardo sat up, his color returned and a smile on his face. "Gracias, La Patron. Gracias," he said. He met Silas gaze. *"I tried to quit the drug on my own, I don't want it in our pack. It knocked me down, in truth I thought I was dying. How can I tell them to stop the use when it devastates us so?"*

"The sample was flown to my lab in the States this morning, give them another two or three days. Once we have the solution, then take them off."

Ricardo nodded and stood. He looked at the other three Alphas who came to his aid, embraced them and offered refreshments.

"Biggest wolf I've ever seen," a pack member said.

"Never felt that much energy before either," another whispered.

"I bet no one ever challenges him," someone said.

Silas ignored the chatter and searched for the pack members using the drugs. He identified 22 in the immediate area and asked Ricardo how many users were in his pack.

"Around 52," Ricardo said.

"Which means whoever controls the drug controls those members," Silas said. *"Franz is the only supplier?"*

"Si."

"Surround yourself with members who don't use the drug, expect Franz to make a power move by calling the 52 who depend on him to either serve him or start another pack. Prepare for war in your pack," Silas said.

Ricardo's eyes widened. *"He's human military."*

"He's been setting this up for a while, he wants what he cannot have, to be a full-blood and human. Leading a pack of drugged full-bloods the next best thing." Silas paused. *"Of course, I cannot allow it."*

"Por favor, please do not destroy them, my niece, nephew work closely with him, so many others who took the drug because of me, I ask for mercy on their behalf," Ricardo begged.

"Once the antidote for the drug arrives, everyone will be given a choice to take it and be rid of the poison. Those who don't cannot be allowed to disrupt the pack." Silas spoke through the links to all the Alphas, Angus and Hawke. The Alphas nodded slowly and looked at Ricardo who eventually agreed.

"This is my fault," Ricardo said.

"Therefore, you will lead with the solution. Admit your mistake, share your plans for a brighter future and lead. No Alpha is perfect, we're still human. As long as your pack knows you have their best interest at heart, and you're working to make life better for them, they'll forgive mistakes."

The other Alphas clapped Ricardo on the shoulder in a show of solidarity, while pledging their support.

"What's going on?" Lucian asked as he strode across the floor, his gaze flicked from Silas to Ricardo and then to the other Alphas.

Raven followed and stopped next to Silas. "Greetings La Patron, would you care for refreshments?"

Silas smiled and touched her shoulder to send healing energy through her. He could tell she wasn't feeling well.

"Oh," she jerked and smiled up at him. "Thank you, Sir."

"What?" Lucian spun around, looking at her.

"Nothing, I just feel better, that's all." She looked at Silas and the others. "I'll bring refreshments." She left the room.

Lucian watched her back for a few seconds and then looked at Ricardo. "Are you alright? I got a message you were sick."

Ricardo patted Lucian's shoulder with a genuine smile that reached his eyes. "La Patron, Alphas, Angus, Hawke, my brother's pup, Lucian. The sweet one who left is his litter-mate, Raven. Plus two more, Duke and Tasha." He looked at Lucian. "I decided to stop using the drug, the side-effects are brutal, knocked me over." He nodded toward Silas. "La Patron healed me, I'm better now and working on antidote for everyone to stop taking the drug."

Lucian glance at Silas and back at his Uncle. "Really?" He touched his Uncle's cheek and stared into his eyes. "No more drugs, you are out of that business?"

Ricardo nodded. "The pack is out of that business. I'll allow them to take the drug a few more days until La Patron's lab sends the antidote." He looked at Silas who nodded.

Lucian hugged his Uncle. The Alpha's eyes watered as he accepted the embrace and clapped Lucian on his back a few times. "We will be a pack again, my brother wanted it and I want it."

"Gracias," Lucian said looking at Silas.

Raven entered with a tray with drinks. Another pack member followed with two platters of meat.

Hawke took a platter of meat, placed it on the table and started eating. Angus joined him.

"Have you spoken to Duke or Tasha about this?" Lucian asked his Uncle.

"They left when I told them I was off the drug. I haven't seen them since." He shrugged. "Franz will be banned from pack lands and properties. No more drugs, I will make the announcement in two days."

Lucian nodded. "Good, I never liked him."

Silas smiled at the exchange. "*Alphas from the other countries visited me today,*" he told the other Alphas. They all turned and looked at him. "*They will be competing against you tomorrow.*"

"*Good,*" Pedro said. "*Our packs need to see us fight for them.*"

Silas appreciated the sentiment and hoped it gave the Honduran Alphas an edge. He looked at Hawke and Angus. "*Franz and other full-bloods are coming. He does not leave this place until we know the ingredients of the drug and his intentions.*"

Hawke nodded, stood and walked outside. Angus walked over and stood behind Ricardo.

"*Incoming,*" Silas told the other Alphas. "*No bloodshed.*" Ricardo tensed.

Lucian looked toward the door, frowning. Conversation stopped as Franz, Tasha, Duke and at least 20 pack members entered the room.

"Shit," Raven muttered and crossed her arms.

Silas bit back a grin and watched Franz cross the room with utter confidence and stand in front of Ricardo. "I heard you were ill, my friend and came to check on you."

"I didn't take the drug today, just to see what would happen. It wasn't good. Whatever that is, it's poison for us," Ricardo said.

Franz glanced at Silas and then at Ricardo. "It's not poison, we've discussed the side-effects and are working on corrections. You know that, agreed to it."

Ricardo nodded. "In ignorance and greed, I agreed. Sold out my pack. It was wrong. I made a bad decision and hurt a lot of people. I'm working with La Patron and the other Alphas to correct my mistake." He looked at the pack members who walked in with Franz. "In a few days, La Patron will provide an antidote to this drug that will set you free from its influence without the side-effects I went through today." He glanced back at Silas. "Believe me, if it weren't for him, I would still be going through withdrawal. It felt as if my wolf was dying which would kill me." He took a deep breath. "Once the solution arrives, you'll have a choice. Get off the drug or leave the pack. There will be a zero-drug tolerance policy in this pack."

Franz' jaw tightened. "Just like that? You terminate five years of business like this? Without talking to me first? Without sharing information that could fix the problem? This is how you treat me?"

Tasha walked forward, took Franz' hand while staring at her Uncle and kissed the back of it. "Don't worry about him. As soon as they leave, he'll be begging you for a hit."

"You're pathetic," Raven said.

Tasha moved toward her.

"Don't." That one word from Lucian stopped Tasha in her tracks. "You don't have to be addicted to the drug Tasha. You can break free, shift again, run in the woods."

"I don't want to shift or any of that. Some of us like being the baddest wolves in town," she sneered.

"Really?" Angus said stepping to the side of Ricardo. "Show me how bad you are." He looked at the other full bloods with her. "All of you, show us how tough you are," Angus challenged.

"I don't have to show you shit," Tasha snapped.

"Yes, you do," Silas said and triggered their aggressive natures. One by one they became more feral, snapping and making threatening moves.

Angus smiled at Silas. "May I?"

"Yes, but we promised Ricardo no loss of life," Silas said watching a relieved Ricardo take a step back along with the other Alphas as Angus walked in front of them all.

"So this is the power you get from the drug?" Angus asked looking at the 20 standing in front of him. "La Patron will you seal the room so they can't run away?"

Silas sealed the room with a chuckle as Angus charged into the group with blazing tornado-like fury. Fists flying, feet kicking, pack members flew through the air, hit the side of the bubble and slid to the ground. Tasha jumped in yelling and was hit by an airborne pack member. They both landed on the floor several feet away. Duke and a couple others landed a few punches which unleashed Angus fury. He didn't shift to his next level but he hit harder and moved faster. His last hit knocked Franz on his ass sliding across the floor. When they all lay groaning on the floor. Angus shifted to his two-footed beast, howled and then to his third and largest beast.

The room went completely silent.

"Show off," Hawke said.

Silas laughed.

Angus morphed to human and walked off. "You don't need drugs, you need to learn to fight."

The Alphas surrounded Angus with questions regarding the fight and his various beasts.

Raven stepped closer to Silas. "My brother can do that."

Silas looked down at her. "Lucian has a two-footed beast. No one else does. It's one of the reasons no one messes with him or any of us." She bit her lip. "Is it common in the States?"

"Alphas mostly. Angus is my litter-mate," Silas said.

"Oh, I see. Hawke?"

"He shifts bigger than anyone I've ever seen, it's best not to ever threaten his mate or make him angry," Silas said wryly.

Hawke picked up Franz and walked out the room while the others were still on the floor trying to get up. Silas and Angus spoke to the pack but offered no assistance to those who disrespected their Alpha. If Tasha had been a member of his pack he would discipline her as publicly as she'd behaved. But it wasn't his call.

Franz stumbled back inside 10 minutes later and sat on the floor. He looked as if he'd had one glass of liquor too many to drink. Tasha noticed him and sat by his side, holding his hand with a defiant look.

Hawke returned, took a seat and grabbed another plate of food. *"I sent the drug ingredients to Passen. I'd guessed most of them, now Passen has everything to counter it. Won't take long, he was almost there anyway. He said he'd overnight it as soon as he capsulized them."*

"And Franz' plans for all this?" Silas asked.

"He'd worked in General McNeill's office during the time Tyrese was sent on that mission in Lyrill, and learned about full-bloods. He's grabbed every bit of research he could find and infected himself with one of the Liege's serums. It didn't kill him, gave him extra abilities and he wanted more. A part of him wanted to help the pack, another part wanted to belong but felt he needed to bring something to the table no matter what. He suspected the drug was harmful and really wants to fix it. Franz's unstable, though. His thoughts flit all over the place. It took a while to get just that bit of information. One thing for sure, he loves the bitch. She was uppermost in his thoughts, almost to an obsessive level. He wants to heal her very badly," Hawke said.

Silas stood in the middle of the room.

Ricardo's pack surrounded him asking questions regarding the new direction their pack would take.

The other Alphas continued talking to Angus. Lucian, Raven and Duke stood in a corner talking.

"Jasmine?"

"Silas what are you doing up this time of morning?"

He explained what happened.

"Busy day."

"Just five more to go," he said as he signaled to Angus and Hawke it was time to leave.

"I'll keep the light on for you."

"As long as the light is next to a place I can sink into you, that's perfect." She laughed as he intended.

"Good luck on the challenges later today, everyone," Silas said and walked out.

CHAPTER TWENTY-SIX

General Crall called during a late breakfast. Silas wasn't surprised the Joint Chiefs would have Crall contact him since he refused to talk to them directly.

"Good morning, Sir," Crall said in an upbeat voice. *"I understand you're in Honduras."*

Silas sat back in his chair and pushed away the empty plate. *"Yes. I'm here as the Goddess' Emissary."*

"Really?" Crall asked seriously. *"This isn't a finger to the Joint Chiefs?"*

"I don't have that kind of time to spend days here dealing with an out of control pack. There are easier, more comfortable ways to aggravate those assholes. What did they do to you when you returned with my Knights?"

"Asked questions, wanted to know how I knew where to go, who was involved, your take or anger level, that kind of thing. I can only speak of what I know which is very little. I did tell them

you sent me there, which shocked them into silence. They thought you believed whatever they told you. Came as a shock you have a poker face."

"Hmm." Silas wasn't interested in them at the moment. Crall would be perfect in Mexico. *"How much longer until you retire?"*

"I reach 30 years next year, Sir. I can retire then."

"Don't reenlist, I'll need you for another assignment. Seems I've been derelict on my duties to the Goddess and have recently been reminded I have more to do. I want you involved with that, Miller too. Look for other full-bloods to rise in position, let me know who you recommend and I'll call in some favors to have them moved up."

"Yes, Sir."

"What did they want you to say or do?" Silas asked to get it over with.

Each day the Honduran full-bloods operated more and more like a pack. Hector and Pedro sent word that they were having portable bleachers delivered to the park this morning so members could sit and watch the fights. They would leave security to watch the place. Angus left to set up the two fighting rings and make sure everything was in order. Concerned about security, Hawke went out looking for items he could put together to assist in handling the crowd. They had a lot on their plates today and little time to deal with the Pentagon.

"Apologize for General Lee who acted alone, without their knowledge or approval."

Silas snorted.

Crall chuckled. *"They know I can smell a lie, that's probably why the Admiral I spoke with wasn't involved and was genuinely upset. Not all of them knew what was happening, I'd bet it was just one other. I can look into it if you'd like. At this point, you hold all the cards. They want the Knights back."*

Silas wasn't sure which direction he wanted to go. To expand into Canada and later Mexico he'd need his Knights and some KnightForce. Eventually, he might allow a small group to serve but they would never have the full battalion as before.

"Go ahead, expose the traitor and let me know who it is. What happened to Lee?"

"He was formally charged the same morning I left. Shipped back to the States shortly after. He's being held in DC. From what I've heard the Admiral and General questioned him for several hours trying to get a name of who helped him, he never told. He pleaded guilty and awaits trial."

"When you discover who helped him, I want him exposed publicly. He doesn't deserve that kind of loyalty," Silas said.

"Agreed. I'll let you know what I discover and tell the Admiral we spoke and you're still angry?"

"Yep, still pissed they didn't know what was going on in their own house. Also tell them I refused to discuss what I'm doing here, let them stew a bit. Also, I'm shutting down communications until I return to the States. That should give you a break."

"Thank you, Sir. Much appreciated. If you need me for anything, I'm here. Good luck with your mission." Crall signed off.

Silas wondered how anything got done with all the backroom deals and buck-passing. If any group needed an Alpha, it was the US Military.

"Silas, we have a problem," Angus said. *"Solo's gang was attacked and left him in the middle of the street bleeding out."*

"Is there a doctor? Someone to look him over?" Silas strode into the bedroom to dress and find Solo.

"Not for full-bloods," Angus sounded confused. *"How are they surviving? I'll contact one of the Alphas, see what they can do."*

"If any of them have a doctor, someone who helps their packs heal, I want to meet them today," Silas said disgusted by the lack of basic necessities in the area.

"On it," Angus said.

Silas dressed and left the hotel with Umi after securing their floor. He arrived at a run-down building at the edge of town surrounded by other buildings in similar states. That pack members lived in such conditions pissed him off. He'd need to have Jackie and Quinn look into the costs of providing a hospital and school for pack members in this area.

Solo lay on a bed in the back room. Angus knelt next to him with his hand on his shoulder. Silas had been feeding him energy to help heal the pup.

"What happened?" Silas barked to the other young men standing out front.

They started talking at once. Silas managed to gather the gist of what they were saying. "The gang member he competed against last night did this?"

Angus stood and sighed. *"Yeah. The guy was jealous and embarrassed for losing to someone he considered inferior."* Angus stroked his goatee. *"I also picked up the gangs have been on the sidelines so far, but they plan to change that today. Something's going to happen at the fight this afternoon. Solo and these guys don't know exactly what, but they overheard the other gang talking about it. The Red Wolves are leading it."*

"I'm getting tired of them. If the three who used the explosives show up I will hold them and pass judgment."

"Good. What about Solo? He still wants to compete today." Angus looked down at the healing pup.

"Let him. I'll work on him a bit before we leave." Silas moved next to the bed. "Solo, how are you feeling?"

Solo looked up at Silas. "Mucho better, Gracias." Strain surrounded his eyes as he tried to sit. Silas placed his hand on the pup's shoulder and sent healing energy into him. Solo's eyes widened as he stared into Silas' eyes.

In this young man, Silas saw himself when he was much younger. No guidance, no pack, just a desperate desire to survive. Solo had heart, strength and if properly molded would make a strong leader one day. Once the pain cleared from Solo's eyes, Silas removed his hand with the full realization he'd given the pup a little extra juice to fight today.

"Better?" he asked as he stepped back.

"Mucho." Solo held Silas' gaze until he left the room and searched for Angus.

"La Patron?" Solo called.

Silas turned and waited.

"Is that what Alpha's do? Help? Heal? Protect?"

"That's a part of what we do, Solo. The gifts from the Goddess are to help the pack survive, grow stronger and healing is just one. Preparing for the future is another that is important." He wanted to be sure the pup understood the responsibility.

Solo nodded. "Si. Thank you." He turned and walked back inside.

Angus and Silas entered the car and headed for the park

#####

Silas and Angus met Hawke at the park tinkering at the far edge with several pieces of pipes and wires. The bleachers and fighting rings were in place. Silas threw an opaque bubble around the area, much larger than the previous night and secured it.

"What about the doctors?" Silas asked Angus.

"Two, one with Pedro, the other will come with Hector."

"Have all the Alphas checked in?" Silas wasn't sure Franz would back off and leave Ricardo alone.

"Yes, wished them all luck this morning," Angus said.

"Did you tell Hawke about the gangs?"

"Just told him. He wants to handle walking the grounds with a few pack members and deal with the gangs if they show up. Each Alpha promised five men to assist with security. That's 25 plus Hawke, should be good."

Silas thought about it. If they couldn't communicate mind to mind they'd need another way.

"Radios," Hawke said when Silas questioned him about it. *"Crude, on a human level, but that's all they have right now until the Goddess restores their abilities to mind link."*

Silas stepped inside the arena and scanned the area. He stepped outside the bubble as people arrived. Angus took the challengers to a corner where chairs had been set aside while Silas and Hawke scanned each person before allowing them to enter.

Hawke and Silas both looked up at the same time. Hawke leapt forward, Silas covered him with a frontal shield, just as gunfire erupted. The bullets bounced off the shield and flew in various directions. People dove to the ground covering their heads. Hawke landed on the driver of a moving jeep, ripped one weapon from the full blood in the passenger seat, swung it and knocked the other pup in the back holding an automatic out of the car.

The jeep slammed into a tree, throwing Hawke forward a few feet. He grabbed the full-blood who had fallen out the jeep and broke his neck. Returned to the dazed gang members in the jeep and broke their necks as well. In less than three minutes the four-armed gang members were dead. Hawk searched them for weapons and destroyed each one so they couldn't be used again.

He left the car and the bodies behind as he returned to his post.

"That says don't mess with pack," Hawke told Silas.

"Yes, I believe it does." Silas greeted the Alphas from Nicaragua, El Salvador, and Guatemala who arrived with several members from their pack. He explained their people could only enter if there was space available after the locals were inside since it was more important for them to see their potential Alphas in battle.

"Of course," the Guatemalan Alpha said and spoke to the group who seemed disappointed but stepped aside. "They will wait and accompany me home later."

Silas nodded and continued scanning and allowing pack members to enter.

Jorge ran to Silas with a look of horror pointing in the direction of the dead gang members. "Is it true? Did you kill those pups?"

Silas' brow rose. "What's true is they fired semi-automatic weapons at pack members attending an Alpha challenge officiated by me. Hawke jumped in front of bullets that would've hurt innocent pack. For that, they forfeited their lives. No one and I mean no one messes with pack. Learn and understand that clearly right now, Jorge. If the gangs want war, war I'll give them. Believe me when I say I won't lose."

"But... they're just —"

"Murderers, thieves, criminals with no regard to pack life. Pack comes first, Jorge." Silas' voice rose. Winds of heated energy swirled around him as his anger rose. "Do not defend anyone who fires bullets into a crowd of pack members, don't do it."

Jorge realized a crowd had surrounded him and bowed. "I apologize, Sir and make no excuses for their behavior. But if we respond in the same manner as they behave, how are we different?"

Silas lifted Jorge by his neck and held him in the air. Their gazes met. Silas' eyes itched, no doubt blazing blue. "You think defending pack is the same as what those cowards who fire weapons as they run away from the consequences of their actions, did?"

The crowd murmured no and called the gang members names.

Silas read Jorge's mind and knew he genuinely hated the loss of any life. But there would be bloodshed, change often required it.

"No. It's not the same... I just wish." He hung his head as Silas brought his feet back to the ground.

"You wish they'd just do the right thing, but they've had decades to make changes and haven't. They're not going to just accept a new Alpha, that's why the Goddess must choose Her champion and empower him or her to bring order."

Jorge looked at Hawke, and shook his head. "This is...I'm sorry you were shot."

"I protect the pack at all costs," Hawke said causing people to look at him and the blood on his shirt. "No one messes with pack, no one. Until everyone believes that with every fiber of their being, your pack will be fragmented." He waved the next person forward, scanned and allowed them entry.

CHAPTER TWENTY-SIX

The end of the first rounds of eliminations surprised Silas. Hector had been eliminated by Solo which sent shock waves and then wild applauds through the crowd. As a farmer, Hector hadn't been a skilled fighter and the Alpha position had been bestowed upon him because of his ability to provide for his pack. He shook a surprised Solo's hand and returned to his seat.

Solo nodded to Silas and Angus as he took his seat in the area reserved for those proceeding to the next level of eliminations. Tonio and Jose won their matches and were slated to fight a Guatemalan and Nicaraguan Alpha, respectively. Silas sensed tension between the men but didn't mention it.

Ricardo and Pedro won their first rounds and were slated to fight Alphas from El Salvador. Silas had been impressed with Pedro's brawling style in the ring, it reminded him of a Berserker. Pedro completely changed when on the attack, he decimated his challenger in record time. The crowd loved it. Ricardo was skilled and fought well. He lacked Pedro's ferocity, still he did a good job in dealing his opponent a loss and winning support from the crowd.

The next round would pit the four Alphas and Solo against foreign Alphas. Silas stood in the middle of the rings, waved the noise down to announce the next rounds and what it all meant when sustained gunfire erupted outside. Screams from outside penetrated the bubble. Hawke and Angus ran out while Silas demanded order inside. He released the Alphas to go out and assist.

Anger bubbled beneath the surface at the idea of pack, full-bloods, attacking full-bloods. It made no sense and showed the need of an Alpha. He calmed everyone inside, spoke of the need to come together as pack, to live among humans while being proud of their dual natures. He spoke of midnight runs in the mountains, the pleasure of worshiping the Goddess, Her love for them and what She expected, while listening through mental links to reports of those injured outside. Hawke and Angus worked with the Alphas and doctors to treat anyone who needed it. Most importantly, Hawk had caught the scent of the perpetrators.

Silas announced the time for the next round of challenges and dismissed everyone. Outside, pack members supported each other and left hopeful of change. Hawke and Angus assured the Alphas that the matter of the shooting would be handled and wished them the best for the final rounds.

Hawke looked at Silas. *"I can track them."*

Silas nodded and they took off jogging. Initially Silas thought they'd be heading into Tegucigalpa, the capital, but they turned off before reaching the city and ran up and behind it toward more sparse housing.

They'd run a little over 15 miles before Hawke stopped. *"It's that house there. I'm not sure how many heartbeats…"* He looked at Silas. *"Twenty? More?"*

Silas inhaled and listened intently. The punks were celebrating, bragging over the fact they'd shot people, shut down the Alpha talk. *"This is them, makes no difference how many there are, none of them will be leaving."* He threw a power shield over the house and walked slowly toward it. They would see the three of them approach and not be able to do anything about it. If they fired a weapon, it wouldn't penetrate the shield and would, in all likelihood, hit one of them. They couldn't leave, couldn't hit and run like they did before. They were trapped like the cowards they were. After a few attempts to leave, and failed shots, the stench of fear and desperation leaked from the shield.

Silas stood in front of the house. "These punks have no idea what an Alpha is, I'm thinking to teach them a lesson." He looked at Hawke who shook his head slowly and morphed to his largest size.

"They shot pack, meant to hurt them. They don't deserve a lesson, Alpha. They broke the rule and deserve to die."

Fear ratcheted at Hawke's words and display.

Angus morphed to his two-footed beast and swung his fist. "Death for hurting pack."

Silas looked at Angus and then Hawke. "What if we only destroy the ones who fired their weapons into the pack? Can we extend that mercy?"

For several seconds, neither responded. "Not all of them are bad, if we can save a few to serve the Goddess, wouldn't that be worthwhile?" Silas asked knowing the gang members were listening.

Hawke flowed to his two-footed beast. "Yes, Alpha."

Angus pawed the ground as the scent of fear grew stronger. "Death for hurting pack."

Silas took a deep breath. "No one hurts pack. You're right, I'll send out the ones who pulled the triggers." Silas walked through the shield and faced the full-bloods. Most of them were older, and not young teens as he had originally thought. A few lay bleeding, others watched him with curious expressions and others sneered. Silas dealt with the three sneering ones first by grabbing their beasts, forcing the change and pushing them outside to Angus and Hawke. It happened so fast the others in the room had no time to act.

They stared at him and backed up as he inhaled. One by one he identified the shooters and pulled their wolves. No one spoke as seven wolves were pushed out the energy field to be handled by Hawke and Angus.

"Come here." Silas looked at the remaining 11. They moved closer with their eyes on the ground. He activated his bracelet and touched each one. Three were hardened criminals who would never serve an Alpha. Even now two were wondering how to take him down. Rather than leave them for the incoming Alpha, Silas snapped their necks. The others backed away and didn't want him to touch them.

Silas compelled their wolves forward and continued searching all eight of the remaining gang members. He doubted any would follow the new Alpha but was reluctant to terminate them. They feared him and it was possible they might fear whoever the Goddess chose to lead.

"No one hurts or hunts pack," Silas said in a hard tone. "You're alive because you weren't with the others when they shot at pack members at the challenge. Most didn't know that's what they were going to do, yet you participated in the celebration." He paused and stroked each of their wolves. These were new recruits without much experience. Several handled domestic details for the gang, finding food and keeping the place safe. Lost pups with no real guidance.

"Do you know about the Goddess? Your history as full-bloods?"

"No."

"Si."

"Some."

Ignorance was a killer. He gave them a brief history lesson on how they came into being, the Goddess' role in their lives, Alphas and the need for them. One being to teach pups and remind everyone of the rules of the Goddess while maintaining pride in who they were.

He sensed his words fell on deaf ears for a couple and they probably wouldn't live through the end of the week. But the majority listened and seemed surprised by most of what he shared.

"If you want to live, you will change. I will leave the destruction, the rest of the destruction of your gang to the new Alpha. He'll be able to do this as well." He pulled all of their wolves, leaving them in wolf form. "If any of you harm or try to harm a pack member again, I'll personally terminate your life, is that clear?"

He removed the energy shield and dragged them outside. Hawke and Angus stepped close, surrounding the shaking wolves. Silas shifted to his beast and walked amongst them until they stopped shaking. He wanted them to experience being in the presence of an Alpha and hoped it would helped them change their way of thinking. After a few moments, Angus shifted to his beast and started playing with a couple pups.

Hawke morphed to human and watched over them. A few pups crawled to Silas and laid their muzzles on him.

"How much time before the next challenge?" Silas asked Hawke.

"Hour and a half, I'm hungry."

"Okay, pity we can't go for a run," Silas said looking at the green forest as he stood and shifted. The wolves surrounded him, yapping and looking happy. "We have to eat and then Alpha challenges."

Angus shifted. Smiling he rubbed the belly of the pup he'd been playing with. *"Good I'm starving."*

The wolves shifted. None of their earlier angst appeared on their faces. Instead they held expressions of wonder and gratitude as they gathered closer to Silas.

"We have a place where you can eat, it belongs to pack. You'll enjoy it," the pup Carlos said. Tall, thin and the youngest of the group, he had taken a liking to Angus and hung near his side.

"How far?" Angus asked him.

"A couple miles down the mountain, before town."

Silas nodded.

"Who's got the keys?" Carlos asked looking at the others.

"We'll walk," Silas said and took off jogging. Angus and Hawke caught up. The others followed them. When they reached a dirt road, Carlos veered to the right. Silas and the others followed him. They passed several homes in sad states of disrepair, something the future Alpha would need to handle. A large, one story wood house stood at the end of the road. Several full-bloods sat at tables outside and stared at them as they arrived.

Eager to announce their arrival, Carlos yelled. "La Patron, Angus and Hawke are here to eat." The full-bloods outside looked surprised as Silas nodded, spoke greetings and walked inside. A tall dark woman leaned over a counter to stare at them.

"La Patron? Here?" she sounded confused.

"Si," Silas said and smiled at her. "We heard the food was good here and we're very hungry. What are you serving?" He looked around for a table and menus.

"Please have a seat." She waved to the table which Carlos rushed to clean and wiped the chairs.

"Something smells good," Hawke said looking at her. "I want some of whatever that is. Lots of it."

Silas and Angus laughed. "Just so you know, we'll probably eat whatever you have left in your kitchen while you cook more."

Her white teeth flashed from a wide smile that lit up her face as she realized they were serious. "Let me get you started with chicken baleadas." She clucked her teeth and went in the back. Moments later, Carlos and several of the eight placed platters of folded tortillas filled with chicken, cheese, refried beans, sour cream with slices of avocado on the side. A plate of plantains and bottles of cold water were placed on the table.

"Appetizers," Carlos said. "She's cooking for you." He rubbed his stomach and walked off.

Silas checked the food to ensure it was safe and then took a bite. It was good. He'd remember to tell Jasmine about this later today.

They had just finished their meal and pushed back from the table when a full-blood who'd been outside when they arrived approached them.

"La Patron, may I ask what happened to the others?"

"What others?" Silas asked as he placed three times the amount owed for the meal on the table. It had been worth it.

"The ones with Carlos, the ones who terrorized our community, where are they?" He looked over his shoulder and then at Silas. "Are they coming back? No one knows."

Silas placed his hand on the man's shoulder and activated his bracelet. "They won't be back. Soon there will be an Alpha who'll protect and make sure the pack is provided for. It won't happen overnight but with the Goddess' help life will become better for all pack members. You won't be on your own. Pack helps pack, remember that."

The full-blood's eyes watered as he nodded slowly. "Thank you, it's been… life has been hard. Real hard"

Silas nodded and walked toward the door with a heavy heart. One of the older gang members who Silas personally terminated had been this full-blood's son. The gang member beat his sire and mam regularly, took their money and shot up their home. They lived in fear of him and the others and were helpless.

"We were told not to come, not to be involved with your meetings, so we stayed away. It's good you came today. It's good to see an Alpha and know the Goddess hasn't forgotten us." He opened the door for Silas and stepped aside. Outside, there were three times the amount of people watching him as it had been when he arrived.

Silas was unsure what they wanted, so he smiled and waved as he walked through the crowd.

"La Patron. La Patron. La Patron." The cheer started with the older full-blood he'd just spoken to and spread quickly. By the time Silas and the others reached the road, the chant had gained momentum and he felt compelled to change the direction. He held up his hands.

They quieted.

"Thank you for the best food I've eaten since coming to your beautiful country."

They cheered.

"The Goddess' concern over you and your wellbeing is why I'm here. In Her infinite wisdom, She has decided you need an Alpha, similar to the one in the States." He bowed.

They clapped and cheered.

"There are Alpha challenges in progress but being able to win a physical battle is only a part of the job. The Goddess will search the heart of each candidate. Only someone who cares or has the capacity to care about you, your life, your problems and heartaches will be your Alpha. Trust the Goddess, pray to Her for the best Alpha and once he's chosen, pledge your loyalty. Never forget, pack takes care of pack. That's why I'm here, in the end, we're all members of the Goddess' pack, Si?"

"Si," they yelled.

Silas waved, turned and walked down the road before breaking into a run toward the park.

CHAPTER TWENTY-SEVEN

Silas watched Angus and Hawke scan the entrants into what he hoped would be the final rounds of competition. They'd done a lot in two days. They might leave the country before the seventh day. What they'd once thought impossible was coming together fast. The pack wanted change and was ready to embrace the Goddess and a new Alpha.

Tonio and Jose nodded as they took seats in the challenger's section. The Alphas from the other Central American countries arrived and took their seats. Solo and Hector entered, talking, and laughing like old friends.

Silas smiled and hoped the two could work together to strengthen the pack. Pedro entered, nodded and headed toward the challenger's section.

"Have you seen Ricardo?" Angus asked Silas.

Silas saw Raven and Lucian in the stands and searched for Ricardo. He tried to contact the Alpha through their link and got a weird feeling in the pit of his stomach. *"Something's wrong with Ricardo. Deadly wrong."*

"What?" Angus asked. *"Deadly wrong?"*

"His link's been severed."

Hawke turned and met Silas' gaze. *"Can you determine where he is?"*

Silas tried to find the Alpha but couldn't pinpoint him. *"No. I can't find him either. Which isn't good."* He released a frustrated breath and stared at Lucian until the pup met his gaze. He waved him forward. Lucian and Raven met Silas in the middle of the ring.

"Where's your Uncle?" Silas asked. His gaze flitted between them both.

Raven frowned. "We had a late meal together, and he said he'd see us here." She looked at Lucian. "He left before we did. I'm surprised he's not here." She looked around.

"Was he going somewhere? Other than here?" Silas pressed.

"No. At least I don't think so, he was excited about still being in the competition. He wouldn't miss this," she said sounding nervous.

Silas placed his hand on her shoulder and sent calming energy through her.

"Has something happened to him?" Lucian asked, his gaze direct.

"I don't know. I can't contact him. He's not responding to me."

"You're linked to him?" Lucian sounded surprised.

"To all the Alphas here," Silas said and then told the others what Raven said.

"Want me to search for him?" Angus asked.

Silas didn't want to see what happened to the Alpha. He knew the end result and didn't want to deal with more death or the fallout this soon. *"Yes, take Lucian."*

Silas sent Lucian to Angus and Raven back to her seat, even though she wanted to go with her brother. Hawke remained at the entrance and soon the place was full. Silas was happy to see the full blood from the restaurant and the cook, both waved as they took their seats.

When the time arrived to start, Silas reminded everyone of his mission, the Goddess' love for them and the need for an Alpha. He introduced the contestants, but when he got to Ricardo's name he added, "or his representative." The crowd murmured and looked around but no one challenged his statement outright.

With just five fights, Silas allowed them one at a time. They were brutal. Tonio lost to the Nicaraguan Alpha, his brother won against the Guatemalan. Solo won against an El Salvadoran Alpha.

Parts of Ricardo's body had been found. According to Angus, the Alpha had been ripped apart by several beasts. Angus had their scents, and suspected Lucian realized it had been his own pack who killed his Uncle. Lucian's grief had been instant, followed by his anger. He wanted to track down the missing pack members and destroy them and would have if Angus hadn't implored the pup to think first. Angus and Lucian searched the house and grounds and found no one. Those responsible had disappeared.

Angus and Lucian arrived during Pedro's fight. Silas sensed the pain, and frustration from the pup and hoped he'd channel it into something positive.

Pedro's match with another El Salvadoran Alpha became the highlight of the evening due to its ferocity and brutality. The two were evenly matched and neither gave an inch. In the end Silas believed Pedro wore down his opponent and stopped short of delivering a death blow when Silas stepped in.

The last El Salvadoran Alpha waited for his match. Silas prepared to tell everyone that Ricardo wouldn't be returning for the challenge when Angus stopped him.

"I think Lucian wants to take his Uncle's place. He asked questions about it on the way here. He wants his Uncle remembered or something like that."

"He needs to talk to me now before I make the announcement," Silas said looking at the remaining challengers.

Angus waved to Lucian, they spoke for a few seconds before Lucian walked toward Silas. "Sir, I'd like to stand for my Uncle if it's permitted."

Silas placed his hand on Lucian's shoulder. Waves of grief, pain, and anger rolled off him. He genuinely cared about his den. "Let me explain to the audience why I'm allowing this, go with Angus to prepare."

Lucian nodded and returned to Angus.

Silas cleared his throat, quieting the room. He took a moment and looked at the expectant gazes. "A great Alpha was taken from the pack today. Alpha Ricardo was attacked by cowards on his way here and was murdered." Silas let the words hang in the air.

Raven wept. The person next to her pulled her close.

"We're not sure what happened but we've got the scent of the perpetrators and will be visiting them soon."

A cheer erupted from the crowd.

"No one hurts pack," Silas said, his voice rising above the crowd. "No one." He went on to speak of Ricardo, their short association and the vicious attack.

"One of his own, his pack, his kin, wishes to step in to complete his Uncle's challenge and I'm granting it under the circumstances." Most in the crowd cheered.

Silas called the last El Salvadoran Alpha to the ring. The large, muscular man strode forward with confidence. Next Silas called Lucian.

Raven stood clapping and cheering louder than anyone else.

Lucian's determined gaze told its own story. Heartache and the need for vengeance would go a long way in bringing down his opponent. The two charged. Lucian surprised everyone by how fast he moved, how hard his punches fell and high he jumped over his opponent to flip him on the floor. It quickly became evident that the pup had innate skills none of the others had.

"Didn't see this coming," Angus told Hawke and Silas. *"Thought we'd be peeling him off the floor."*

Silas and Angus looked at each other. *"Reminds me of Rese and Rone,"* Angus said.

"He's fast like Damian," Hawke said. *"Did you check to make sure he's not enhanced?"*

"Yeah," Angus said. *"No metal, no weapons, although looks like he doesn't need any. I can still hear how hard he knocked that one on his ass a few minutes ago."* The Alpha staggered a few steps with blood dripping from his nose and lip. Lucian

remained poised for an attack but Silas was sure the fight was over.

The Alpha attacked. Lucian sidestepped and punched him beneath the chin, sending him flying out the ring into the side of the bubble and sliding to the floor. He didn't move.

A second later the crowd erupted.

Solo and Pedro stood whistling and clapping. Eventually the other challengers clapped as well.

"You explained what winning meant, right?" Silas asked Angus.

"Yes, well not directly. He knows this is an Alpha challenge," Angus hedged.

"And if he wins he'll be interviewed to become Alpha, right?" Silas asked.

"No, I didn't go into all of that."

Silas cursed. *"He'd better be willing to go all the way or all of this is for nothing,"* Silas snapped.

"I'll talk to him during the break. If he doesn't go to the next round, just explain the fight was a memorial kind of thing for his Uncle," Angus suggested.

"That's bullshit and you know it. Get him on board and do it now," Silas said.

Silas started the next round of eliminations. Those who won the first two fights were the first to start. During that time Angus spoke with Lucian regarding the challenge. The pup understood what this was all about but was unsure he was capable or qualified to become Alpha. Especially if he had to mete out justice to his litter-mates if they had knowledge of his Uncle's death.

Angus assured him that Silas would be the one deal with those who killed an Alpha. And no one would escape his justice, even if they hid behind a uniform. In the end, it was knowing the Goddess would determine the Alpha that eased Lucian's mind.

Solo won against the Nicaraguan Alpha, surprising everyone with his fast, lethal moves in both human and beast form.

Pedro and Jose were next to fight. Silas thought both were savage fighters. Pedro's feral nature reminded him of himself when he was younger. Jose was cunning, flexible and reminded him of Angus. The battle was as brutal as he thought. Neither fought as hard against the other as they had against the foreign Alphas but the crowd loved it. In the end, Pedro won and Jose held up his opponent's hand to the crowd.

Solo was called to fight Lucian. The crowd grew quiet as the two entered the ring. Solo leaned forward and said something to Lucian which appeared to surprise him.

Silas wondered at that exchanged but explained the rules to the crowd and the opponents. Whoever won this round would challenge Pedro. He stressed that the Goddess would interview the champion or all the challengers, it wasn't his decision. Ultimately, She would choose the Alpha and enable him to lead the pack. These challenges were for the pack. He turned, reminded the two men of the rules and stepped away.

The two fought and it was an exciting match. Solo did flips and avoided direct hits. Lucian did the same. It became apparent the two of them had no intention of battling in the same manner they had done before. Nevertheless, the crowd loved their brand of fighting.

"I'll stop this soon, call it a draw," Silas told Angus and Hawke.

"They're not going to fight, not really fight each other," Hawke said. *"They have heart."*

"If Solo flips any higher, he'll hit the ceiling. How many times have they actually made contact?" Angus asked.

"No more than five," Silas said. *"I'll give them a few more minutes and call it."*

"Pedro isn't going to go easy on Lucian or Solo," Hawke said.

"And he shouldn't," Silas said. Minutes later he called the fight a draw. Since Lucian had only fought one opponent, he and Pedro were next.

As Hawke predicted, this fight was completely different from the one between Lucian and Solo. It was apparent in Pedro's demeanor, and his feral gaze that he wanted to be known as the one who won against all challengers even if he didn't become Alpha.

Silas hoped Lucian was up to the task.

Pedro didn't disappoint. He shifted to wolf, a large brown beast with white stockings. Lucian flowed into his animal, black with one white front stocking. Silas and Angus looked at each other, wondering if Lucian was part of the Black Wolf line. Didn't seem likely but who knew? Grandfather's seed had spread far and wide, perhaps down to Central America. Lucian's quick, lightning fast reflexes, Pedro's ferocity, held the crowd in thrall. It was unclear who they preferred but they all enjoyed the fight.

Pedro drew first blood across Lucian's eye.

Lucian flowed into his two-footed beast and backhanded Pedro so hard he flew across the floor. He didn't get up. The stunned crowd roared their approval. Lucian was the champion if the Goddess agreed. Lucian pushed through the crowd of well-wishers on his way to Pedro. Solo tended the downed Alpha and made a space for Lucian.

"Hey, you're tough Alpha," Pedro said through a cracked lip that was healing.

"Are you okay?" Lucian asked.

Silas, Hawke and Angus watched the pack gravitate toward, Pedro, Solo and Lucian. *"Black wolf in Honduras. Think he's the only one?"* Angus glanced at Silas.

"Who knows? Grandfather or the Goddess never mentioned this one," Silas said slightly irritated over being kept in the dark. *"Wonder what's next?"*

"He's a natural," Hawke said watching Lucian help Pedro to his feet.

"Lucian's the one who rescued me in the mountains," Silas reminded them. Nothing ever happened by coincidence, he should've made the connection then.

Angus nodded. *"Everything's connected in some way."*

"It's been a long day," Silas said. *"I need to address what happened to Ricardo."* He looked at Hawke. *"Did Passen overnight the pills?"*

Hawke nodded. *"Yes, Umi will pick up the box from the station and bring it to the hotel to save time."*

"Good. The sooner we get these pups off those drugs the better."

Lucian, Pedro and Solo approached them.

"Well done, Lucian, Pedro and Solo. As I said before the challenge was for pack, to see and know your leader's abilities to protect and defend is important. Prepare for an interview with the Goddess. I can't say when, where or how, but be in a position of expectancy. She will contact you in Her own time."

Smiling widely, Solo slapped Lucian on his back.

"All of the challengers should be in a position of expectancy," Silas said looking at Solo and then Pedro since the others had left.

"Yes, Sir," Solo said, the smile slipping.

Pedro nodded, turned and waved a large truck closer. "They'll take the bleachers, now."

Silas nodded as workers swarmed in and within minutes removed equipment, leaving the area clear.

"Any ideas where the Sup's disappeared to?" Silas asked Angus as they headed out the clearing.

"Town? A club or bar? They own a couple."

Silas didn't want to search through crowds. *"Back to the hotel first to decompress and think this through."* He didn't relish the idea of spending more time here than necessary, but he couldn't allow the death of an Alpha, especially one linked to him, to slide.

CHAPTER TWENTY-EIGHT

Silas and the others sat at the dining table in his suite, eating a steak and pork loin meal Umi prepared. After the fight, he'd walked in, kicked off his shoes and stripped down to his boxers, prepared to unwind from the long day. He had reached out to Jasmine, talked to her for a few moments when the scents from Umi's meal cart drew his attention. Jasmine suggested they talk after he filled his belly and he agreed.

Platters overflowing with meat disappeared, leaving rolls, and cheesy potatoes, which Hawke scooped up. Satisfied, Silas stretched and finished a bottle of water.

A nap would be nice. Better if Sweet Bitch were here. *"Jasmine?"* He stood and walked to his bedroom, leaving Hawke and Angus at the table.

"Finished? That was fast," she said.

He told her what Umi provided and added. *"This place is beautiful, you'd love the waterfalls, the green mountains, lots of water-sports at the lake."* He paused, appreciating the natural, unspoiled beauty of the country.

"Is that an invitation for me and the kids to meet you there?"

Had he been thinking of that? Sure, he missed her, wanted to touch and share some of the things he'd seen. But there was danger here too. Someone had blown up the house he'd been staying in, he wouldn't forget that.

"Not really. Just missing you."

"Miss you too. But it sounds like a lovely place to visit. I've never been to Central America."

"Maybe after the Alpha's chosen, we'll return for his installation ceremony or something like that."

"Who won?" she asked.

He told her of the last contests and what happened. She commiserated with him over Ricardo's death but was happy the challenges were over.

"Have you talked to the Goddess about what's next?" she asked.

"No, not yet." His mate knew better than most how the Goddess worked, to say more would only add fuel to the fire of her growing discontent with his belief.

"Hmm, as long as you're still coming home on time."

"As far as I know, this is over and I'm back in seven days." He didn't add "if the Goddess doesn't change plans," that was a given, at least in his mind.

An erotic memory of a time they'd been wrapped in each other's arms, kissing to the point they broke apart gasping for air filled their link. Blood raced to his cock, making him hard in an instant.

"Miss you," she said again, her voice deeper, a sensual caress that sent his mind into overdrive.

"Miss you, too," he said as images of his face between her legs replaced the one she'd sent moments before. Sounds and sensations flooded their link, along with his ravenous need for her.

She gasped.

He exhaled and placed his hand on his cock. Damn boxers prevented him for feeling his rock-hard flesh. He slipped them off and grabbed his dick as her breathing labored.

"That felt so good," she whispered. *"I couldn't breathe, my body shook so hard, just like…. Like now,"* she gasped and screamed.

Triggered by her excitement and release, he stroked faster. *"Open wide for me, let me feel what you're feeling,"* he said, panting as his need built. Waves of pleasure flooded their link carrying him on a tide of eroticism he hadn't been expecting. His heart raced in anticipation.

Faster, harder, he stroked, lapping the energy from her orgasmic explosion. Higher. Tighter. Almost there.

"Argh," he yelled as ropes of jizz flew across his belly and chest.

"Thanks, Wolfie." She sounded like a satisfied cat. *"That memory is my favorite when I need a quickie."*

He laughed as he headed to his bathroom to clean up. *"Glad I could oblige. Every time I'm with you, every taste, stroke and orgasm I wring from your delectable body becomes my favorite. Any will send me over the edge."*

She snorted.

"True," he said. *"In person is best. Always. Nothing beats the way you feel when I sink into you. The way your walls hug me in greeting and tighten on your release. It's the best homecoming a man can ever experience."* He stroked his hardening cock.

"Agreed, but in a pinch, memories of riding your sweet cock will get me through. I needed that tonight and you delivered."

He loved when she forgot herself and talked nasty. *"And thoughts of your sweet, juicy, pussy will keep me sane for another night. I need to get back home to you."*

"Silas stop," she moaned.

He grinned. *"What?"*

"The kids are in the living room and you've got me touching and rubbing…"

Her words were kryptonite to his fragile peace. *"Me too, Sweet Bitch. You're never alone with this need, never."* Images of her riding him filled their link. He leaned against the wall, stroking his cock, pulling, squeezing, trying to emulate the feel of her. Nothing worked but he was too close to quibble.

Her moans grew louder.

In his mind's eye, he watched her lean back, sliding up and down him, slamming hard on the down stroke. Maybe they'd cum together this time. His need ratcheted as he imagined her face, flushed, beads of sweat on her brow. Her tongue licking her lips. Her pussy tightening around him. Tighter. Tighter.

He wasn't sure who released first.

Her scream drowned his or vice versa. His toes curled on the tile as pleasure shot up his back, lifting him higher and then releasing him to the cosmos. He took a moment to catch his breath. Watching her control her pleasure on top of him was his favorite position.

Her eyes would be at half-mast right now. She'd be trying to catch her breath, possibly push off him and roll to the side. Or if she were really tired, she would collapse on his chest until she could speak. He loved that option the best.

What was she doing without him?

"You okay?" he asked hoping she'd share.

"One... sec..."

He smiled and turned on the shower.

"That was... wow."

Warm water ran from his head to his feet, removing the evidence of their sexual play. *"It'll be better when I get home,"* he promised.

"Of course, but like I said, this works in a pinch."

He chuckled. *"I hope we weren't too loud... with the kids in the other room.*

She sighed. *"You're bad."*

He laughed. *"They're all grown and know how pups are made. They know I adore you, can't keep my hands and my cock off you."*

"Silas."

He laughed. Their interlude was over. Decorum had returned. Every aspect of her personality delighted him. *"Okay, I'll behave."*

"I've got to shower."

"Wish I could wash your back."

"Don't start, Silas."

He laughed. *"What? Just saying I want to serve you in every way."*

"Hmpf."

"If I were there, I'd wash your back and anything else that needed... cleaning."

She laughed. *"Stop. Don't you have to find some people or something. Go take care of that so I can deal with our pups. I can only imagine what Bella must think hearing me scream,"* she muttered.

"No doubt she recognized it as a similar sound my son pulls from her," he said.

"Bye, Silas." She disconnected.

He laughed. Feeling better, and more alert, he finished showering. Ten minutes later, dressed, refreshed, he re-entered the empty living room. Umi had cleared the dining room table and left a couple cakes and a bowl of fruit on the table.

Silas took a banana and headed toward the sofa. *"La Patron, this is Pedro. We need your assistance."*

"What do you need?" Silas asked and then took a bite of fruit.

"Lucian, Solo and I tracked the gang to a research lab located near the foot of the mountains near Soto Cano, the military base," he added. *"They will not allow us to enter."*

Of course not, Silas thought. Things would never be that easy and the place was restricted. *"How did the Sup's enter?"*

"I don't know, Sir," Pedro said. *"We tracked them here."*

"What are your plans for them?" Silas asked while looking at the clock. It was shy of midnight, Hawke and Angus were probably connecting with their mates the same as he had with Jasmine.

"I have a cárcel on my lands where we can hold them temporarily while they are questioned," Pedro said. *"We brought the truck to carry them."*

"Move back, remain with your truck, give me some time to work on something, I'll get back with you."

At least Pedro had a jail to take them, that was a step in the right direction. Silas wondered how bad he would wreck his budding relationship with the Honduran President by calling him this time of night. He would say it was an emergency, the pups might be infected with something. The whole lab might be in jeopardy. Explain they would need to be in wolf form when they exited the building without explaining how he would accomplish that task. Silas tossed ideas back and forth. Weighed his remaining time in the country with political expediency. The last thing he wanted was to be told to leave before he finished his assignment.

Unless he had one of the others use the bracelet to take on a high-ranking official's body, they couldn't access the high security facility again. He pulled out his phone and made the call.

####

Silas experienced a sense of déjà vu when he, Angus and Hawke arrived at the research lab a couple hours later. Had it been a few days ago his Knights were held captive here? Seemed much longer. The conversation with the Honduran President had been tense. There were moments Silas didn't think the man would grant his request to open the doors and allow the full-bloods to be released to his care. The President wanted details and information Silas couldn't share with any human, regardless of their position.

In the end, money closed the deal. Silas agreed to make a sizable donation to a charity the President choose, which would no doubt line his pocket personally, before the end of the month. Pleased with Silas' word, the President agreed he could take the full-bloods from their haven of safety. Once he received permission, Silas and the others left the hotel for the lab.

"Pedro, we're here." Silas had his vehicle park a significant distance from the truck and walked over. *"Open the back."*

Lucian opened the back of the truck. Hawked jumped on the bed and inspected it to ensure nothing would harm the pups. He nodded to Silas.

Silas inhaled and focused. He sought the beasts inside the lab. There were several he didn't want. It took time to zero in on the Sups. They were in a room on the first floor which made everything easier. Although Silas had permission to enter the lab, he preferred not to.

Locked in on the 28 pups, Silas pulled their wolves. In an instant, they shifted from human to wolf and they weren't happy.

Next, he called them to him. Some he had to drag, others came willingly. Those he suspected weren't on the drugs. Security had been informed to open doors so they could exit and not tear the place apart. When the front doors of the lab opened wide, wolves bounded out the building and headed toward him.

"Jump into the back of the truck," Silas told them as he pointed. Most jumped up, walked around or sat watching him. Three were dragged outside, their feet slid against the concrete floor of the lab and then the asphalt parking lot. Silas glanced at Hawke. "They're going to hurt themselves."

Hawke and Angus picked up the three wolves and put them in the back of the truck. A smiling Lucian closed the door and locked it as howls of discontent rent the air.

"We'll follow you," Silas told Solo, and Pedro who lagged behind Lucian who'd already entered the truck.

"Yes, Sir," Pedro said as he swung into the driver's seat.

Angus started the car. Silas and Hawke entered and pulled onto the road.

"More than I anticipated," Hawke said from the back seat.

"Yeah," Silas said thinking the matter through. "Were they that many at the kill site?" he asked Angus.

"No. I scented a few Sups, nothing like this."

"So why did Franz send them all there?" Hawke asked. "Something to do with drugs? Experiments? Or to muddy the waters? Because he's at the root of all this. Ricardo was killed by his order."

Silas agreed. Taking care of Franz and the Red Wolves who blew up the house would be his gift to the new Alpha he decided. Those Red Wolves were laying low, no doubt waiting for him to leave before showing their hand. Same with Franz, Duke and Tasha. They all needed to be dealt with before he left.

####

Pedro's jail faced the sea from a high cliff. High powered lights surrounded the facility, giving it a surreal glow from the distance. Stone walls topped with barbed wire discouraged uninvited guests. Inside, the pups followed Silas, who followed Pedro, to a large room. Angus and Hawke brought up the rear to ensure all pups were accounted for. Lucian and Solo flanked Silas, and occasionally looked over their shoulders at the pups.

"Have Umi bring the package here when it arrives," Silas told Hawke.

Hawke nodded and pulled out his cell.

Silas had the pups sit on the concrete floor. "Who's questioning them?" he looked at the three men.

"Angus said you'd take care of it," Lucian said frowning.

"I will deliver judgment to whoever was involved, but this is your idea to bring them here for questioning." Silas read Lucian's uncertainty. "Would you like me to question them?"

"Yes, Si, I would. Gracias." He spoke fast and stepped to the side.

"Find out if any of these were involved with Ricardo's death or had knowledge of it," Silas told Angus and Hawke. He turned to Pedro. "Could you bring us something to drink?"

Pedro's skin flushed. "My pardons. Of course, what was I thinking?" He turned to leave.

Silas looked at Lucian and Solo. "Go and help him. We'll need a lot to feed the pack."

The two nodded, and left to find Pedro.

Silas threw up an opaque shield to stop anyone from seeing Hawke or Angus touching the heads of each wolf. He went to the three he had dragged out the lab, stooped in front of them and one by one, touched their heads, sent warmth through them and read their memories.

Done, he stepped back and waited for Angus and Hawke's report, although he doubted the 25 had any knowledge of Ricardo's death.

Silas released the shield as Angus released the last wolf. Hawke finished a few moments later. None of the wolves were aware of Ricardo's death, except the three reluctant wolves. They knew of the ambush because they had stood guard. The three wolves who tore Ricardo apart had fled to El Salvador. Silas would have them returned for justice. In the mean-time they had a pack to heal.

Lucian, Pedro and Solo returned with drinks and food. They placed everything on a long table leaning against the wall. Even though he wasn't hungry, Silas took a bottle of water and a piece of meat. The pups whined as they watched.

"I'm going to return them to human," Silas told Lucian. "Once they're settled, make the announcement regarding your Uncle's death. Talk to them, tell them what happened and the challenge. They may not know."

Lucian frowned. "I tracked someone from my Uncle's attack to the lab. One or more of them have to know about it."

"We'll take care of those three." Silas nodded to Hawke and Angus. They moved in position to take the ones with knowledge of the murder.

Silas released their wolves, forcing another shift, this time to human. Bones popped, realigned. The more inexperienced wolves were naked. Angus grabbed one of the three wolves next to him and tied rope around his wrists while Hawke did the same to two others. They placed the three men back to back, forming a triangle. Silas placed an energy band around the three to hold them in place while Lucian talked to the pack.

Lucian held up his hand for quiet. Pedro and Solo stood behind and to the side of him watching. Silas, Angus and Hawke stepped to the side out of the way to listen and observe the person who may be the future Honduran Alpha. Lucian had the heart for it if not the desire.

In short order, Lucian told them about the death of their Alpha, how it happened and that members from the pack had been involved. The initial shock gave way to rage as the pack turned toward the three men in the back, and demanded death to those involved with Ricardo's demise. Lucian strode to the three and asked Silas to release them.

"Ask your questions first," Silas said.

"Who killed our Alpha?" Lucian shouted and morphed to his two-footed beast.

The three looked up at him and named names. "They left the country."

"Who told them to do this?" Lucian asked.

The three looked down at the ground.

"Please release them so I can kill them," Lucian said. The pack was in full agreement.

"Don't you want to know who's behind all of this?" Silas asked. If Lucian's litter-mates were involved, they would die as well and he knew Lucian didn't want to deal with that.

"Last chance," Lucian said, hovering close to their faces. His long claws left marks on their cheeks. Silas smelled their fear and wondered if Lucian did as well.

"On whose order did those cowards ambush our Alpha? Who told you to help them?" Lucian yelled.

"Tasha."

"Tasha."

"Tasha."

Lucian jerked as if slapped. "You lie."

"You can smell a lie," Silas said into the silence. "Do you smell one now?"

Solo looked away.

Pedro frowned.

Seconds passed. Lucian morphed to human. "Tell us what happened."

The three haltingly told how Tasha was afraid she would die without the drugs Franz provided, even though Franz told her it wouldn't happen and that the antidote would be worth a try. Her wolf was growing more and more out of control one of the three said, earning a glare from Lucian.

"Are you sure she told them to kill him?" Lucian asked again, disbelief and pain evident in his voice and posture.

"Yes. Either her or Duke would lead the pack afterward." That comment left the room silent.

"What did you do?"

"Made sure no one stopped them. Gave them time to run, to leave the country. Then spread the word to go to the lab to meet with Franz. He let us in and then left."

Lucian turned and looked at Silas. "What can I do?"

"The death of an Alpha, this Alpha in particular because he was connected to me, falls under my jurisdiction. If you're satisfied with the answers, then I'll handle it from here." He paused. "You should know, everyone connected with Ricardo's death will be dealt with. This cannot be allowed a pass."

Lucian met his gaze for a few moments. "I cannot kill my litter mate."

"No, you cannot. Be grateful for the Goddess' wisdom in that," Silas said. "But Tasha will forfeit her life for her role in Alpha Ricardo's death." He wanted to be sure they all knew what would happen to her.

"My brother?" Lucian asked Silas.

"Ask them." Silas pointed to the three shaking in the middle of an angry pack.

Lucian gathered himself, turned and asked. "What was Duke's role in this?"

The three frowned. "Duke? I never saw him. Was he there?"

The other two demurred. "Never saw him. Don't know if he was involved."

Silas sensed a weight lift from Lucian. "What about Raven?" Silas asked stepping away from the wall, ignoring Lucian's shocked scowl.

"No, she wasn't involved. They didn't want him or her to know." The wolf tipped his head toward Lucian.

"Good," Silas said. "Now we've gone through all the people Lucian cannot exact punishment on." He pointed to the three and released them. The moment they moved, the pack attacked.

It wasn't pretty.

CHAPTER TWENTY-NINE

Tired, in need of a hot bath and several hours of uninterrupted sleep, Silas and the others were on their way back to the hotel the next day. Umi had delivered the antidote pills to Pedro's early this morning. All 25 former Sups readily took the regiment and were finally sleeping. It had been a rough night without the drugs.

According to Dr. Passen, they needed to take the pills for two days to counter the addiction. Lucian asked Pedro to allow the pack to remain as his guests until they were free of both the effects of the drug and Franz. He shared his fears with Silas of Franz making another attempt to snare the wolves. He wanted to secure their pack land borders against his litter-mate and Franz.

Silas didn't bother reminding him that neither would be a concern for long. He'd sent word to the Alphas in the rest of Central America regarding the rogue wolves who turned on their Alpha, and killed him over drugs. Disobedience to your Alpha meant exile, murder cut your life span to the moment you were found.

Just before they entered town, the brothers, Tonio and Jose, contacted Silas. *"Last night the Goddess came to me in a dream. She was beautiful. Glowing, kind. I am honored beyond measure.*" They constantly talked over each other as they recounted the conversation. Ending with a long drawn out sigh, as if they'd just experienced the most satisfying event in their lives.

Silas understood. *"I'm glad you had an opportunity to meet Her."*

"Si. And thank you for your patience and coming to help us when we could not help ourselves. She will return to us as we return to Her. We will heal and grow strong as a pack," Tonio said with confidence.

"That's what's important," Silas said as they turned into the hotel parking lot. *"Soon we will know who She names as Alpha."*

"We look to work with him," Jose said.

"Si, She says we must all work together to survive," Tonio added.

Angus parked near the back entrance. Hawke stepped out first. Silas disconnected from the brothers and exited the car. He stopped, spun and jumped in time to miss an attack.

Hawke and Angus watched as the female hit the wall, bounced once, turned and stalked toward Silas with her finger pointed at his chest.

"Where are they?" she demanded. "What did you do to my pack?"

Silas met the red striated gaze of Tasha and realized she had finally lost control. This aberration was the culmination of the drugs she had taken. He sensed no fear from her. No pain over the fact she'd just hit a wall or that blood ran from her nose. The drugs made her oblivious to reality.

She flew forward, knocking him back a bit and punched him in the stomach. When she tried to hit him again, he blocked every blow she tried to land. She was fast, her hits had some weight. Curiosity got the best of him. He wanted to see what the drugs could do and allowed the attack to continue.

Yellowish drool ran down the side of her mouth which she couldn't close because her fangs had lengthened a few inches as if she had shifted. A line of hair sprung from her forehead, down her neck, like an out of control Mohawk. Her gaze sharpened as she tried to claw him.

Silas grabbed her hands, held them high in one of his as he scolded her. "None of that. Do what you feel but if you put a mark on me, my mate will be furious and you don't want that." He pushed her backward. She stumbled a few feet and fell to one knee, staring at him.

Angus and Hawke leaned against the car watching. *"Where's Franz? Or Duke?"* Angus asked.

"She must've ditched them somehow," Hawke said.

"They should be here by now," Angus said scenting the air. *"I think Duke's here."*

"Where the fuck are they?" She asked in a guttural voice. "What did you do to them?"

"Killed them for killing their Alpha, what else?" Silas said in an up-beat tone.

Her screech sent chill bumps across his arms. She leapt toward him with arms, and claws outstretched.

Silas side stepped at the last moment, grabbed her by the neck, flipped her over, and slammed her to the ground. She jumped up and charged again. The whites in her eyes were almost completely red giving her a demonic appearance. Silas didn't bother stepping aside this time, instead he punched her in the chest, knocking her back a bit. He followed that punch with several more until she staggered.

She pulled out a knife, threw it at Hawke. It embedded into his shoulder. Thinking Silas distracted she leapt forward again. He batted her cheek with the back of her hand sending her flying into a nearby car. Even though the knife wouldn't hurt Hawke, Silas was done being nice. He moved quickly, grabbed her by the head, twisted and broke her neck. He dropped her to the ground as Duke ran forward.

"Nooooo," he cried dropping beside her body. "It was the drugs. She could've been helped, she could've been helped."

"Maybe, but the moment she conspired to kill Alpha Ricardo, her fate was sealed," Silas said in a hard tone. "Did you have anything to do with Ricardo's death?"

"Huh? What? Death? No." His horrified gaze met Silas. The scent of truth filled the air.

"What do you know about it?" Silas pressed.

"Nothing. Not until we were at Franz' retirement party on base. Tasha mentioned she'd heard something about his death. But she was lying, I could tell. I just didn't know what part she lied about." He stroked her hair a few more seconds. "The drugs changed her. She wanted to be Alpha. That's all she ever wanted." He looked at Silas. "She didn't have the heart to care about pack, I told her that. She started the gang, talked Franz into searching for something to make her, us, the best." He shook his head. "Nothing was ever good enough. She always wanted more. Franz spoiled her, gave her whatever she wanted. But he would never be her mate, in her own way she despised him for being human, even though he took drugs to change. If he hadn't retired, who knows what would've happened. The military would've found out soon enough and kicked him out. Physically, he's as messed up as the rest of us."

"The others are on the antidote, recovering. They aren't messed up anymore," Silas said.

Duke's eyes widened in surprise. "What? The stuff you promised my Uncle? You were serious?"

Silas nodded.

"Where?" Duke wiped his mouth and looked at his dead litter-mate. "How can I get some?"

Hawke moved forward and offered him two pills. Duke's gaze flit from Silas to Hawke and back to Silas. "This is it?"

"Yes," Silas said.

Duke took the pills and swallowed them. "How long before I'm free?"

"Give it two to three days," Hawke said as he extended his hand to assist Duke to his feet. He wiped the moisture from his eyes with the back of his hand while staring down at his sibling. "I'll miss her."

"Call Raven and Lucian, they're still here," Silas suggested.

CHAPTER THIRTY

Silas and Angus entered the hotel after sending Hawke to take Duke and Tasha's body to Lucian and Raven on their pack lands. He suspected Lucian wouldn't be happy, might balk over the Alpha's position. If it was up to Silas, he'd pick Solo. The pup had heart and a loyal streak a mile wide. He simply needed training and a cause. Pack leader would provide both.

Heading toward the elevator he hoped he could leave before the seventh day and wondered what the Goddess' plans were for him now that the challenges were done.

Umi met the elevator as he always did when Silas returned. "Would you prefer to eat before your rest, Sirs?"

Silas glanced at Angus. "Food, a conversation with my mate and then sleep," he said.

"Same here," Angus said as they entered Silas' personal suite where they had their meals and planning sessions. "*Watching you fight takes a lot of energy.*" He chuckled and headed for the table.

"I'll bring your meals right away," Umi said.

"Hawke had an errand and will be here later, make sure there's plenty for him," Silas said to Umi's back.

"Yes, Sir."

"Obvious red demon effects aside, did the drug make her stronger than a Knight or KnightForce agent?" Angus pulled out a chair while watching Silas.

Silas thought about it. *"She was strong, that's for sure, but nothing like those teams. Or my Alphas, or even some half-bloods. We're supposed to be one with our beasts because we tap into their energies for cunning, strength, and sensory skills. It seems the drug enhanced the human side at the expense of her beast."*

"So even if she gained extra skills, she lost her beast's abilities which made her slightly better than the others but not much." Angus paused. *"Maybe that's all she wanted, a slight edge."* He shrugged. *"If she'd developed her beast better who knows. She could've been a great Alpha."*

"She didn't care about pack," Silas reminded him. *"She ordered her Uncle killed. Raven said they moved in with him after the death of her parents. No, she wasn't Alpha material or even pack material."*

"I think Lucian will get the job," Angus said leaning back as Umi placed a large empty plate in front of him. Silently, Silas agreed but wasn't sure.

Aromatic smells of meats, breads, and other tasty bits filled the room as Umi removed the covers. He placed two platters filled with various meats on the table. Another with breads, and another with bowls of rice, beans, sauces and veggies.

"Enjoy your meal, Sirs." He bowed and left the room.

Silas and Angus each took a platter of meat. He used his empty plate for the other stuff. Soon the only sound in the room was the scraping of forks on plates. When he finished, he pushed back from the table with a satisfied nod. "He's good."

"Can we take him home?" Angus asked with a devilish grin.

"Ask Jasmine," Silas said.

Angus grunted and turned aside.

For several moments, neither spoke. "When you… when you were hit with the explosive," Angus said looking at his clasped hands resting on his knee. "There was this void." He moved his hand in a circular motion in front of his chest.

Silas didn't know what to say and remained silent.

"I wasn't sure what was missing until I came out of the darkness or whatever that was. Hawke told me about the explosion, the damage done, Rese, Rone, Jasmine and Shyla had been working on me for hours, feeding my beast energy so I could heal."

Silas' chest tightened at the retelling, somehow they'd never gotten around to this before.

"I remember lying down, looking up at the ceiling feeling so lost." Angus cleared his throat. "I didn't really understand it at the time but you're the last of our litter. We're the last, I mean. Without you, there's this empty spot no one else can fill. Scared the shit out of me. Not being able to find you, blood calls to blood and I couldn't find you." The look of pain and sadness on his face spoke of the difficult time he experienced.

"Grandfather must have blocked it," Silas said, hoping to ease his brother's pain.

Angus nodded. "Probably. They don't think what we're going through during times like that. I needed to know you were alive and healing." He shook his head. "It was a constant demand in my mind, and heart, more than you being my Alpha."

Silas nodded. "When you disappeared to follow Shyla, I was not in the best frame of mind either. I knew you were alive, but I couldn't find or connect to you. Drove me crazy, which impacted everyone around me." He paused to allow his words to settle and add comfort. They'd both had similar experiences. "Nothing made my heart happier than hearing from Grandfather that you were mending, once I saw for myself, I was finally at peace."

Angus nodded. For several moments neither spoke. "Try not to do that again, it's difficult on my mate," Angus said without looking at Silas.

"I'll try," Silas said dryly. "When are we going home? My pups returned to the Compound for a visit, I want to spend time with them before they leave."

"Adam and his mate?"

Silas nodded.

"There's one thing I'd like to do before we leave," Angus said in a serious tone.

"What?"

"Those assholes who blew us up, I want them."

Silas read the deathly determination in Angus' eyes. *"Without starting an international incident?"*

"No one will ever find them."

"But they'll be missing."

"People go missing every day. They think they've gotten away and are just waiting for us to leave to continue their reign of terror."

Silas bit back a smile. Angus leaned towards the dramatic when he wanted something. *"Reign of terror?"*

Angus snorted. *"Call it whatever. I still want them to pay with their lives for what they did to us."* He looked at Silas. The need for vengeance rolled off him in waves.

"Do you know where they've gone off too?" Silas asked. Those three were bad news, even the Honduran President had heard of the explosion and asked Silas if he planned to deal with it.

"I'll find them."

Silas didn't doubt Angus for a second. *"Okay. Make sure there's no trail back to us. I want to leave as soon as the Goddess releases me.*

Angus' face lit into a wide, feral grin. *"I'll rest later."* He left the suite humming.

Silas chuckled and headed to the bedroom.

"Franz is here, he's wired and claims he has plastic explosives in place all over the pack grounds. He's unhinged over Tasha's death. Is it possible they were mates?" Hawke asked.

"Anything's possible. What does he want?" Silas asked.

"Tasha. Once he saw her body, he lost it. Threatening to kill everyone with a push of the button."

Silas released a sigh and shook his head. *"Seems every time I break a neck, it sets off serious repercussions."*

"She killed her Alpha." Hawke's voice was implacable.

"Yes. I should've waited for Franz, took care of them both at the same time. I'm slipping."

"She attacked you, Sir. There was no waiting for someone else. Her condition had deteriorated to the point she couldn't

have stopped and waited. Death, yours or hers, was the only objective at the time."

"Yes, but that doesn't help save pack lives."

"In her mental state, chances are more pack lives would've been lost. I've contacted the other Alphas to come. They'll remove the pack members from the area while we remain here. They should be here soon," Hawke said.

"Good."

"How's Raven and Lucian responding to Tasha's death?"

"They're upset."

"Are you in danger?" While Silas regretted Lucian and his litter-mate's grief, he wouldn't tolerate anything happening to his men.

"Other than the bomb strapped to Franz' waist and threats of more bombs on the grounds… no," Hawke said.

"What is it with this country and plastic explosives?" Silas asked preparing to go to Lucian's.

"Not sure, Sir. Franz knows a lot about them it seems. He's screaming he'll blow up the whole country."

"Over Tasha's death?" Silas asked, curious.

"Possibly."

"I'm on my way," Silas said.

"Are you sure? You're the main target of his anger, it might trigger him to do something stupid."

"Yes, I'm sure. I started it, I'll finish it."

"Yes, Sir. I'll let your arrival be a surprise."

"Right." Silas thought about the volatile situation for several moments.

Jasmine wouldn't handle it well if he arrived at Lucian's without a plan. Her reaction would mirror his if she had recently recovered from being hit with explosives. Hell, he wouldn't want her anywhere near Franz. He ran his hand through his hair, thinking hard on how to handle this.

Moments later contacted General Crall. "We have a situation and this is what I want you to tell the Joint Chiefs."

####

Silas arrived at Lucian's 30 minutes later, 15 minutes after the military who were currently sweeping the area for bombs. Hawke had contacted him the moment the MP's arrived and knocked on the front door. Franz had been so removed from reality he instructed Lucian to open the door, so they could attend Tasha's memorial service.

So far nothing happened. The only explosives were strapped around Franz. Either he lied about more explosives or his drug induced reality made him think he had spiked the area with bombs. Regardless, Silas and the others breathed easier knowing the pack and their homes were safe from this maniac.

"He's close to the edge," Hawke said. *"He keeps looking at Tasha, says things like he wants to be with her and asking her to wait for him."*

"Damn."

"There's eight people in here, the ones he couldn't see or sense left and met Solo and Pedro. They're on the way to meet the other pack members recuperating at Pedro's place," Hawke said. *"If I didn't want to break his neck for providing weapons and explosives to gang members, I'd feel sorry for his pathetic ass."*

"Franz is the supplier?" Silas should've known.

Just one more thing to land on the Commanding Officer's desk which should be overflowing by the time the Admiral and General finished with him. The man had been caught unaware when the call from the Pentagon came informing him on what happened in his back yard. He had been quick to dispatch soldiers to the area to help contain the situation.

Franz belonged to them and as such Silas held the military responsible for his actions.

The Joint Chiefs agreed and unleashed their fury on Franz's Commanding Officer.

"Yes. He admitted it and a few more sins. He apologized to Duke, Lucian and Raven for their Uncle's death. He didn't order it, and found out afterward but had to help her cover it up. Sounds like he loved her crazy deep."

Silas understood that kind of love. He'd have done the same thing in an instant if Jasmine had committed a crime. *"Should I come in?"*

"Can you create an energy field to contain him? To keep him from detonating?"

Silas thought about it. He rarely used his abilities on humans, usually they couldn't handle it. *"I should. If I start now, from a distance he'll only feel tingling. The closer I am, the stronger it is."*

"Can you get a fix on him?"

Silas scanned the house. *"Yes. I sense him."* He sent energy and loosely wrapped it around Franz, allowing freedom of movement, for now, so Franz wouldn't notice.

For several moments, Silas concentrated on building a strong, impenetrable box around Franz to absorb as much of the impact from detonation as possible. Once he had it in place, he moved toward the house.

"How can you even consider blowing up this place?" Raven demanded. "We're her family, litter-mates. This was our home. How can you say you loved her and think about doing such a wrong thing?"

"I… I don't want to live without her." Franz sounded hurt and confused.

"That doesn't mean you have to do this," Duke said in a calm tone. "Tasha loved you, we all know it. But she would never allow you to hurt us. Never. You need to stop and get some rest. You look tired."

Silas moved closer and nodded to the MP's on the porch.

"She should be Alpha," Franz said.

"He's moving around again," Hawke said.

"Which Alpha?" Raven asked.

"The main one. They didn't want her because she was a woman," Franz. "They stole her dreams."

"That's not true. Women competed to be Alpha," Raven said, obviously gambling on the fact Franz didn't know the truth. No women applied for the Alpha spot.

"Tasha told me they refused her request to fight in the challenge because it would make the others look bad if she hit them too hard," Franz said.

Silas marveled at the lies Tasha told as he tightened the energy field around Franz.

"Hey!" Franz yelled trying to move. "What's going on?" he looked like a lost puppy when Silas entered the room and ushered everyone out.

Duke placed his arm around Raven and walked toward the front door, along with the others. Hawke moved to stand behind Silas. Solo, Pedro, Hector, Tonio and Jose entered and stood near the wall.

Lucian stepped in front of Franz and stared at the man for a few moments. "As Alpha of Honduras, I ban you from all pack lands from this day forward. The Goddess has been merciful in sparing your life." He looked toward the front porch. "Come inside and take him away from here," he told the MP's.

Silas heard Lucian's announcement of his position. Did that mean he could go home now that his assignment was complete? He and Hawke stepped outside onto the patio to allow the military to do their job.

The MP's shot Franz with some type of sleeping agent, incapacitating him and removed the detonation devices. Then they took him away.

"Did you know?" Hawke asked.

"No, I wasn't informed of Her choice but I'm not surprised. Lucian has a heart for people, and with the Goddess' training he'll make an excellent Alpha." Silas looked at the green countryside. *"They should buy land, lots of it and build schools, hospitals, stores, grow food and make clothes for pack. Maybe there's some kind of industry they can do on the side to increase their bank accounts. The need here is great."* He thought of the poor housing, non-existent medical care, lack of educational facilities and wanted to help.

"Grandfather suggested you send Cain and Abel, they have extensive experience in start-ups like this," Hawke reminded him.

Silas nodded. *"Yes, they do. They helped me."* He would talk to Jasmine, get her opinion on what to do here.

"La Patron?" Lucian said as he walked toward Silas and Hawke. No longer did he appear like the unsure man afraid to hear his sister had committed a crime. There were still traces of grief, which was to be expected, but Lucian's entire countenance was different. He stood taller, straighter, with confidence as he approached with his hand extended.

Silas took and held it for a few seconds.

"Thank you. I would not have been able to do what was necessary. The Goddess explained a lot of things to me, now I understand why you had to handle the matter, everything in fact, the way you did. I and every pack member in this country are grateful for your assistance."

Silas nodded and released his hand. He wasn't able to read Lucian which meant the Goddess' seal was upon him.

"If I can intrude on your graciousness a little longer. There are a lot of things I'd like to discuss with you, Angus and Hawke." He looked around. "Where's Angus?"

"Searching for the three Red Wolves who used the explosives on the humans." Silas made no apologies for not seeking permission.

Lucian's brow rose. "Cleaning up?"

Silas nodded. "It's the last bit of it."

"Once again thank you. There are many things I must do, the Goddess asked me to spend your remaining time training with you. I hope you don't mind."

Silas' hope of leaving tonight fizzled beneath the smile he offered Lucian. "Yes of course. We will assist as best we can."

Lucian took a deep breath, closed his eyes and shook his head. "I never dreamed of this day. Grandfather said I wouldn't be a runt forever, that I was destined…" He looked at Silas. "I'm rambling when we should discuss territories, rules and order. Please, come with me, the Alphas are in the office waiting."

"*Did he say Grandfather?*" Hawke asked Silas.

"*Yes, he did. That wily old man spread his seed far and wide,*" Silas said as they re-entered the house. Solo, Pedro, Hector, Tonio and Jose, stood when they entered and offered a toast. Silas took a glass and joined the toast to the new Alpha of Honduras.

The planning session was intense. They assigned territories, with Hector remaining Alpha over his pack, and Solo taking over the area surrounding the Capital. Duke would take over for Ricardo.

Silas mentioned buying land, schools, hospitals, stores, a solid infrastructure for pack. He mentioned they could be designed as private, for family members only to keep out humans. They all agreed on the idea but understood the challenges in such a poor country.

"Make an offer on a thousand acres before I leave, then hire pack members only to clear portions of the land for those buildings. There will be enough money for salaries and supplies," Silas said after agreeing to Lucian's long-term loan specifics.

"What about theft?" Pedro asked. "Humans will try to steal our supplies."

"What if we send a few Knights to work on security and train your best men as security?" Silas offered thinking of a few who spoke Spanish and would blend in well.

"That would be great," Lucian said. "Now to find qualified professionals to work in the hospital and schools."

"Education is the backbone of any pack. Teach pups the rules when they're young and it'll solve most of your disciplinary problems in the future. Plus, our mission is to live amongst humans without revealing our true nature. Which means pack must be literate, and educated to compete for the best jobs in every arena of life. You want pack on the police force, in government, military, owning stores, developing businesses so that you have a solid voice to live in peace."

"That makes much sense," Solo said. "I've never given much thought to school but now I think to focus attention there. Maybe I'll take some online classes, learn more to help."

Silas nodded his agreement. "Once the building is in place, we can work out a trade. I'll send some teachers here and you'll send your applicants to us for training. We can rotate them in and out until your schools are fully staffed. We'll do the same for the hospitals. I'll send a team to make sure the medical center is correctly set up for pack." He eyed Lucian. "You must pay them. Include salaries your professionals can live on in your budget.

They can either buy a home on pack lands or in town. You want the money to circulate within pack businesses first. I will help you with that."

"Gracias. Gracias, your generosity… it's unbelievable," Lucian said. The other Alphas murmured their agreement.

"The Goddess has blessed us, and who knows, maybe it was to be able to help other packs. Rebuilding your pack won't be easy, but we'll help in any way we can," Silas said.

Hours later, Silas called for a break and walked outside to take a breath of air.

"*It's done,*" Angus said as Hawke and Silas were returning to the planning session.

"*It's been almost four hours what took so long?*" Hawke asked.

"*They left an interesting trail into the mountains, but I found them. No one else will, though.*" He sounded satisfied.

"*We're at Lucian's, the new Alpha could use your expertise,*" Silas said.

"*On my way,*" Angus said.

CHAPTER THIRTY-ONE

Jasmine stepped into the living room and faced her children. They'd arrived a few minutes earlier for lunch and to spend time with Silas who arrived home around 4:30 that morning. He'd been exhausted but happy to be home. After a few hours of rest, she woke with a hungry wolf between her legs. Now they both needed to rest.

When the new Alpha had been chosen, she and Silas thought he would leave Honduras early. But after listening to Silas, sitting in on a couple planning meetings and speaking to two of the Alphas mates regarding setting up a network of women, she understood why he needed every second of those seven days. Her heart melded with the courageous Honduran pack who had a long way to go. But she was glad to have him home.

"He's in the shower and will be out in a bit. Go set the table and put out the food," she instructed hoping no one would comment on the love marks on her arms or neck. No such luck.

Renée and Jackie pulled her aside smiling. "What time did Daddy get home?" Renée asked. "Thought he was tired."

"Not that tired," Jackie said smiling.

"Never that tired." Jasmine winked and walked off. Behind her the girls laughed.

Adam and his mate Bella were the last to arrive. Jasmine liked the lovely girl and thought she suited her head strong son perfectly. Adam followed Bella like a love-sick puppy, something that surprised all of them.

"Bella, Quinn, have Renée show you where things are in the kitchen," Jasmine said including her expanded family. This lunch would just be the kids, their mates and kids. Tonight, she planned a larger meal with the Knights, and everyone else. For now, she wanted to spend time with just her kids, so they could all thank God and the Goddess for Silas' safe return.

Quinn had just taken the rolls out the oven and placed them on the table when Silas entered the living area dressed in black jogging pants and a short sleeved gray tee.

He smiled at everyone. Jasmine could've warned him, maybe she should have but didn't. He needed to understand before he left the next time. And with everything on his plate, she was certain there would be a next time.

Renée ran and jumped into his arms holding him so tight around his neck, crying, before David peeled her off so the others could greet him.

"I'm okay, Princess. I'm fine." He looked at Jasmine who dabbed away the moisture from her eyes.

Jackie looked him over, her eyes filling with tears before she hugged him tight around the waist. "Daddy, I was so scared," she whispered holding him tight. Quinn walked over placed his arm around her shoulders and shook Silas' hand.

"We were worried. Thank the Goddess you're alright," he said.

Silas clasped Quinn's shoulder. "Thank you for taking care of her." He nodded toward Jackie.

"She is my heart, I cannot live without her," Quinn said simply and moved Jackie aside.

In a rare show of emotional distress, David wrapped his arms around Silas and held on tight for several moments. It was such a shock, no one moved or interrupted as Silas stroked David's back and murmured words of comfort. Jasmine could see it shook Silas. Of all the kids, David normally remained unaffected by most things.

David backed off and stood next to Jasmine, reaching for her hand. She took his, offering comfort until he stopped shaking. Adam introduced his mate. Bella hugged Silas and wiped the tears from her eyes as Adam stepped close and hugged Silas tight for several seconds. His shoulders shook as he cried unashamedly over the close call they all received when hearing Silas had been involved in an explosion.

Silas met her gaze and she could tell it finally hit him how they'd suffered over the news of his possible demise. He hugged Adam and Bella close for a few moments, whispering words of encouragement. Tyrese, Danielle and their pups stood to the side watching, with wet eyes.

Rose and Tyrone stood back, wiping tears and holding their pups until it was their turn. Jasmine wondered when Cameron and Lilly would arrive, they should've been here by now.

Danielle lost it and openly wept against Silas' shoulder. Tyrese took several deep breaths to keep from breaking down. He held onto Silas a little longer and stepped back with his head down.

Rose walked forward with her arms outstretched and tears rolling down her face. "Padre, you scared me. I'm so happy you're here, alive and well. Bless the Goddess," she sobbed on his chest.

Silas met Jasmine's gaze again as he held Rose who worked as his personal assistant. The two were very close. Tyrone and their boys waited a few seconds more before they hugged and kissed Silas. Tyrone dabbed the tears from his eyes as he stepped back, saying how grateful he was to see his father and Alpha again.

Unable to speak around the thick ball of emotion in his throat, Silas extended his hand to Jasmine. She released David and took his hand. He kissed the back of hers and then kissed her softly.

"You kept this from me, I had no idea."

"At the time, you didn't need to know, now you do. Angus had to promise he would take care of the those who set off the explosives to keep the kids from flying over and handling that matter themselves."

"Angus did take care of them."

"Good." She paused. *"Don't ever forget this, how we feel. How much you mean to us and how your health and well-being impacts our lives."* She shook his hand. "To the table everyone."

He pulled her back. *"I love you so much I can't express it. If I'd known all of this, I'm not sure… I don't know what to do with it."*

"Accept it. Accept we love you and just as you'd give your life for family, family will drop everything to be here for you. You mean the world to us, never forget that," she stressed.

He read the truth in her eyes and thought of his near brush with death, the new mission and the days he spent sharing ideas and implementing a new pack structure with Lucian in Honduras. Everything had been interconnected, even his homecoming. Often, he spoke of the meaning of pack and how they looked after each other, but never gave much thought to his den being a pack. Not until today. With the Goddess' reminding him of his initial instructions to take this continent, he would need the support of his den and national pack more than before.

"Thank you, Sweet Bitch," he whispered as he brushed a kiss against her lips. "You're right as always. Let's go, our family's waiting for us."

Her smile lit her face as they walked hand in hand into their future.

Hello,

I've been writing about Silas and Jasmine since 2013 and they keep talking to me. It's delightful watching them grow stronger together, raise their family and remain a solid unit. Silas Knight is one bad Alpha and his mate, Jasmine, is tough as well. Together they lead millions of people (dual-natured) in the US. But that's about to change.

The Goddess is calling Silas to complete his original task to lead the North American continent. That won't happen easily or overnight. Book one kicks off the Rise of the Wolf Nation. More to follow soon. Threaded with that new series is the completion of La Patron's Den. Two more books, Renee and David's stories which are integral to the Rise of the Wolf Nation.

You're invited to journey with me through all the books in this series. If you like fast paced action, suspense and great love connections like me, you won't be disappointed. Feel free to drop me a line, SydneyAddae@msn.com or join my Facebook group, La Patron's Den, where discussions regarding Silas and the Wolf nation abound. Also, you can find me at my website, SydneyAddae.com.

Knight Chronicles is a newsletter for my Readers Group from the characters of the series to keep you informed of what's going on in the Wolf Nation. Each issue has a personal message from Silas Knight, La Patron, or his mate, Jasmine. Character profiles with in-depth interviews and thoughts you won't find anywhere else. Also works in progress, new releases and special give-aways in every issue. If you would like to receive **Knight Chronicles** click this sign up link! Thank you. (http://eepurl.com/bb3csz)

La Patron, the Alpha's Alpha is my first paranormal series and I'd like to ask a favor. When you finish reading, **please leave a review**, whatever your opinion, I assure you I appreciate it.

Thanks again
Sydney

BirthRight

BirthControl
BirthMark
BirthStone
BirthDate
BirthSign
Sword of Inquest
Sword of Mercy
Sword of Justice
La Patron's Christmas
La Patron's Christmas 2
La Patron's New Year – Catherine Marsh, Leigh West
KnightForce 1
KnightForce Deuces
KnightForce Tres'
KnightForce Damian
KnightForce Ethan
Angus

La Patron's Den
Jackie's Journey
Adam: Alpha Awakening

Booksets
La Patron Series Books 1-6
La Patron Series Books 4-6
Sword Series